Calmly, Carefully, Completely

By Tammy Falkner

Night Shift Publishing

For Diane, because she read 1001 different versions of this book and never once complained (where I could hear her).

With special thanks to Kayla Gardner who let me borrow her horses and then helped me give them life.

Pete

Nobody fucks with you in prison when you're all tatted up.

Not a single, solitary soul.

It could have something to do with being big, too. I haven't asked. I've just enjoyed it.

At home, it's a completely different story. At home, everyone fucks with me. I am the youngest of five, all brothers. They're all as big as me, if not bigger, and they have even more tats than I do. You don't get any points for being adorable. At my house, all you get points for is being a good person, contributing to the household, and supporting your family in every way possible.

It's too bad I sucked at all the requirements. I fucked things up royally two years ago.

I never should have done what I did. But I did it, and I did my time behind bars. I just hope that they can forgive me at home and not hold it over my head.

A hand clapped onto my shoulder jerks me from my internal dialogue. I look up and see my pro bono attorney, Mr. Caster. "Good to see you again, son," he says as he sits down across from me. He opens a file folder in front of him.

"Why are you here?" I blurt out. I wince immediately, realizing how rude that sounded. But his brow just arches as he shakes his head. "I mean, it's good to see you, sir."

He chuckles. "Nice to see you, too, Pete," he says. He takes a brochure from the folder and turns it so I can read it. "I have an opportunity for you."

My oldest brother, Paul, says opportunities are other people's problems. "What kind of opportunity?" I ask hesitantly. I open the brochure. There are pictures of horses and children and climbing structures and a pool with lots of splashing going on. I look up at him.

"This is a brochure for Cast-A-Way Farms," he says.

"And?" I ask.

"The opportunity," he says. "I talked to the judge and told him you would be good for this program." He raises his brow again. "I hope I'm not wrong."

I hate to sound like a numbskull, but... "Not following, Mr. Caster."

"I need a few good young men to help out at the Cast-A-Way camp for five days this summer." He starts to reload his folder and closes it. "I read your file. I liked what I saw. I think you have potential. And you have the skill set that I need for this particular camp."

Skill set? All I can do is ink people. I work at my brothers' tattoo shop when I'm not behind bars. I don't know how to do much else. "You want me to tattoo them?"

He chuckles again. "I need your signing ability," he admits. "We have a camp every year for special needs kids. We have a very special boy this year who has MS, so he has a tracheostomy tube. He can't speak. He signs. His mother's going, but she can't be with him 24-7. So, I thought you might be able to come and help." He shrugs. "There will also be a small group of boys there who are hearing impaired. You might work with them some, too."

I look at Mr. Caster's forearms and think I see a tattoo creeping out of his short-sleeved dress shirt. He follows my gaze and shrugs.

"You think you're the only one who wears your heart on your sleeve, Mr. Reed?" he asks, but he's smiling.

I shake my head. "Your opportunity sounds interesting," I say. "But I'm on house arrest for a year. I can only go to work and/or approved activities."

"I already talked to your parole officer," he says. "He's in favor of it." He crosses his arms in front of him on the table and leans on his elbows. "Only if you want to, though. No one is going to force you."

I pick up the brochure and start to read. It actually looks kind of interesting.

"You'd be doing me a big favor," he says. "I need another man present who can be a good role model for the boys we'll be taking from the juvenile detention facility. They'll be there working, getting service hours. I need someone to help me with them. That's why I need you." He narrows his eyes. "You're big and scary looking enough." He grins. "And your file looks good."

"You'll have the youth offenders at your camp? Working with the kids?"

He shakes his head quickly. "They'll interact some with the kids. But not much. They'll be there more to help with the daily living tasks— feeding the horses, moving hay, stacking boxes, doing odd jobs, helping with meals…"

I've never been afraid of manual labor. My brothers have drilled it into me from day one that I am going to work hard at everything I do or I'll have to answer to them. I heave a sigh. I'm slowly talking myself into this.

"There's a perk," he says. He grins.

"Do tell," I say. I sit back and cross my arms in front of me.

"If your time spent at the camp goes well, I can ask for leniency with regard to your house arrest, based on merit." He looks into my eyes. "If you earn it, that is."

Wow. I could get leniency? "It's for five days?" I ask.

He nods. "Monday through Friday."

I heave a sigh. "When do we leave?"

He grins and holds out a hand for me to shake. I put my hand in his, and he grips it tightly. "We leave tomorrow morning."

"Tomorrow?" I gasp. I haven't even gone home yet. I haven't gotten to spend any time at all with my brothers.

He nods. "At oh-dark-thirty." He smiles again. "You still up for it?"

"It can really shorten my sentence?" I ask.

He nods. "Maybe. It's up to the judge. And depends on how things go at camp." He sobers and looks directly into my eyes. "Pete, I think you could help with the boys I've invited to the camp. With all of them. You can help with the hearing-impaired boys, the ones who can't talk, and the ones from the youth program. I think you can do brilliant things. I believe in you, Pete, and I want to give you an opportunity to prove you're better than this." He makes a sweeping gesture that encompasses the room.

Better than jail? Am I better than what I have become? I am not so sure.

"Do we have a deal?" he asks.

I nod and stick out my hand again for him to shake. "We have a deal."

"Do you need for someone to pick you up in the morning?" he asks.

I shake my head. "I can get here."

"I'll see you at six a.m." He claps a hand on my shoulder and points toward the door. "I believe your family is waiting outside."

My heart trips a beat. It's been so long. I can't imagine what it's going to be like to be with them again. To feel normal.

I nod and bite my lower lip. But I steel my spine and walk out the door. The guards lead me by the guard station and toward the door, where they give me a bag of my belongings and ask me to check it. I slide my wallet into the back pocket of my jeans. I put my watch back on my wrist. I drop my piercings into my pocket. I might be able to get at least some of them back in later.

"Ready?" Mr. Caster asks. I don't realize he is right beside me until I look into his eyes. Very softly he says, "Stop worrying so much. They're the same family you left two years ago."

They might be, but I'm the one who's different. I nod my head, though. I can't speak past the lump in my throat.

I shove against the door, pressing hard on the lock bar, pushing, and then I find myself outside the walls of the prison for the first time in two years. I take a deep breath and look up at the sky. Then I see my brothers waiting at the end of the walk and the lump in my throat grows twice the size. I blink hard, trying to squeeze back the emotion.

Paul, my oldest brother, is standing beside Matt, who has the biggest grin on his face. His hair has grown back, and it's gotten longer than I've ever seen it on him. He told me in a letter that he had decided to let it grow out now that he knows what it's like to lose it all to cancer. He's recovering. I missed it all because I was behind bars. But that's one of the reasons why I was there. I thought I could help him and just ended up getting myself in trouble.

Logan is standing with his arm draped over his girlfriend Emily's shoulder. She looks up at him like he hung the stars and the moon. He points and smiles toward me, and she looks up and yells. Then she wiggles out of Logan's arms and runs toward me full force. She hits me hard in the chest, her arms wrapping around my neck. I lift her off the ground and spin her around as she squeezes me. She murmurs in my ear. "I'm so glad you're coming home," she says. "We missed you so much."

I look around. Someone is missing. "Where's Sam?" I ask. Her face falls, and she looks everywhere but at me. Sam's my twin, but he's not here. My gut clenches. I really hoped he would be.

"He's stuck at school. You know how tight school schedules can be." She won't look me in the face, so I know she's lying. I put my arm around her for a second and walk toward my brothers, but it's only a few steps before Paul jerks me away from Emily and wraps me up in a big bear hug. He squeezes me so tightly that my breath jerks out of me.

"Let me go, you big ox," I grunt out, but when he does, he grabs my head in his hands and runs his fingers through my prison cut. My hair's so short it's not much more than fuzz on the top of my head.

Logan punches me in the arm, and I turn to look at him. Logan's deaf, and he uses sign language. But after eight years of silence, he started to talk right before I went to prison. He signs while he speaks.

"Somebody scalp you while you were sleeping?" he asks, pointing to his hair. It's so strange hearing words come out of Logan's mouth. He went so long without speaking. But Emily brings out the best in him, including his voice. "It looks like you went three rounds with a weed eater. And lost."

Before I can answer, he's pulling me in for a hug. Logan's special. He's wicked smart, and he's ultra talented. Emily's his and everyone knows it. They're meant to be together forever, and no one doubted it from the first night he brought her home with her ass tossed over his shoulder and her Betty Boop panties showing.

Logan lets me go, and I look at Matt. He looks so healthy he's glowing. "Speaking of haircuts," I say, pulling on a lock of his hair. "When do you think you might get one?"

He cuffs me gently on the side of my head and pulls me into his shoulder. God, I have missed them.

"We're going to start calling you Goldilocks," I warn. We're all blond, and some of us are more blond than others.

"Try it, asswipe," he jokes as he punches my shoulder. "It's been a long time since we've had a good match."

Emily wraps her arm around my forearm and squeezes. "I think you're bigger than when you went in," she says.

"Not much else to do but work out and read." I shrug.

"I can still take you," Logan says. He flexes his muscles. It's so good to hear him speak.

Logan was injured in a car accident right after I went to jail, and he almost died. I wanted to go to him so badly. But they wouldn't let me out. "I heard you're an old man with a limp now." I duck when he tries to grab my head for a noogie, and I dance away from him.

"Nothing about me is limp," he says with a chuckle. "Right, Emily?" he says, grinning. She punches him in the arm. He bends at the waist and tosses her over his shoulder. She squeals and beats on his butt, but he pays her no mind. He never does when they do this. He starts toward the subway so we can go home. The rest of us follow.

Emily gives up and dangles there over Logan's shoulder. She's right by my face, so I lean in and kiss her on the cheek. "You all right?" she asks quietly. It's fucking ridiculous the way she's just bobbing there.

"It's good to be going home," I admit. "Strange, but good."

She wraps her hands around her mouth and whispers dramatically. "We have beer at the apartment! For your birthday!"

I grin. I spent my twenty-first birthday behind bars. But I had a feeling they wouldn't let it pass by without some kind of celebration. "Just beer?" I whisper back playfully.

She winks. "There might be some other stuff, too. Like wine."

My brothers don't do anything more than drink occasionally. "Is there cake?" I ask.

She nods. "Sam made it." Sam's the baker in the family. It's too bad he had to play football to earn his way into college because he'd make a damn fine baker. And he'd be happier doing it.

"So he was home this weekend?" Hearing that he was home this weekend but he's not there now is like a knife to my gut. It fucking hurts. I can't say I blame him, though.

She nods, and she does that thing she does where she doesn't look me in the face. She'd be terrible at poker because she can't lie worth shit.

"How long do you think he'll avoid me?" I ask.

Matt looks over at me, his face searching mine, but he doesn't answer my question either.

Reagan

I sit in my dad's truck and drum my thumb on the steering wheel along with the music. I dropped Dad off an hour ago, and he sent me on an errand because he hates the idea of me sitting outside a prison by myself. I finished his errand, and now I'm waiting. He can't fault me for that, can he?

I freeze when I see three tatted-up men walk by where I'm parked. They're blond and huge. But one of them is holding hands with a girl, a pretty lady with dirty-blond hair. I sit up taller and watch them. They're friendly with one another, and you can almost see how happy they are to be together. The one holding hands with the girl slaps her on the bottom and runs from her, and she streaks off after him until she can jump on his back. She leans forward and kisses him on the cheek. He puts her down because she's signing something to him. My heartbeat stutters. This is the family. I'm almost certain of it. They're Peter Reed's brothers.

Peter Reed is someone I have wanted to meet for two and a half years. He saved me one night when I really needed saving. He found me huddled in a room in the back of a frat house after the unthinkable happened.

I'm huddled by the wall, still shaking from what happened. He turned out the light when he left, so I sit in the dark with my teeth chattering so hard that my jaw hurts. My panties are still wrapped around my ankle, dangling there like the useless piece of cloth they are. One side is broken from where he ripped them off me, but I can't make my arms unwrap from around myself long enough to pull them up. Or off. My skirt is hiked up around my waist. He didn't bother to even pull it down when he was done. He just whispered in my ear about how no one would ever believe me if I told and how I better keep it to myself if I knew what was good for me.

My phone dings beside me, its bright face a beacon in the darkness, and I look down at it. I want to pick it up. It's probably one of my friends wondering where I've gone off to. But I can't unwrap my arms long enough to reach for it, either. If I unwrap, I'll fall apart. I can't fall apart. I just can't.

The door opens, and a sliver of light tumbles into the room. A young man laughs at someone as he closes the door in a girl's face. He flips the light on and leans back against the door, cursing playfully. I crawl on my hands toward the shadow in the corner. Maybe he won't see me. But he does. I can tell when he freezes and curses for real.

My teeth are still chattering, and I can't draw in a complete breath. He drops down to squat in front of me. "Hey, are you all right?" he asks. He reaches a hand toward me. An animalistic sound leaves my throat. It's one that scares even me, and he jerks his hand back like I'm a rabid dog and he's afraid I'll bite. The guy who just left, he wasn't afraid of me at all. After a few minutes of really nice kissing, I was ready to stop, but he pushed me down, tore off my panties, held me still, and raped me.

I look into this man's sky-blue eyes, and they're so different from the brown ones that hurt me. I open my mouth to speak, but only a squeak comes out. My phone dings again, and I look toward it.

"Do you want me to get it for you?" he asks softly. He reaches for it and then puts it within my reach. I take it, jerking it from his hand as I crouch further into the corner. He pulls back like I scare him. I look down at the screen.

Rachel: Where are you, hussy? I saw you locking lips with the douchebag. Did you leave with him?

I need to reply. But my fingers are shaking too much.

"Do you want me to do it?" the man asks. He gently takes the phone from my grasp with a twisty tug, and I let it go. It's of no use to me. I'm shaking too badly to use it.

"What do you want me to say?" he asks.

I swallow hard. I screamed when it started, before he covered my mouth with his hand, right before he banged my head on the bathroom countertop, and now my throat hurts. "Help me." The words are a whisper, and he leans closer because he can't hear what I'm saying.

"What?" he asks softly.

"Help me," I say. He looks at my face. He doesn't look down at my exposed body. He just looks at my face, like I'm not sitting here with my skirt hiked up above my hips, like my shirt's not torn open. Like I wasn't just raped. Defiled. Used. I tug at my skirt, and he looks around the room, opens a cabinet, and lays an unfolded towel over me. I start to adjust my clothes beneath it. He looks down and picks up my shoes, which I must have kicked off when I was flailing. He sets them next to my feet. He sees my panties hanging over my ankle, and he reaches for them, lifting my leg gently so he can pull them off my foot. "I need those," I say. I really, really need them.

He shakes them out and holds them up, as if I was putting them on. "They're torn," he says.

"I need them," I say again. A tear rolls down my cheek, and his face softens. He finds the scraps of fabric where the man who hurt me ripped them at the hip, and he ties a knot in them. He holds them up, like I'm two and need his help getting dressed. I put my feet in them and stand up, unsteady on my legs. He reaches out to support me. My hands are shaking so badly that I can't pull them up. He helps me. He hisses in a breath when he pulls them past the blood on my inner thighs. He lifts his gaze, looking into my face as he pulls them over my hips, and then he tugs my skirt down to cover them. I lower the towel, and he closes my shirt with gentle fingers. He bends over and picks up my phone where I dropped it.

"Can I call someone for you?" he asks.

I nod. But I can't think of who. I can't call my parents. I wasn't supposed to be at this party. I was supposed to be in my dorm room studying.

"Call Rachel," I say. I lean against the counter, feeling like I can't hold myself up anymore.

He scrolls through my contacts until he finds her name. He calls, and I can hear the faint ring through the phone. "Hello, Rachel?" he asks.

"Who are you and why do you have that hussy's phone?" I hear Rachel ask.

He looks at me. "Do you want to talk to her?" he asks me over the phone.

I shake my head.

He closes his eyes and says, "My name is Peter Reed, and I'm here with your friend…" He stops and looks at me, his eyebrows scrunching together. "What's your name?"

"Reagan," I whisper.

"I'm sorry," he says. And he really looks like he is. "I can't hear you." His tone is soft and much more sympathetic than I deserve.

"Reagan," I bark. I groan inwardly at the way I said that. It was a spurt. But he heard me. That's what matters.

"I'm here with your friend, Reagan. She needs you."

"Where?" I hear Rachel say.

"J-just tell her the party. M-master bathroom, I think." I look around.

"Do you want me to just go find her?" he asks, looking at me over the phone.

My gut clenches. "Don't leave me," I whisper. My jaw quivers, and I hate it. But this man makes me feel safe.

He reaches out and very gently lays his hand on the side of my head. I jerk back, and he immediately realizes that touching me was a mistake. "I won't leave. I promise," he says. He turns back to the phone. "We're in the back bedroom, in the bathroom. She's hurt." He looks at my face while he says it. Not at my abused body. His eyes stare into mine. "She's strong," he says. "But I think she needs you." He looks down at the phone. "I think she hung up on me."

I nod. "Thank you," I say.

"I'm going to stay with you," he says to assure me. "I'm not leaving. I promise."

I nod and lean against the counter, crossing my arms beneath my breasts.

"I'm going with you so I can be sure you go to the hospital," he says.

I shake my head. "That's not necessary."

He looks into my eyes. "A rape kit is necessary."

Oh, I'm going to the hospital. I need to be tested for STDs. And get a morning-after pill. And do all the things I never thought I'd have to think about, much less do. "I know. I'll go."

"I'll go with you."

I shake my head. He's already seen enough of my shame.

"I can't walk away and leave you like this."

There's a quick knock on the door, and he calls out, "Who's there?"

"It's Rachel," says a muffled voice. My soul cries out for her. I nod, and he opens the door. She rushes in and stops short. Her face contorts, but she bites it back quickly when she sees a tear roll down my face. "What happened?" she croons. She wraps her arms around me and pulls me in tight. I sob into her shoulder as she holds me. I look up at him through the curtain of her hair and see that he's blinking furiously. He sniffles and straightens his spine when he sees me looking at him.

"She needs to go to the hospital," he says quietly.

"I'll take her." She looks around. "How can we get her out of here without everyone seeing her?" she asks.

He pulls his hoodie over his head and walks over to me. He bunches it up like he wants to put it over my head, but he asks for permission to do it with his eyes. I nod, and he drops it over me, and his scent wraps around me. It's like citrus and woodsy outdoor smells combined. It wraps me up and holds me close, still warm from his body. I tug it down around my hips. Rachel wets a corner of the towel he gave me earlier and wipes beneath my eyes. "You have scratches on your face," she says. Then she sees my neck. "Did he choke you?" she gasps. But she quickly recovers. I cover my neck with my hand. That's not the worst he did.

A growl starts low in Peter's belly, but I can hear it. He's angry for me. "Thank you," I whisper to him as she leads me to the door, her hand holding tightly to mine.

"Can I come with you?" he asks.

Rachel looks at me for confirmation, but I shake my head.

"Can I at least check on you later?" he asks. "How can I find you again?"

"We need to go," Rachel says.

He follows us down the hallway and through the noisy kitchen and the even noisier living room. He shields my body with the width of his and opens the door for us so we can walk in front of him. Rachel's hand is in mine, but I feel the need to reach for his, because he represents strength for me. "Thank you, Peter Reed," I whisper.

"You're welcome," he whispers back. He opens the car door for me, and I gingerly sit down. I'm sore so I hiss. He stiffens. "Are you sure I can't go?"

I nod. I lay my head back and close my eyes. And let Rachel drive me to the hospital.

A shriek jerks me from my memories. I watch as a blond man walks out of the front of the jail, and the girl who was with the three men launches herself at Peter Reed. I know it's him. I haven't seen him since that night, but I am completely sure that my savior just walked out of the prison.

A knock sounds on the passenger window, and I jump. I look over at my dad, who makes a face at me through the glass. I unlock the door, and he gets in. He looks at the scene in front of us. "Are you happy now?" he asks.

My dad's an attorney, and he took over Pete's legal needs when I found out where he was. I went looking for him a few weeks after the attack. I asked around campus until I finally found someone who knew one of his brothers. Pete was in jail for a foolish mistake. So, I asked my dad to help him. He's been working to have him freed ever since.

My dad's well known in this town for his work with the youth detention program, and he does a lot of pro bono work for people who can't afford representation. Dad found out that Pete had legal counsel that someone else set up for him, so he asked to assist in the case. Pete still had to go to jail, but he got a much lighter sentence because of Dad's help. Pete doesn't deserve to be in jail. He deserves to be given a medal of honor.

I look at Dad and smile. "Yes, I'm happy now. Did you get to ask him about coming to the farm?" I ask it very shyly because my dad reads me like I'm a book.

He nods.

"And?" My insides are flipping around, and my heart is racing.

"He's coming."

I lay a hand on my chest and force myself to take a deep breath.

"What do you hope to get out of seeing this boy?" Dad asks.

"I just want to thank him, Dad."

Dad grins and rolls his eyes. "I was thinking you might want to have his babies."

I snort. "Not yet."

I'll see Pete tomorrow. I can't wait.

"Hey, kid," he says softly. "He's been in jail two years. He may be a little harder than that boy you met that night so long ago."

Dad talks about it like it happened years ago. But it happens again and again in my head, every single night.

"He still saved me, Dad," I say quietly.

Pete

I don't want to be back here. I didn't miss jail at all last night. Not for a minute. And I don't plan to be on the wrong side the bars again. Ever. But here I am, back where I never wanted to be. I'm outside the prison but still… I'm wearing jeans, sneakers, a T-shirt, and a tracking bracelet on my ankle. The boys standing in line are still in prison garb. They haven't been officially released from the youth program yet, but this volunteer program is their first step toward that.

Doors open in front of me, and I step onto the bus, sliding into the front seat, pushing myself close to the window. I put my backpack with my meager belongings in it on the seat next to me, hoping the bus isn't so crowded that someone has to sit with me.

A young man behind me sits forward in his seat. "You going to the farm, too?" he asks. His breath smells like he's been eating the ass end out of a mule.

"Dude, sit back," I grumble. I admit it. I'm a little hungover.

He leans back, and I lay the back of my head against the window and stretch my legs along the length of the seat. But then his nose pops up near the crack between the seat and the window, right by my face. "You're going to the farm, right?" He breathes heavily right by my ear. And it was two mules. Not just one ass that he ate. Good God, somebody better get him a Tic Tac. I reach into my backpack and pull out a roll of breath mints and pass him one. He pops it into his mouth and smiles.

"Yeah, I'm going to the farm," I say quietly.

"Me, too. Cool, isn't it?" He grins. He's even younger than me. I'd guess he's eighteen, compared to my twenty-one.

"Yeah, cool," I mutter.

"What were you in for?"

They know I was in prison? For some reason, I thought I was coming as a mentor of sorts. Not as an ex-con.

"Lie back and get some sleep," I say, closing my eyes.

I really want to know what the kid was in for, but I would never ask. That would just be rude.

"I killed somebody," he says. I open my eyes and see that he's smiling. His eyes are a little maniacal, and they bounce from one place to another.

"Sure you did," I mutter, but fuck it all… Now I'm intrigued.

"No, really," he says. He's suddenly excited, and he rubs his hands together. "Deader than a doornail." He holds up his finger like it's a gun and points it, then makes a *pfewww* sound with his mouth.

"Mmm hmm," I hum, closing my eyes again.

"Have you been there before?" he asks. He's kind of like a puppy. A puppy that can kill people. Maybe a cocker spaniel. Those always were fucked-up little dogs. My neighbor, Mrs. Connelly, had one, and I used to walk it. That thing would bite you as quickly as it would look at you.

"Where?" I ask.

"The farm," he says, getting all excited again. I hear him moving in his seat like he can't sit still.

It's actually called Cast-A-Way Farms, based on the brochures I saw yesterday. I force my eyes open. "No. Never been."

"Me, neither. But I know someone who went last year. He said it was nice. Except for the sick kids and the ones who are retarded."

I fucking hate that word. "They're not retarded," I say. "They're deaf. And some have MS. And some have autism. And lot of other things that make them special. But they're not retarded." I fucking hate labels. My brother, Logan, the one who is deaf, has been called more names than I can count.

"Oh, okay," he says. He nods. "Okay." He repeats himself.

"Don't use that word again," I warn.

"Okay," he says. He nods, his head bobbing like a dashboard dog.

The bus driver gets on the bus, and my parole officer enters, carrying his clipboard. He sits down in the seat opposite me and flips through his paperwork. He's big and beefy, and he's packing. He's dressed in a V-necked shirt that stretches tight across his shoulders and khaki pants. He looks over at me, and his eyebrows draw together. "You Reed?" he asks.

I open my eyes. "Yes, sir," I say. We actually met at the prison, but he must not remember.

"How'd you score this program?" he asks.

I shrug. "No idea." I have a good idea it had something to do with Mr. Caster, but I don't know what happened. He acts like this is an honor or something.

My parole officer's brows pucker again, and he reaches for his clipboard. "You're the one whose brother is deaf."

I glare at him. "Yep."

He nods and sets his clipboard to the side. "There will be a few hearing-impaired kids at the camp. And there's one boy who has MS and has a tracheostomy tube, so he can't talk. You'll be working with him as a translator."

I nod. "Sounds good."

"How long have you been signing?" he asks.

My brother lost his hearing when he was thirteen, and that was ten years ago. "About ten years?" I say. I'm not completely sure. I've been signing so long that I don't even realize I'm doing it most of the time.

He turns so that his knees are facing me. "What were you in for?" he asks quietly.

I nod toward his clipboard. "You already know," I say. I close my eyes again.

He grabs my foot and shakes it. I jerk my leg back. That's something one of my brothers would do. "I'd rather you tell me."

"Possession with intent," I say quietly. I really don't want Tic Tac behind me to hear me.

He extends a hand to me. "My name's Phil," he says.

I grip his hand in mine. "Pete."

"You're not going to be any trouble, are you, Pete?" he asks.

"No, sir," I reply. No trouble at all. I want to go home when this over.

He nods. "Fair enough. I may need for you to help me with some of the younger kids." He jerks a thumb toward the back of the bus.

I nod. I'm the oldest one here, aside from Phil.

Phil gets up and sits down across from Tic Tac and goes through the same drill. I see him do it with everyone. There are about ten young men on the bus, all under the age of eighteen, if I had to guess. There's one younger boy who doesn't look older than sixteen.

I heave a sigh and close my eyes. I cross my arms over my chest and try to sleep. If I'm correct, we have a few hours to go until we get to Cast-A-Way Farms.

Reagan

The pool is wonderful. It's too bad it's surrounded by assholes. I squeal and cover my head when another one jumps into the water right beside me, drenching me with his splashing despite the fact that I specifically said I didn't want to get wet. I have somewhere to be when I leave here.

Chase pops his head up out of the water and rests on his elbows right beside my head, his nose almost touching mine. "Didn't get you wet, did I?" he asks. He looks at me just long enough to make me uncomfortable. Or make me want to punch him in the nose. I shrug to myself. Whichever comes first. He has been dropping these sexy hints ever since I went out to dinner with him two weeks ago. If I could do it with anyone, it wouldn't be Chase Gerald. Besides, he doesn't know what happened to me my first semester at college. Nobody knows about it except for my family, Peter Reed, Rachel, and the man who turned me off sex forever.

I want to tell Chase to fuck off, to tell him that he can just stop trying because I'm never going to be the easy girl who will fall into bed with him. But I can't tell him I was raped because then he'll look at me with pity. That's the last thing I want.

I pretend like I didn't hear his comment about getting wet. The type of wet he's talking about isn't even in my vocabulary. Chase grunts and pulls himself from the water. I don't know why I invited him over. He brought his buddies, and I don't know which one of them gives me the creeps more. Even worse, they brought their girlfriends. These are the same girls who look at my little brother like he's some kind of carnival sideshow.

Chase stands over me and shakes the water from his hair. His kneecap is directly beside my head. With a leg swipe, I could take him out...

His eyes narrow, and I hear the rumble of a bus coming up the driveway. I stand up and grab my towel, dry off really quickly, and then I pull my clothes on over my bathing suit. "Sorry, Chase. I have to go."

"Are those the camp kids?" he asks.

I twist my hair up into a messy ponytail.

"Yep." This is my favorite part of the summer. My dad has been holding his camps here since my brother was three, when we realized there wasn't a safe place to send him to camp where he could be who he is— a normal little boy with autism.

The first year we did it, we invited only kids with autism. Through the years, it's grown. Now we have kids with challenges like Down syndrome, autism, processing disorders, and this year there's even a group of young boys coming who are deaf. I'm excited. These boys need me. And they don't threaten me. I don't have nightmares about them hurting me... Not like the others.

"Is that a prison van?" Chase asks.

"Yep," I say.

Every year, my dad invites young men from the local youth detention center to come and volunteer at the camp. They're not violent young men and are screened carefully, and they'll come with their own director. But they all do have a criminal history. They get community service hours at the camp.

"Are you sure that's safe?" Chase asks.

"Yep," I say. I'd be more worried about Chase than I would them. "You guys can see yourselves out, right?" I ask over my shoulder, not really caring about their responses.

I step into my flip-flops when I get to the gate, and I see my dad coming toward me. "You ready to go meet the new campers?" he asks, dropping his arm around my shoulders. He's one of very few people I allow to touch me. If anybody else grabbed me like he does, I would have to take him out. Dad smiles at me and kisses my forehead.

My mom comes around the corner of the house and catches up with us, and she has my brother Lincoln in tow. Link doesn't like to hold hands with anyone, and he rarely looks anyone in the eye, but he looks like your average kid in every other way. Only he's not average. He has autism. He speaks when he wants to speak, and when he doesn't... Well, there's not much of a chance of getting anything out of him. We've had a lot of kids with autism at the camp, and they all have different challenges, and not one is like another. I hold out my hand for Link to give me five. He grins in that sideways way he does, and it still makes my heart turn over even after all these years.

"The prison bus is here," my mom warns.

"I'll go talk to them," my dad says. "You go unload the kids and help them get settled."

I really want to go find Pete, but instead I have to help settle kids into their cabins. Some of them have caregivers. Some of them don't. Some of them have a parent with them. The ones who don't will have a camp counselor assigned to their care. They'll sleep with the boys and hang out with the boys and make sure they eat, drink, take their meds, and shower. The counselors are all from the local hospital. Some are medical students. The youth offenders won't be responsible for the kids' needs at all. They'll interact with them but in a very small way.

My mom gives me a clipboard, and we pin color-coded name tags to all their shirts so we will know who the nonverbal ones are at all times. I read through the descriptions, see what their challenges are, and make notes in my head about each of their special needs.

The boys are always fun. We had girls here last month, and the girls are more of a challenge. They always have drama. Boys are just boys, and they want to ride the horses and swim in the pool and have a good time. They want to be boys in the most basic sense of the word. And this is where they can do it.

When the kids are all settled, I go to find my dad. He's sitting on the top of a picnic table with his elbows on his knees, his hands dangling down between his thighs. He's giving them the speech I've heard every year since I was eleven.

"You've been given a lot of responsibility, and I just hope you're up to it," he says. He holds up a single finger. I stand behind a tree and smile because I know this part of the speech. "I have one rule," he says. "If you break it, I'll send you back to the center immediately."

The young men all look at him with expectant faces. "My daughter is home for the summer from college. If you touch her, if you look at her, if you talk to her, if you think inappropriate thoughts about her, I will chop your nuts off while you sleep." He picks up a hatchet he had on the picnic table for dramatic effect and slams it into the wood. He waits for a minute, and I see the young men all ball into themselves. I cover my mouth to hold in a laugh. It's always the same routine. He threatens, and then they spend the week avoiding me.

I stand there a little longer, until I feel like he's done, and then I get ready to go talk to my dad. He's with the parole officer so I wait. I turn and lift my foot to take a step, but the tip of my flip-flop gets caught on a tree root and I trip, my hands flailing as I careen toward the ground. But before it happens, strong arms catch me, and I tumble into something solid.

I roll over and look down. I brush my hair back from my face. I'm lying halfway across Pete, and he's holding his hands out to the side to keep from touching me. I scamper to roll off him.

"Shit," he grunts as he lumbers to his feet. "Ten bucks says you're the daughter."

I close my eyes for a second and try to control my breaths. I have wanted to talk to this man for almost two and a half years. But he looks at me like he doesn't know me.

"And there go my nuts."

My gaze slices to meet his. His eyes twinkle.

He jerks his thumb toward my father. "He was serious about the hatchet, wasn't he?"

He looks so worried that I feel a bubble of laughter building within me, replacing the hurt that came with him not recognizing me. "'Fraid so," I say, biting back a grin.

"Figures," he mumbles, and he walks toward his cabin, shaking his head. I watch him walk away. He doesn't remember me.

Pete

Reagan. Damn, she's pretty. Then again, she's the first girl I've had my hands on in almost two years. She lay there on top of me for a second, looking down at me, and I immediately knew who she was. I'll never forget her. But the last time we met…it wasn't a good night for her. And she would probably be uncomfortable if I brought it up. I don't want to get sent back to the city. I want to be here. I want to work with these kids. I want to have this damn tracking bracelet off my leg so I can go back to some semblance of a normal life. I just want to be Pete.

I wish the fuck I knew who Pete is. I had a pretty good idea of what my life would be like until my brother Matt got sick. Then things got all fucked up.

Then I did what I did and ended up in jail. It was all my fault, and I take full responsibility for it, but that doesn't mean it doesn't suck ass.

She has green eyes and the same freckles I remember across the bridge of her nose. Shit. I can't even think about things like that. If I were at home, I would ask her out to dinner. I would tell her about how I know her. I would find out if she's all right. Then I would ask her out on a date. But here, I'm nothing. Nothing but a man who would get his nuts chopped off for talking to her. I have no doubts that her father was serious. Dead serious. I adjust my junk and keep moving.

But then she looks over at me, glancing over her shoulder. Her face colors, and my heart starts to do a little pitter-patter in my chest. I'm an ex-con who's still on house arrest, and she's looking at me like I'm a real live man? She licks her lips and turns away to talk to someone else. I want her to look at me again.

Her blond hair is damp, and it's tangled up into a messy knot on top of her head. She's not wearing any makeup. The women I know paint their faces until they're almost unrecognizable when they get out of the shower. This one is all natural. And I like it. I shouldn't. But I do. I could look at her all day.

There was a second when she fell on top of me that she looked fearful. Was that because of what happened to her? Does she even remember me?

But then a motorized wheelchair zips toward me. "Hold on there, Speedy Gonzales," I say, stepping in front of him. "Where are you going in such a hurry?"

The young man is blond and fair, and he has a piece of plastic sticking out of his neck. He signs to me, but his movements are jerky and off balance. They're not fluid like sign language usually is. *Marshmallows*, he spells with his fingers. He jerks his crooked finger toward where someone is lighting a campfire.

I wonder if this is the boy I'm supposed to work with. An older woman runs up behind him, her breaths heaving from her. "Sorry," she pants, clutching her side. "He's hard to keep up with in that chair." She extends a hand. "I'm Andrea. And this is my son, Karl. Karl's excited to be a camper this year." I shake hands with her and drop down in front of Karl.

"You can hear, right, Karl?" I ask, signing to him. He nods and smiles, but it's jerky and crooked. He's so damn excited he can barely sit still in his chair.

I can hear, he signs. *I just can't talk.*

I nod. I get it. "How old are you?" I ask.

Fifteen. He looks around me toward the campfire. I think he really wants to get to where the other kids are congregating.

"Such a lovely age," his mother says, rolling her eyes.

He's fifteen? He can't weigh more than a hundred pounds. I step out of his way. "Go get 'em, Gonzales," I say, nodding my head toward the fire. He grins and rolls away from me, stopping beside where Reagan is now setting up chairs by the fire.

"I think he already has a crush on Reagan," she admits.

"Reagan?" I ask. My Reagan?

Reagan stirs up more emotion in me than I know what to do with. I shake it away, and I look at Gonzo's mom. "Can you tell me a little about his challenges so I know what I'm working with?" I ask.

"Not *what* you're working with," she corrects. "*Who* you're working with."

"That wasn't what I meant," I start.

She lays a hand on my arm. "Where did you learn to sign?"

"My brother is deaf," I say. She nods, taking in my tattoos and my piercings, which I couldn't even get back in after I got out of jail. I had to get re-pierced last night, and they're still sore. At least I don't feel naked anymore. "I didn't mean to insult your son," I say. Now I feel bad.

"Karl's only limitations are that he's in a body that doesn't do what he wants it to do, and that he can't speak." She looks at him across the clearing, her eyes full of love for her son. And exhaustion. "He still has all the desires and urges of a fifteen-year-old boy. There are just some things he can't do." She heaves a sigh. "He gets frustrated easily. That's the hardest thing for him. His mind is sound, and his body just won't cooperate."

I nod. I know what it feels like to be out of control. "Why don't you take a break for a half hour or so?" I say. "I'll go hang with Karl."

Her eyes widen, and she looks so excited that I wish I'd made the offer as soon as they arrived. "Really?" she asks.

I nod. "Have fun. I'll take care of him."

Tears fill her eyes, and I realize how much this woman desperately needs a break.

"I'll see you in thirty," I say.

She nods and walks toward her cabin. She's tired, and I can tell.

I walk to the campfire. The sun has just barely set, and there are only a few kids out here. "Hey, Gonzo," I say to Karl. He turns around and looks at me, his grin big and goofy and so fucking adorable that I already love this kid. "You giving Reagan a hard time?" I drop down to sit on a log that rims the fire.

She's really pretty, he signs. He looks up at her, blinking his blue eyes, his face tilted toward hers. She smiles at him.

"What did he say?" she asks.

"He says you're really pretty," I translate.

He throws up his hands in protest. *You're not supposed to tell her!*

Sorry, dude, I sign back, trying not to grin. *If you're going to talk about her, I'm going to have to tell her what you say.* I grab his shoulder and squeeze. This is a rule my brothers came up with, and we always stand by it. You don't get to use sign language to talk about people. It's for communication. *So, unless you want her to know it, you better keep it to yourself.*

Traitor, he signs. But he's grinning.

Reagan blushes, but she says, "Thank you, Karl. I think you're kind of cute, too."

I've never seen a kid grin quite so big. She looks down at him. "Do you want to go with me to find some sticks for the fire?"

He nods, and he's already moving before she's even ready to go.

"You think we should bring your mouthpiece?" she asks, nodding her head toward me.

He signs to me. *I got this. You stay here.* He waggles his eyebrows at me.

Not a chance, dumbass, I say back. He laughs. It's the first sound I've heard him make. *She's too old for you.*

Maybe she likes younger men.

I look around like I've lost something. *I don't see any other men here. I see a pretty lady and a boy who's hoping to get some action.*

He grins and nods.

I laugh. *She's too old for you. So lay off. We'll find you a different one. One more your speed.*

My speed is faster than you think.

Apparently.

She turns back from where she's been walking in front of us. "Are you talking about my ass?" she asks. She doesn't even crack a smile.

Gonzo points to me as if to say, "He was."

She laughs and blushes again.

Traitor, I sign when she turns back around.

He laughs, jumping in his chair a little.

Now all I can do is stare at her ass. She's cute. Like a fairy princess walking in the woods, picking up sticks. When her arms are full, she looks at Gonzo and says, "Can you be my hero and carry these back?"

He nods and lets her fill his lap up with sticks. He turns to take them to the fire and leaves us standing there, gathering more of them. "Hurry back," I call to him. He turns back and signs, *Hands off my girl.*

I hold my hands out to the side and then give him a thumbs-up.

She turns to me and extends her hand. "I'm Reagan."

She doesn't remember me. Should I even remind her? She probably works hard on a daily basis to forget that night.

I take her hand in mine and heat shoots straight through me. And it's not because it's been two years since I've had a woman in my arms. There's something about this girl. She jerks her hand back and looks into my eyes. I want to ask her if she felt that. She wipes her hands on her jeans, and I realize she was just pulling back because my hands are sweaty. I'm an idiot.

"Pete," I say.

"Why do you call him Gonzo?" she asks.

"Why not?" I continue to pick up sticks.

"He's a sweet boy," she says.

"He's a hormone on wheels," I correct.

She laughs. "At least you see him as a normal young man. Most people see the chair." She shakes her head and looks up at me. I feel like she's looking directly into my soul. "What makes you different?" she asks.

You mean aside from my tats, piercings, and the fact that I came from prison? I shrug. I look in his direction. He's already on his way back. "I just see a boy who wants to be treated like one." I call to him when he gets close. "Hey Gonzo," I say. "Can you take some more?" He grins and nods. We load him up, and he leaves again. I turn to her. "So, what makes you different, Reagan?" I ask. I want to touch her, but I don't dare. So, I just look at her instead. I watch her lips and wait for her to explain the meaning of life to me.

Reagan

He has the bluest eyes I've ever seen. It's a little distracting because his piercings draw your attention away from his eyes and then you have to find your way back. He has tattoos all the way up his arms, from his wrists to where his T-shirt breaks up the designs. Then they start again and go all the way up his neck. He's broad and tall, and he's a little intimidating. But he's not, all at the same time. He saw me at my most vulnerable point, and he did exactly what I needed.

"I don't think I'm different," I say. "I'm just like every one of those kids." She nods toward the cabins. "No better. No worse. Same fears. Same drives." I shrug.

He nods slowly and starts to pick up sticks again. He has a tattoo on the back of his neck. The words *Sam* is written in gothic, chunky letters.

"Is Sam your girlfriend?" I blurt out. I immediately want to bite the words back, but they're already out there.

"Sam?" he asks.

I rub the back of my neck, then point to his. "The tattoo."

He smiles. "Oh, that."

But he doesn't elaborate. I feel like a dummy for even asking the first time. I'm not going to ask again.

"So, you're home from college?" he asks. I can't believe he doesn't remember me.

I nod.

"Where do you go?" he asks. He looks at me, waiting for my answer. And I don't think I've ever had this much attention from a man that I actually want to talk to. He really cares about what I say. Or at least he wants me to think he does.

"NYU," I reply. "Junior this year."

"My brother goes to NYU." He smiles. "Logan Reed?" he asks. But it's a big school. The chance of me knowing his brother is small. But I know about all his brothers because I asked a lot of questions when I was looking for him.

I shake my head.

"He's deaf."

I shake my head again. The only time I have seen him was outside the prison yesterday, never at school.

"All tatted up, like me." He looks down at his arms, and I take the opportunity to look at his tattoos.

"Can I see?" I ask. I don't want to be rude, but I really want to look at him. I don't want to touch him, but I want to look.

He grins. "You can look, but you can't touch," he teases. It's like he read my mind. My heart starts to thud. I'm the last person he has to worry about touching him. "Because I like my nuts exactly as they're hanging."

My face floods with heat, but I don't let the opportunity to study the drawings on his skin pass me by. I look at the cross that has the word *Mom* written inside it. "What's this one for?" I ask.

"My mom died a few years ago."

He also has the word *Dad* with wings attached. "Your dad died too?" I ask.

"He left after our mom died." He stills. He's suddenly tense, and I hate that I asked.

"I'm sorry," I say.

"I don't want your sympathy, princess," he says.

I snort. "Princess?"

He nods, his gaze lingering on my eyes, then my lips. He licks his and draws his lip ring into his mouth to play with it with his tongue. "Princess," he says slowly.

"You couldn't be further from the truth," I say. He has me pegged all wrong.

"I doubt it." He looks at me for a minute too long. My stomach flips.

Suddenly, I hear the crash of boots stomping through the woods. I look up and see my dad walking toward us, a scowl on his face, and he has the hatchet in his hand. Pete immediately crosses his hands in front of his lap and steps away from me.

"Go help with dinner," Dad snaps at me. He glares at Pete.

"Yes, sir," I say. I take the sticks Pete has in his arms and smile at him. "See you later," I whisper.

"Don't go," he whispers back. "Who's going to protect my nuts?"

"Princesses don't do that." I grin at him and walk away. It's hard to do, but I don't even look back over my shoulder.

Pete

Shit. Now I'm in trouble.

"You had one rule," Reagan's dad snaps. He holds up a finger. "One rule!"

"Yes, sir," I say. "I remember."

I won't be surprised at all if fire shoots from his mouth and his eyeballs pop out. "If you remember, then why were you alone in the woods with my daughter, Mr. Reed?" he asks. He's really close to being in my face. But my brothers have done worse. This is nothing compared to when they try to throttle me.

"Pete," I say.

"Beg your pardon?" He glares at me.

"My name is Pete," I say. "We should probably be on a first name basis if you're going to get intimate enough to chop my nuts off." I motion to his hatchet.

He blows out a quick breath, grins, and shakes his head.

"We were just gathering sticks, sir," I say.

He narrows his eyes and glares at me. "Can I trust you?" he asks.

"I want to go home when I'm done here, sir," I say. I want this fucking bracelet off my leg.

"Nice manners," he mutters. "Who raised you?" he asks. "The system?"

"No, sir," I say. "I have four brothers."

"Where are your parents?"

"Gone."

"I know your story, but why'd you end up in jail?" He's blunt. I kind of like that.

"Stupid choices I made." I kick at a rock in my path to keep from having to look at him.

He nods. "At least you know they were stupid."

I heave a sigh. "Sir, I've done my time. Don't send me back. I promise I won't bother your daughter, and I won't let anyone else bother her, either."

He looks into my eyes. "I believe you." He starts to tug on a leaf hanging near his head. "My daughter…she's special."

I don't respond because I don't really think he wants me to. I agree with him, though. She's too fucking special for someone like me.

He motions for me to follow him. He walks back toward the fire, where Reagan is sitting on a log beside Gonzo's chair. He's looking at her like she's the first girl he ever laid eyes on and she's looking back at him like he's a real fifteen-year-old. I mean, he is a real fifteen-year-old, but I doubt he gets treated like one very often. She looks up at her dad and smiles. "Dad, this is Gonzo," she says. She grins, but Karl doesn't correct her. I think he likes the nickname.

Her dad extends his hand, and Gonzo reaches out to shake. I don't think the kid gets this often, either. He looks almost honored, and I realize right then and there that I will do whatever it takes during camp to make sure he has a good time. He deserves it. Five days to be a normal boy.

"Reagan," her dad says, cupping the back of her head in his big hand. She looks up him expectantly. "You met Pete?"

She nods and nibbles on her lower lip. "Briefly."

"Don't let me catch you in the woods with him again," he says.

"Dad," she complains.

"And don't go into the woods with Gonzo, either. He looks even more dangerous than Pete." Her dad scowls.

Gonzo grins.

Her dad points a finger at him. "Do you hear me, young man?" he asks. "Hands off my daughter." He leans down and kisses her forehead. "I know she's pretty, but she's off-limits." He points at me and back to Gonzo, going back and forth a few times. "I got my eyes on you two."

"Yes, sir," I say, trying to look serious.

Her dad walks away. I sit down on the log beside her and stare into the flames. The sun has completely set, and the golden purples have faded into a dark sky filled with stars. "You want a marshmallow?" Reagan asks.

"I'm a city boy. We don't roast marshmallows." I shake my head.

"Gonzo?" she asks. He nods and rubs his chest to say *please* in sign language.

"He said please," I tell her. He grins.

She puts a marshmallow on a stick for him and holds it out so he can grip it. His chair keeps him from getting too close, and his stick isn't long enough. He visibly deflates. So I take two sticks and bend them together, making one long one. I pass it back to him. "Do you want me to do it for you?" she asks.

He shakes his head. *I can do it.*

I lay my head back and look up at the stars. But then another group of kids arrives, and some of them are deaf. I'm busy for the next hour, just trying to translate for them all. The time flies, and it's later than I thought it was. "Gonzo, you're going to turn into a marshmallow if you eat one more," I warn. Either that or he's going to be sick.

One more? he asks, holding up one finger.

"If you get sick, I'm not cleaning it up," I warn with a laugh. Reagan threads another marshmallow onto his stick. He refused to give it up, even when other kids were waiting to toast marshmallows. I didn't have the heart to take it from him.

The rest of the kids have gone to bed. Gonzo is one of the oldest ones here. I see his mom walking up from the shadows. She came to check on him after the half hour was up, but he was having so much fun that I sent her away for a little longer. Her hair is now down, and her face is soft. She has her hands stuffed in her pockets. It's getting chilly out. "You about ready for bed, Karl?" she asks.

G-O-N-Z-O, he signs. I laugh and shake my head.

"Oh, it's Gonzo now, is it?" She punches her hands into her hips. "You have a perfectly good name. I don't know why you would want to be called that."

I punch him in the shoulder. "Dude, that was our secret." I sign to him. *You're not supposed to tell your mother everything.* I hold up my hands as though to say, *what the heck.* I know full well that his mother knows sign language.

He laughs. *Thank you for tonight.* He looks directly into my eyes. He's kind of jumpy the rest of the time, but right now, he's telling me something without even using words or sign language, and he's so still and serious.

I look at Reagan. "He said thank you for tonight."

She smiles and nods. "You're welcome."

He points at me. *Don't make out with my girl when I leave.*

I hold my hands up. "I promise not to try to make out with Reagan after you leave. I'll only put the moves on her when you're here."

Traitor, he signs.

"Dude, I warned you." But I laugh. Reagan ducks her head and doesn't meet anyone's gaze.

"Good night, you two," his mom says. Gonzo waves and speeds off behind her.

"You're really good with him," Reagan says quietly.

"He's easy to like."

She picks up the stick he left and feeds a marshmallow onto it. She holds it out to me. "Here you go, city boy. Your first marshmallow roasting."

"Well, I'll be damned," I say, taking the stick from her. "You got one of my firsts."

She freezes.

Shit. I made a mistake. "I was just kidding," I rush to say. I'm watching her face, and she looks everywhere but at me in the firelight. "I shouldn't have said that. Out loud."

I haven't stuck the marshmallow in the flames yet. She reaches out tentatively and wraps her hand around mine. She turns her wrist and moves my hand closer to the flames. "Like this," she whispers. She's trembling, but she doesn't let go.

"Are you okay?" I ask softly.

She smiles at me in the darkness. "I'm fine."

I draw in a breath. I don't know how to ask. "No," I say. She looks at me. "After that night. Are you okay after what happened that night?"

She stiffens beside me. "You do remember me," she whispers.

"I think about you all the time, wondering what happened that night after you left."

She exhales slowly, like she's fortifying herself. "Thank you for what you did."

"You're welcome." I don't need her thanks, but I feel like she's been waiting to tell me this. I watch as the marshmallow roasts, its creamy skin turning brown. A purple flame engulfs it, and she jerks our hands back, raising the marshmallow toward her lips so she can blow out the fire.

Her lips purse and she blows, and I feel it deep in the center of me. I want to kiss her so bad that I can already taste her. "I know I don't know you, but I feel like I do. After that night, I feel like you're a part of me." My words are so foolish that I bite back any further stupidity that might fall from my lips.

"I feel the same way," she says. "I don't know if that makes you feel any more normal."

At least I'm not alone in my thoughts. "I would give just about anything to kiss you right now," I say softly. Shit. Did I say that out loud, too?

She smiles, but she still doesn't look at me. She seems almost...regretful? "I would give just about anything for you not to," she says quietly. She leans the stick so that the marshmallow is closest to me.

She may as well have punched me in the gut. It's been two and a half years. "You haven't let him steal everything from you, have you?" I hope she hasn't. If she has, he wins. He raped her, and he took even more than that.

"I looked for you after that night," she says.

"I asked my brothers to check up on you, when I went to prison," I admit. I look into her eyes when they shoot up to meet mine. "Not in like a creepy stalkery way."

She laughs. "You going to eat that?" she asks, nodding toward the marshmallow.

"It's burned." She doesn't want to talk about that night, and that's all right with me.

"Some people like them like that." I watched enough kids eat charred marshmallows to know she's telling the truth. "If you're not going to eat it, I am." She raises an eyebrow at me.

"Go for it, princess," I say. She pulls it from the stick, peels off half the outer coating, and passes the rest to me. She talks around the hot goo.

"Try it," she says.

I'd do just about anything she asked me to do right now.

I eat the marshmallow. "I don't understand why people like these things. That wasn't that great."

"Tomorrow night, we'll make s'mores." She rubs her hands together like she's excited.

"What the fuck's a s'more?" I ask.

She laughs, throwing her head back. Her hair falls down her back, and I want to gather it up and wrap it around my hand to see if it's as soft as it looks. "A s'more is a cooked marshmallow, a square of chocolate, and a graham cracker, pressed together to make a sandwich."

"Anything is better with chocolate," I say. My mom used to say that. I don't know why I felt the need to make that comment out loud.

"True." She doesn't speak.

We're quiet, the crackling flames the only sound aside from crickets and the occasional kid crying out to ask caregivers questions. Before, when I was with girls, it was all about trying to get them out of their clothes. It's been two years since a woman has taken me inside her, and right this second, I can't imagine enjoying that any more than what I'm doing right now.

"I'm sorry if I made you uncomfortable asking for a kiss," I finally say.

She snorts. "At least you asked."

"Glad you like that because I might keep asking until I get one." She laughs as she shakes her head.

"You promised Gonzo you'd only put the moves on me when he's around."

"Let's go wake him up, then." I make like I'm going to get up, and she reaches for my hand to stop me. I feel that tremble again. I sit down, but this time, I'm a little closer to her.

She's quiet for a moment. "This is nice," she says.

I reach up to tuck a lock of her hair behind her ear, and she flinches. "Do I scare you?" I ask. I did just get out of prison. But it's more than that, I'm sure. With what happened to her, she probably has a lot of intense shit in her head.

She shakes her head. "No. You wouldn't hurt me."

She picks up a stick and starts to draw in the dirt, her arm clenched around her knees until she's folded into a ball.

She looks up, her green eyes bright in the firelight. "I just don't like to be touched." She shrugs. "That's all."

"Can we work to get around that, princess?" It comes out more like a whisper.

Her eyes fill up with tears, and she blinks them back furiously. I want to touch her, but I have a feeling that would be the wrong thing to do.

"It's me," she says. "Not you." She waits a beat. "I'm sure you're a perfectly amazing kisser. And I'm missing out on one of the best experiences ever." She lays a hand on her chest. She's teasing me now. This is better than a moment before. It's easier to deal with. But I almost long for the quiet, emotion-filled whispers. "You've kissed a lot of women?" she asks.

Ouch. I'm sure she doesn't want the truth. "A few."

"A few hundred? A few thousand?" She laughs. It's a tinny, hollow sound.

"A few," I repeat.

"Does it get more common feeling after a while? Like your heart stops feeling like it's going to beat out of your chest after you've done it a few thousand times?"

I chuckle. "Not if you're doing it right." I adjust my body, hunching over my lap a little. Her whispered words and heat-filled glances are affecting me, and I'll be damned if I want her to see it. "You feel like yours is going to beat out of our chest when you kiss a man?"

She shakes her head. "No."

"Then why are you asking?" I ask.

"I feel like that now," she says. She gets up, and I want to grab her and pull her to me. "I had better get to bed." She stretches, and I can see the little strip of skin between the bottom of her shirt and her jeans. I reach up and tug her shirt down. She covers her belly with her hand, like she wants to block my touch.

She stares into my eyes. She doesn't say a word. "Can I kiss you yet?" I blurt out. God, you'd think I'd never seen a girl before.

"No." She laughs.

"Can I keep asking?"

She nods. It's a quick jerk, almost imperceptible, but she's biting her lower lip and smiling. "Good night," she says.

"Good night," I call to her retreating back. She walks into the darkness until it swallows her up.

Reagan

My knees are still wobbly when I get to the house. I go in the kitchen door and find my parents sitting at the table with cups of coffee. They're talking quietly.

"Have fun?" my mom asks. She stares at me over the rim of her coffee cup. She looks a lot like me, with her dark-blond hair and her sun-kissed skin. My dad says she looked just like me when they met. Her hair is completely straight like mine, and she's tall and willowy like me, even after all these years.

I nod in answer to her question. "We were roasting marshmallows."

She quirks an eyebrow at me. "That's what they're calling that now? When I was young, it was just called flirting."

Heat creeps up my face. "I wasn't flirting."

"Mmm hmm," she hums. But she's smiling.

"Let her be," my dad growls playfully.

"What's his name?" she asks.

I'm purposefully obtuse. "Gonzo."

My dad snorts. "Gonzo is the fifteen-year-old who was hanging out with Pete, the mentor for the boys from the detention center."

"Pete, huh?" Mom asks. Mom knows that Pete's the one who found me. "What's he like?"

I shrug.

Her eyebrows draw together. "You get any strange vibes from him?"

"Mom," I warn. "Leave it alone."

"Pete's a mentor? Or is he an ex-con?" Mom looks curiously at Dad.

Dad nods. "He's out of jail on parole."

Mom inhales quickly. Dad shoots her a look. "He didn't do anything violent, did he?" Mom asks. My heart stops. It trips over in my chest and then stops completely. I don't dare to even breathe until I hear the answer.

"I wouldn't have admitted him if he was violent," Dad says. He points to a stack of folders by his elbow. "I just finished going through his file again, to see if there's more I can do to help him." He jerks his head toward it. "Want me to give you an overview?"

I shake my head. "I don't need to." I'd much rather hear it from Pete. "He seems nice." I glare at Dad. "Even though Dad threatened to chop his nuts off."

Mom snorts into her coffee.

"Hey, it works," he says. But he's grinning.

Mom bumps my elbow. "How are things going with Chase?"

I shake my head. "He's not my type."

My dad says in a singsong voice, "But Pete's her type."

I pick up the stir stick he discarded on the table and throw it at him, but a grin tugs at my lips. "He was very nice. And I promise not to get pregnant." I get up quickly while he's still rolling that around in his head. "Good night," I chirp as I start up the stairs.

"It'd be hard for him to get you pregnant if I chop his nuts off!" Dad yells to me.

I laugh and shake my head.

I stop at the top of the stairs and listen. "They were awfully close there by the fire," Mom says. "I was watching out the window." There's a quiet pause. "Did she let him touch her?"

"No, but she touched him." He heaves a sigh. "She didn't even try to punch him in the throat."

Fine. I can be a little aggressive. It all started after my attack with some self-defense classes. Then I realized I'm really good at martial arts. I can't help if it some people make me want to drop-kick them.

"That's a start," Mom hums.

I shake my head. I'm not starting anything. He's just a man that doesn't make me want to run in the other direction. That's all he is. He's nothing more than that.

It's strange, because if I judged him based solely on his appearance, I'd be running away as fast as I could.

"He's a good kid, it looks like," Dad says on a heavy sigh. "He made a stupid mistake."

"He's kind of hot with all the tattoos," Mom says. She giggles, and I hear my dad growl. She shrieks, and I walk away. They don't need an audience for that part.

I stop by Lincoln's room on the way to mine and knock on his doorframe. "Enter," he calls, even though the door is open. He's sitting on his floor stacking blocks to make a tower. But Link's towers are not like other towers. They are complicated works of art based on numerical theories and stuff I don't understand.

"You have fun at camp today?" I ask. We were only there for setup, and camp won't truly begin until tomorrow, but he got to walk around and look at the people he'll see in the morning. I step into his room and sit gingerly on the edge of a chair.

He nods. He looks in my direction, but he doesn't make eye contact. He doesn't look people in the eye often. When he does, it's usually a mistake. And often ends in a meltdown.

"Did you meet any nice boys?"

He nods again. He only talks when he wants to.

"I love you," I say. He looks up, almost meeting my gaze. Instead, his eyes dart toward my ear.

"I love you, too," he says quietly.

Pete

The fire is hot against my legs, making them itch. I scratch, the sting of my fingernails easing some of the discomfort. I have been sitting here since she left, and it's been a little while. For a few minutes there I thought she might come back. Hell, it's probably entirely in my head; she's not interested in me. I look at the big house where she lives. It's fucking perfect. White picket fence. Acres of land. Rolling pastures. A regular Anne of Green Gables. I didn't read the book. I watched the PBS series when my mom was watching it. It came on after Sesame Street. There was nothing else to do but sit with her and watch it. My brothers gave me a hard time about it, but I didn't care.

The log I'm sitting on shakes as someone sits down beside me. My heart leaps until I realize it's just Phil. He runs a hand through his too-long hair and groans. "How's it going, Pete?" he asks.

The fire is just embers now. It's still hot, but it's not flaming. "Going okay."

"You did a good job tonight." He looks at me out of the corner of his eye.

"I didn't do anything."

"The camp actually starts tomorrow." He looks at me. "You ready?"

"I guess." I shrug and kick at a rock with my toe.

"Did I see you talking with Bob?"

I look up. "Who's that?"

He points toward the big house. "Bob Caster. The owner of the farm."

"Oh, yeah." I've never heard him called Bob. "He caught me talking to Reagan." I smile. Just the thought of her makes me grin, and I haven't laid a finger on her.

Phil whistles. "Better be careful. I've seen him take down boys a lot bigger than you."

I snort. I can't see that happening.

"You remind me of him when he was younger. He was a big, scary kid with a whole lot of attitude."

"You've known him that long?"

"Twenty-five years ago, he was you." He nods when I look at him.

"Me?"

"Straight out of prison, full of piss and vinegar, and ready for a fight. He had an attitude bigger than anybody's I ever met." He laughs. "I was his parole officer."

"Wow," I say. "What did he do to end up in prison?"

He shrugs. "Stupid mistake, just like yours."

"And I don't have an attitude," I correct. I've behaved myself pretty well. My brothers will kick my ass if I'm disrespectful. Particularly Paul.

"You have a real talent with kids. Particularly special needs kids. You ever consider social work? You could help a lot of people."

I've never really given it any thought. I've been afraid to plan a future for fear that something or someone would step in my path before I could start walking. "I don't know," I hedge.

"Think about it. You have time." He pauses for moment, but it's not uncomfortable. "What are your plans after this?" he asks.

I shrug. "Maybe college. I don't know." I got my GED behind bars, but college is expensive and we don't have much money. "I work with my brothers at the tattoo shop." I look up at the big house. A light just came on in an upstairs window. I wonder if it's Reagan's room. Phil smiles when he sees the direction of my gaze. "What's going on with Reagan?" he asks.

"Nothing." Yet.

"You like her?" He's like a dog with a bone. Going to gnaw that bitch into submission.

I shrug.

"Be careful with her, okay?" he asks.

"Why? What's wrong with her?" Does everyone know what happened to her?

"She's wary of men."

"Then she's in the perfect fucking place to stay away from them." A camp full of men and boys. That's smart.

"She's here for the kids."

"I'm here for the kids, too," I remind him.

He nods. "Just be careful."

I plan to.

He stands up and stretches.

"It feels odd, being out here," I say quietly. For two years, I've been locked in a cell. "I don't quite know what to do with myself." I look around. "Particularly with all this wide-open space."

For two years, I had no choices. I ate when people told me to eat and showered when people told me to shower. This place is the opposite of confinement, and I'm feeling a little out of sorts about it.

Phil sits back down. "Tell me what you're feeling."

"You going to pretend to be Dr. Phil now?" I bite back a snort. Something about the seriousness of his face stops my next comment.

"How are your relationships with your brothers?" he asks. I'd rather talk about the fucking feelings.

"Fine," I bite out.

"You have four, right?"

I nod. "Three older—Paul, Matt and Logan. And one my age—Sam. My twin. Except he's in college right now on a scholarship to play football, and I'm here."

"Why don't you sound bitter about that?" he asks.

Sam was with me when I got caught unloading that truck. We both were there. We took some odd jobs from a man in our neighborhood. Yeah, it was illegal, and yeah, I got caught. But Sam was with me when it went down. I told him to run. I got caught. I went to jail. And Sam didn't. Sam's playing football and living the life I wanted. "I'm not bitter at all," I grind out. It's not Sam's fault that I was also carrying a backpack full of drugs. I got busted for possession with the intent to sell. I'm going to be a felon for the rest of my life.

Phil nods. The quiet is suddenly oppressive. Not at all like it was when Reagan was out here. "Matt's the one who was sick?" he asks.

I don't like to talk about Matt. He almost died, and it took money to get him into a chemical trial. The trial saved his life, at least for now. He may need more treatment. That's why I was working with Bone, the man who owned the goods I was unloading. He's also the man who gave me the drugs to sell. He's the reason I'm here. Well, *I'm* the reason I'm here. But still. "Yeah, Matt was sick."

"How's he doing now?"

Matt writes to me every week. He tells me all the stories about my brothers and Emily, and he says he's all right. But I have no way of knowing if it was all sunshine and rainbows when I was gone. When I got home last night, things were fine. And Sam was away at college. "Better," I say.

"And the rest of them?"

"Fine." I take a deep breath because he's looking at me like he's waiting for me to tell him my life story. "Logan's getting married." A grin tugs at my lips. "I fucking love his fiancée. She's pretty damn cool. Her name is Emily, and she plays the guitar. She's good for him."

"Their lives went on without you," he says. He doesn't look at me or change his expression.

"Were they supposed to wait for me to get out before living their lives?" I ask, and I know my tone is caustic, but I can't help it.

"Were they?"

I snort. "I love them too much to ask them to do anything like that." I swallow past the lump in my throat.

"How about Sam?" he asks, his voice soft.

Just his name makes my gut twist. He's the other half of me. We've been together since we were born. We shared a room right up until I got arrested. Losing him was like losing a part of myself. "I haven't seen Sam since the sentencing hearing," I say quietly.

"He was there for it?"

I nod. He was there for everything. But I refused to talk to him. I refused to answer his letters, until he finally stopped writing them. I refused to see him when he came to visit, until he stopped coming.

"Why are you mad at him?" He makes a *tsk, tsk, tsk* sound with his mouth. "You *are* bitter about being the only one arrested."

I shake my head. "No, I'm not."

"Then what is it?"

I've never said it out loud. "I'm fucking jealous, all right?" I snarl. He raises an eyebrow at me, but he doesn't shrink away. I heave a sigh and force myself to unclench my fists. "He didn't get caught." I punch myself in the chest with my fist. "I fucking got caught. Stupid, stupid, stupid," I mutter to myself.

"Did he know you were dealing?" he asks.

I shake my head. No one knew. I'd just picked up the bag that night. Hadn't even made a sale yet. I'd just about convinced myself to return it to Bone and then we got busted.

"Why'd you do it?"

I take a deep, cleansing breath. "Matt's treatment was expensive. I couldn't think of any other way to help him."

He nods. It's a slow up and down movement of his head. He doesn't look at me or say anything.

"You don't know what it's like to know your brother's going to die and there's nothing you can fucking do to help him." I force myself to unclench my fists again.

"No, I don't," he admits. "Did you do drugs, too? Or just deal them?"

I snort. "Paul would lay into me like nothing you ever saw if I even thought about doing drugs."

"I think I like Paul," he says. He finally looks at me and smiles. "It sounds like you have a pretty good support system for when you go home." He rubs his hands together quickly. "Five more days!"

I smile. "Five days," I repeat.

"Can I make a suggestion?" he says.

"Like I could stop you," I mutter.

He grins. "True." He pauses for a minute. "Don't be afraid to make plans, Pete," he says. "Make lots of plans. Because it's only when you don't have any plans that you'll forget where you're headed. Write them down. Make them real. Then go for them. Follow through."

I nod. "Okay." I look down at the tracking bracelet that's on my ankle. "While we're here, am I free? Can I walk around and go places by myself?"

He nods. "I'll know where you are if I need to find you. But yes, you can consider yourself free." He coughs into his closed fist. "Just be careful with Reagan," he warns. He holds up a hand when I start to protest. "You're twenty-one years old. And you've been in jail for two years. And I'm guessing you gave up your V card a long time ago." He clears his throat. "Just remember that there's more to it than the pleasure of the moment."

Now I want to fuck with him. "Do tell, Dr. Phil."

"Life's not about the moments of pleasure you, yourself, can experience. It's about the pleasurable moments you share with someone else that really matter."

Shit. That was pretty profound. "Yes, sir," I say.

"What happened to your dad, Pete?" he asks.

"He left after our mom died."

"He missed out on something pretty fucking great with you, kid," he says. "He could have stayed and experienced all those missed moments with you and your brothers, and his life would have been richer for it."

"My life was fine." I doubt it would have been different if he'd stayed. Paul would have still taken care of us. He always has.

"Moments of pleasure you can give to someone else," he says, tapping his forehead. "Ask yourself before you do it who's going to benefit."

"Yes, sir."

He points toward the big house. "Speaking of moments," he says, grinning. "At this moment, someone is sneaking out to the barn." He squeezes my knee as he gets up. "You're welcome," he says with a laugh as he walks away.

I look toward the barn and see a female form walking quickly toward the big building in the distance. I look around. The camp is quiet, and everyone is in bed. I watch her as she slides through an open door and closes it behind her.

I wonder if she could use some company.

Reagan

I try not to look toward the fire as I sneak out to the barn. I know Pete's still sitting there, and he's not alone. There are two males in profile, and I don't know who the second one is. I pat my leg so that my Maggie will follow me. She's old and can't see as well as she once did, but I feel safe in the dark with her. She wouldn't let anyone hurt me, and I love that about her. I don't have to worry about anyone walking up behind me and me not knowing.

I step into the barn and close the door behind us. Maggie circles around me, her black-and-white coat in strict contrast with the muted colors of the barn. I jump toward her, and she dances back playfully. Even as old as she is, she can still run circles around me.

I step up to the stall door and lean over the cord that's blocking the opening. I have a horse that's due to foal any day now. Her name's Tequila, and she's my favorite of all my horses.

She's not lying down or sweating yet, so I'm guessing it's not going to be tonight that she foals. I duck under the rope that blocks her stall door and rub her gently behind her ears. She pushes her face into my hand, and I laugh.

Suddenly, Maggie stills beside me and the hair at the back of her neck stands straight up. A low growl erupts from her throat, and I stop petting Tequila and step closer to the horse. My heart begins to thud in my chest.

"Hello," a voice calls. Maggie hunkers down, and her growl grows even more vicious. God, I love this dog. The shadow comes closer, and Maggie barks in warning. "Oh shit," someone says, and the shadow moves back.

"Who's there?" I ask.

"It's Pete," the voice says.

My shoulders sink, and I force myself to take a deep breath. I don't let go of Tequila's halter, and I don't come out from behind her. "You shouldn't be in here," I call.

"Well, I'll be happy to leave if you'll call off your beast," he says. Maggie crouches and slinks forward, and the sounds that come from her throat are scaring even me. "Please," he says. His voice quivers.

"Mags," I snap. She turns and looks at me. I pat my leg, and she rushes to me. I pet her soft fur. "Good girl," I croon. Maggie takes her cues from me, and she's now wary but she doesn't want to kill anybody.

"Remind me not to ever walk up on you in the dark again," Pete says. He wipes his hand across his forehead.

I laugh. "I doubt you'll need a reminder." I jerk a thumb toward the bathroom at the end of the barn. "Do you need to go and change your pants?" A grin tugs at my lips. I try to bite it back, but it's nearly impossible.

Pete looks down at his shorts. "I think I'm good for now." He bends his knees and squats down close to the floor. He holds out a hand for Maggie to come and sniff. "Now, if she takes off a digit, I'll be singing a different tune." He laughs.

Maggie slinks slowly toward him. She's still wary, but she's calm. I'm not sure I like the idea of my dog getting friendly with a stranger. "Mags," I call, and she rushes back to me. "Don't try to schmooze my dog into liking you," I warn.

He raises his brow.

"She's trained to protect me," I rush to explain. She goes back and forth to my apartment in the city with me, even though I'm sure she likes it more here on the farm. But I need her. In more ways than one.

He nods, leaning against the open stall door. He jams his hands in his pockets. "I saw you and thought you might want some company."

"I already have company," I say. I probably sound like a shrew, but we got a little too close by the fire and I'm feeling the effects of it now.

"What's his name?" he asks, nodding toward my horse.

I smile a completely unbidden smile. "Her name's Tequila," I say, scratching my horse affectionately.

Pete steps closer, and Tequila swishes her tail in his face. He brushes it away, spitting as he wipes his mouth. I laugh.

"You haven't been around horses much, have you?" I ask.

"Can't say I've ever been in a room with one before," he says, picking at his tongue with his thumb and index finger. He spits again and finally looks satisfied after wiping his mouth with his forearm.

"I got another of your firsts," I say. I immediately realize my mistake and try to take it back. "I mean—"

But he holds up a hand and grins. "Hey, if I had all my firsts to give you, I would." His eyes meet mine, and a spark jumps between us.

I close my eyes and take a deep breath. I'd have liked to have had the choice of who to give mine to. But I didn't. And that's over, I remind myself.

"You okay?" he asks, his brow furrowing.

I nod. "Fine."

I step out from behind Tequila. I still have Maggie between us, and Maggie would never let anything hurt me. Tequila's low on water, so I grab the hose and fill her up. Pete jumps when I accidentally spray his shoes.

"Sorry," I say. I really didn't mean to do that. I bite my lower lip and avoid his gaze.

"A little water never hurt anyone," he says with a shrug. I think I hear him mutter something that sounds like "I could use a little cooling off," but that might just be wishful thinking. He grins at me. He's so damn cute. His eyes are bright blue, I know, but in the low light of the barn, they look almost sapphire. They're rimmed by dark lashes that are so thick they're feminine, but there's nothing girly about him. He's all man, from the width of his shoulders to the quirk of his grin. He's about a head taller than I am, but for some reason, I don't feel intimidated by his size. That's probably because he hasn't touched me.

"You should take a picture, princess," he says with a grin. "It'll last longer."

Heat floods my face, and I look away.

"Hey," he says softly. "I was just kidding." He steps toward me, his eyebrows drawing together.

I take a deep breath and force my insides to settle. I feel like there's a Ping-Pong ball in my belly that keeps dropping toward my toes. Humor usually works in these situations, so I try that. "I can't help it if you're made to stare at." I grin.

This time, it's his face that floods with heat if the color on his cheeks is any indication. "You think I'm pretty," he says, smiling. He's all swagger all of a sudden.

"*Pretty* is not a word I would use to describe you," I say, laughing.

He leans casually against the stall door again. "Then what would you use?"

"Full of it," I toss out.

He laughs.

I take another deep breath. "Why are you here?" I ask.

He shrugs. "I thought you might want some company." His gaze searches mine, and it's so intense that I have to break away.

"I figured you'd be too worried about your nuts to come around me again," I tease. Laughter seems to be the best way to get around this man's poignant pauses.

"You let me worry about my nuts." He laughs and looks down. "Well, you can worry about them, too, but I take full responsibility for their safety."

I laugh. He's really pretty funny. "We can both worry about your nuts," I say with a smile. I chance a glance at him, and he's looking closely at me. Too closely. Laughter. I need to say something funny. But nothing comes to me. I bite my tongue because I don't want to say the wrong thing.

"Do you want to go out with me?" he asks. He looks surprised by his own question, and I assume he wants to take it back. But he doesn't. He just looks at me expectantly.

"Define *out*?" I say.

He grins. "You and me on a date."

He doesn't have a car, and he just got out of prison. A date might be kind of difficult. But I can't say that. I'll hurt his feelings. "What kind of date?" I ask instead.

"The kind where you and I spend some time together," he says with a shrug.

"We're doing that now," I inform him.

"Well, damn," he sings. "You're right." He looks around at the horses. "Next time, remind me to take you someplace nicer."

I laugh. He smiles at me.

"That's a beautiful sound," he says quietly.

I look at Tequila and pat her behind. "Did you pass gas, girl?" I ask. I grin at him. "Sorry, but she can be kind of noisy."

He smiles and rubs his chin. I bet it's scratchy under his fingertips, and if I were another person, I would want to touch it to find out. "And she's funny, too," he says under his breath.

I smile and motion toward the door. "We had better get out of here before my dad comes after you," I say. But I'm not worried about my dad. I'm worried about me. Because I like this man. A lot.

"Can I walk with you back to the house?" he asks, cocking his head to the side. He's so damn cute. And he makes my insides quiver. I'm not sure the latter is a good thing.

I nod, and he steps up beside me and then opens the barn door for me. He holds the door open and lets me and Maggie through. His shoulder bumps mine, and I step away from him. He leans his head down close to me. "Do I smell bad?" he asks.

I lean closer to him and inhale. "Not that I can tell," I reply quietly. He smells like citrus and outdoors, just like I remember from that night. And I want to bury my face in his chest and drink him in. But I can't.

"Just checking," he says with a laugh. "Every time I get close to you, you move away," he says casually. But there's nothing casual about the comment. Nothing at all.

I point to my chest. "I've been working all day...and messing with the horses. I was worried that I was the one who smelled bad."

He looks into my face, and I can't draw my eyes away. "You smell like lemons and raindrops." He closes his eyes and inhales. "And all things innocent."

I freeze. "That is where you would be completely wrong," I say.

"You're guilty?" he asks. "Of what?" His blue eyes narrow.

"Of trusting the wrong person," I say quietly.

"I don't want you to trust me," he says. "I want you to be very, very wary of me. And every other man you meet."

I inhale deeply through my nose. "No problem there," I finally say. Most men fight with me to get me to trust them.

"I don't even trust myself most days," he says. I think he's playing at first, but he's dead serious.

"Why not?" I whisper.

"I'm not trustworthy," he says quietly.

I pull a lock of hair from where it's stuck to my mouth and lick my lips. He watches me closely. "I promise not to trust you," I whisper.

"Good," he whispers back, very dramatically.

We arrive at my door, and I turn to face him. "Thanks for walking me back," I say. I lay a hand on my chest. "It was such a long way," I say, trying to sound like Scarlett O'Hara. "I never would have made it by myself."

He grins. "My job here is done."

"Good night," I say.

He closes one eye and looks at me with the other for a moment. "Can I kiss you yet?" he asks.

I shake my head, and my insides do that quivery little dance again. "No," I whisper. "I'm afraid not."

He whispers again, "Can I keep asking?" He grins.

"I'd be disappointed if you didn't," I admit. He smiles. This time, it's not playful. I think it's all Pete. It's all swagger and confidence.

He turns to walk away, calling, "Good night, princess," over his shoulder.

"'Night," I toss back. I look up and see my dad glaring at me through the kitchen window. "Dad," I gripe, as he opens the back door for me.

"Was that Pete?" he asks. Maggie goes to lie at his feet.

I nod. "That was Pete."

He gnaws on his fingernail. "Should I be worried?" he asks.

I shake my head. "I don't think so."

"Okay," he breathes, and he deflates like a relaxed balloon. He leans forward, pulling my head toward his with his beefy arm. "Good night," he says, kissing my temple.

"Good night, Dad," I say. He turns and goes upstairs. I look out the kitchen window at the first man I have ever truly wanted to kiss. But I can't. I just can't. I know this is going to end badly.

Reagan

Sometimes I wake up with the weight of my memories draped over me like a heavy, wet, woolen blanket. One that weighs me down and makes it impossible to get out of bed. But today, I blink my eyes open and there's no sticky blood on my fingertips and my lashes aren't matted together from waking up with screams trapped in my throat.

Today, I wake up…hopeful. I don't even know if that's the right word for it. It kind of feels like Christmas morning. The one you experience even after you know Santa's not real, but you anticipate the warm and fuzzy feelings that come with the holiday. You rip open your presents and watch your parents exchange gifts that mean something to them. That's how I'm feeling today. And I'm not completely sure I like it.

The girls were here for camp last month, and I didn't feel this giddy because of them being here, so I don't think it's the camp that made me want to rush outside today. It's Pete. And I'm pretty sure I'm not supposed to like him as much as I do.

In a perfect world, I could date him. But my world's not perfect. And it hasn't been for quite some time.

I get dressed and pull my hair into a ponytail. We're going to be working with the horses today before it gets too hot. The boys love to take short rides around the paddock. Some of these kids have never been on a horse before.

I walk outside, and I can smell the aroma of bacon on the griddle. My dad tried hiring a catering service, but he really likes cooking for the kids, and it seems to work better when he throws some bacon on a skillet, scrambles eggs, and offers fruit, yogurt, milk, and cereal to everyone.

There's something for every kid, even with some of the boys' bizarre dietary restrictions.

The men from the prison are acting as waiters right now, and they're doing a good job at it. Pete's working in the middle of two tables. He's signing to some kids and joking with others. He's really good with the adolescents. Gonzo says something to him, and I see Pete hold up his hand to block everyone else from seeing it as he shoots Gonzo the middle finger. Gonzo laughs, and I force myself to close my jaw.

Pete looks over and catches my eye. My heart trips a beat. "Morning, princess," he says quietly, his voice lazy and uncomplicated. But that's a lie. Everything about this man is complex. There's nothing that's not complicated about him.

"Morning," I say back. I squeeze Gonzo's shoulder as I walk by him, and he beams at me. "Sleep well, Gonzo?" I ask.

He grins and signs something to Pete. "What did he say?" I ask Pete.

"You don't want to know," Pete says with a grimace. He glares at Gonzo. "Watch your manners, Karl," he warns. His voice is stern, and Gonzo hangs his head. That's the first time I've heard Pete call him by his real name. Pete stands up and goes to get a fork for one of the other boys. He's still glaring at Gonzo, and now I'm dying to know what he said to earn such disfavor from Pete.

"What did I miss?" I ask, looking back and forth between them.

"Some adolescent humor," Pete grumbles, looking at Gonzo from beneath lowered lashes. Pete reaches for a salt shaker for another of the boys. "Which wasn't amusing."

Gonzo signs something quickly to Pete. "I know that was meant for me," Pete says quietly, staring into Gonzo's eyes. "But she's sitting right here, and it's rude to talk in front of her unless I can tell her what you said."

He grumbles something and then says, "And I wouldn't repeat what you just said for a million dollars." He holds up his hands as though he's saying *what the fuck*. "You don't talk like that in front of girls, dude." He jabs a fork at Gonzo. "When we're alone, you can talk all the shit you want. And it might even be funny."

Gonzo taps me on the shoulder so I look at him. He signs something with his fist close to his chest. The color on his cheeks is high.

"He said sorry," Pete grumbles. Gonzo signs something else and then blinks his eyes at me, batting his thick lashes. "He wants to know if you forgive him."

"I'll think about it," I say. I still don't know what he said, so I don't know why I should be offended. But Pete's so serious that I feel like I need to play along.

"Gonzo, go ahead and get suctioned or whatever it is you do so we can be ready for the first activity," Pete says.

Gonzo grins and signs something. But he leaves. Pete shakes his head. More boy humor?

One of the caregivers rounds up the rest of the boys at the two tables Pete was in charge of so they can get the kids ready for the morning. Pete sits down and heaves a sigh. "That kid reminds me of my brothers," he says, but a grin tugs on the corners of his lips.

"You that tough on your brothers?" I ask.

He chuckles. "I'm the youngest. So, it's usually me saying something inappropriate and them trying to make me shut up."

"What did he say?" I ask. I'm dying to know. But something tells me he's not going to tell me anything.

His gaze is hot, his eyes hooded when they meet mine. "If you must know, it had to do with morning wood." He raises a brow at me, and I choke on my own spit. He laughs and raises a brow. "Should I continue?"

I hold up a hand to stop him. "I could go a lifetime without knowing any more about that conversation." I think about it for a minute, though. "Is that something boys talk about?" I ask quietly, just because I'm curious.

He pulls his chin toward his chest and looks down at me. "Don't go there, princess," he warns, his voice suddenly husky.

"I was just curious," I murmur. But I feel the need to explain myself. "My brother's has autism and barely speaks, so I don't know how boys behave." I lay a hand on my chest, slightly abashed at what I'm about to admit. "When girls get together we talk about everything." I look into his eyes, and they're suddenly half-lowered and smoldery. My heart thumps. "About men, mostly." Heat creeps up my cheeks.

His voice is barely a whisper when he says, "Go there, princess." His eyes twinkle.

"Well, apparently, Gonzo wants to talk to you like I'd talk to my girlfriends."

"And he can, when we're alone. Just like I told him." He isn't smiling anymore. He turns to face me. "I'm not going to hurt the kid. I won't even hurt his feelings. But I'm also not going to treat him like he's made of glass. He's had enough of that."

"Okay," I say quietly. I'll drop it. For now at least.

Pete smiles. He nods his head toward where my dad's taking up the last piece of bacon. "Breakfast?" he asks.

"Have you eaten yet?" I ask him.

He shakes his head. "Too busy so far." He looks at me. "Join me?" He leans close and whispers, "This would be our second date."

I roll my eyes and walk toward my dad, who hands me a plate heaping with food. "I can't eat all that, Dad," I complain.

Pete eyes the plate, licking his lips, and my dad shoves it toward him instead. I go to get a bagel, some cream cheese, and a chocolate milk. Pete sits across from me and starts to unroll his plasticware. He eyes my chocolate milk. "Do you want one?" I ask, and then I take a sip of my milk, looking at him over the top of the carton.

He waits until I set it down and reaches for my milk. He says, "Thanks," and then tips it up to drink from it. His lips press where mine just were, and my belly flips. I look away because I am afraid of what I'll see if I look into his blue eyes right now.

"Sorry," he murmurs. "Didn't mean to make you uncomfortable," he says. He gets up and gets another milk, opens it, and hands it to me. I look directly into his eyes and reach past his outstretched arm to take back my original milk, lifting it to my lips. "Jesus Christ," he breaths quietly. He looks over his shoulder to where my dad's standing, talking with some of the men from the prison program. "If your father has any clue what's going on in my head, he'll chop my nuts off for sure."

I clear my throat because I can't talk past the lump in it. "What's going on in your head?" I ask quietly.

He stares at me and shakes his head. "It doesn't matter." He looks down at his plate and takes a deep breath, and then starts to eat. He chews for a minute and then leans forward like he wants to tell me a secret. He pulls back and shakes his head.

"What?" I ask.

"Nothing." He keeps eating.

"I hate it when people do that," I say, more to myself than to him.

He heaves a sigh. "What's going on in my head is even more fucked up than what's going on my pants, if you must know my innermost thoughts, princess." He taps his forehead with the tines of his plastic fork. "Fucked up."

I swallow so hard I can hear it. "Fucked up how?"

He closes his eyes and takes a deep breath.

I repeat myself, in case he didn't hear me. "Fucked up how?" I set my bagel to the side.

He leans close to me and crooks a finger, beckoning me to do the same. I lean toward him.

"You got me so fucking turned on I couldn't stand up if the place were on fucking fire, princess." He points toward my chocolate-milk container. "And all you did was touch your pretty little lips to a fucking milk carton." He rubs his forehead as if he wants to rub the thoughts away. He looks into my eyes. "All I know is if you ever touched me with that mouth of yours, I would go off like a cannon, princess. I'd be the happiest man in the world, but ashamed of myself, because I have no control when it comes to you, apparently." He grimaces and looks down toward his lap, adjusting his pants as he wiggles his hips. "Our situation is messed up for so many reason that I can't even think about going there with you. But all I can think about is *going there* with you." He groans and shoves a piece of bacon in his mouth. His eyes don't leave mine, though. "I got up this morning thoroughly prepared to ignore you today. But then there you were, and you were smiling at me." He looks down at my mouth. "I couldn't ignore you if I tried."

I take a deep breath, trying to rationalize my thoughts. But I can't. I have never, ever felt like this before. My girlfriends have talked about it, but I have never felt it. Even when I go on dates, it's like some part of me shuts down. But with Pete, nothing shuts down. Everything wakes up.

He goes on to say, "I don't want to want you."

My heart stutters. I get it. I don't like it. But I get it. I nod. Nobody likes damaged goods.

I get up from the table and pick up my plate.

"Wait," he calls.

I can't wait. If I wait, he might see the tears that are brimming in my eyes.

"Princess," he calls again. Suddenly, my shirt jerks and I can't walk any farther. I look back and see his hand twisted in the tail end of my shirt. He leans over the table and presses his lips together. "Don't walk away," he says.

But all I see is the hand fisted in my shirt. My heart stutters, and my breaths freeze in my chest. I can't get away. I turn back and punch him directly in the face with the heel of my hand. He jerks, his eyes closing as he winces and snaps his head back. I chop his wrist with my fist. One, two... Next, I'll go for his eyes.

"Reagan!" Dad yells as he drops what he's holding and rushes in my direction. He tackles Pete, who is still stunned from my punch to the face. They drop to the ground, with Pete rolling to the bottom. Dad flips him over and pulls his hands behind his back. "Reagan," Dad grunts. "What happened?"

Pete lays there on the ground. He's not even putting up a fight. He just winces, his eyes shut tightly as a slow trickle of blood streams from his nose.

"Stay down," Dad warns.

Pete nods, and he doesn't move. But his eyes finally open, and they meet mine. I don't how to interpret that look at all or what to say. So, I turn and run back to the house. I run like the terrified little girl I am.

I burst through the back door and land in my mother's arms. She grunts when I hit her in the chest, but it doesn't stop her from hugging me tightly. "What in the world," she breathes as she rocks me. She holds me close, stroking my hair until I can breathe. Then she pulls back, takes my face in her hands, and forces me to look at her. "Tell me what's wrong," she says.

"I think I made a mistake," I sob.

"What happened?" she asks as she leads me to the kitchen table. She points to a chair, and I sink into it.

"Nothing," I squeak, finally able to catch my breath.

I can't believe I did that. I just assaulted some poor man who did nothing but flirt with me and then tell me he didn't want to want me. I can't tell my mother that.

She puts her hands on her hips. "It's not nothing," she insists.

The back door opens, and the evidence of my shame walks in behind my dad and Link. I wince and look everywhere but at Pete. "Can you get Pete some ice for his eye?" Dad asks my mom. Her brow arches at me, and she shoots me a glare that would drop a full-grown man in his tracks.

She starts to fill a zipper bag with ice. "And just why does Pete need ice for his eye?" she asks flippantly.

Dad points to me. "Your daughter hit him in the face."

Mom gasps. "Reagan!"

Mom crosses to stand close to Pete. She looks him over, pressing on the bone beneath his eye with her thumb. He hisses in a breath. One side of his face is dirty, probably from where Dad rolled him into the dirt. Mom passes him a damp cloth, and he wipes gingerly at his face. When it's clean, Mom presses his eye socket with the pad of her thumb. He winces and jerks his head back.

"I think Reagan did enough damage," Dad warns. "Stop torturing the boy." He glares at me, too. I want to hide my face in shame.

Suddenly, I notice the way that Pete is holding his left wrist in his hand. My gaze shoots up to meet his, and I don't see anything but curiosity.

He should be fuming mad. He has every right to be. "Is your arm hurt?" I ask quietly.

The corners of Pete's lips tilt in a small smile. "It's fine."

"It's not fine," Dad gripes. "It might be broken."

"Oh shit," I breathe.

"Reagan," Mom warns.

"Oh shit," Link parrots.

Shit again. Now Link's repeating me.

"Oh shit," Link says again.

I bury my face in my hands. My parents are going to kill me when they get me alone.

"Reagan, I want you to take the truck into town and take Pete to Urgent Care," Dad says.

I lift my head. He can't be serious.

"Oh shit," Link chimes in. Mom grits her teeth.

Dad motions for me to get up and tosses the keys to his truck at my head so that I have to catch them. "Dad," I complain.

"If it makes you feel any better, I don't particularly want to be in an enclosed space with you any more than you want to be in one with me," Pete says. He gingerly touches his eye, his face scrunching up.

I deserve that. I really do. I heave a sigh. "Let's go."

Pete follows me to Dad's truck, and then he opens the driver's-side door for me to climb in. "Thanks," I grumble. He goes around the truck and gets in the passenger side. "Are you sure you're injured?"

"My heart's broken," he says.

My head jerks up. "What?"

His voice drops down low. "It absolutely kills me that you think I would try to hurt you." He turns to face me directly. "I remember the way you looked that night. I would never, ever do anything to hurt you like that."

I start the truck. It's easier to avoid this conversation if I have something to occupy my hands and a reason not to look at him.

"Never mind." Pete grunts, turning away from me. He faces the window and lays his temple against it. He cradles his wrist in his hand and doesn't even look my way.

Pete

I don't know what to say to her. I have no idea how to address this. I know my wrist hurts, but I also know it's not broken. Her dad was insistent that she take me to Urgent Care, so I let him send us off. She's been sitting there in the driver's seat as we go down the road saying nothing for about ten minutes. Every now and then, she opens her mouth like she's going to say something, and then she slams it shut.

Suddenly, she jerks the truck to the right, sliding into a turn-out spot and then slams on the breaks. I brace myself with my hands and instantly regret it when pain steals up my wrist. "Shit," I mutter.

She heaves a sigh and drops her face into her hands. After a moment, she looks up, her green eyes meeting mine. "I'm sorry," she says quietly.

That hurt like a mother fucker, and I'm irritated enough to want her to suffer for a minute. "For which part?" I gripe. I pull my wrist closer to my body and cradle it.

"All of it," she says. She takes a deep breath and tears well up in her eyes. She blinks them back furiously. All of my anger melts at the sight of her tears.

"I'm fine," I grumble. "Don't worry your pretty little head about it." Okay, that was crass and a little demeaning, but I'm still a little sore.

"You're not fine," she interjects. "I hit you." She grits her teeth. "In the face."

Silence falls over the cab of the truck like a wet blanket.

"I still have some issues from that night," she finally says. She lays her head back against the headrest and looks up at the ceiling.

"Where'd you learn martial arts?" I ask. I may as well be sticking her full of pins and twisting them. And not in the good acupuncture way. I should let her off the hook.

"My dad taught me." She looks over at me. She is so fucking vulnerable all of a sudden. "After what happened at college, I took a self-defense class. I realized I'm really good at it, so I kept going and got better."

I press gently at my eye socket. Her face gets soft, and she looks so sorry. But she just left that comment hanging there in the air, and I feel the need to grab on to it. "Does it make you feel safer, knowing you can lay a man out flat?" I ask.

Her face pales, and she looks away. "Not right this second."

"But usually?" I ask. Her face is still pale, and she her gaze skitters everywhere but at me.

"I like knowing that I can get away from danger," she says quietly.

"You think I'm dangerous?" *Lie to me, princess.* Because my gut's already twisting at the very thought of her being afraid of me.

"In that moment," she hedges. "Can we just not talk about it?"

We need to talk about it. But I can tell she really doesn't want to. "Okay," I say, completely unbidden by me. It's all her. It's what she needs. "When I touch you, does your skin crawl?" I blurt out. I need to know what I'm up against here.

She nods and inhales deeply, acting as if I just tossed her a lifeline. "You make my heart beat faster, in a really, really good way." She finally looks into my face. "I know you can't forgive me, but I'm really sorry."

I reach to take her face in my hand, but she flinches and draws back, so I let my hand drop into my lap. "I shouldn't have grabbed you. It's all my fault." I don't know what to say. I don't know how to make this right for her. If it were any other guy, I would be fucking ecstatic that she hit him in the face rather than let him grab her.

"It's not your fault," she protests. "It's my fault." I feel more than hear her say something under her breath that sounds like *his fault.*

"I just didn't want you to walk away until I got to explain," I say. "I grabbed your shirt."

"And I felt like I couldn't get away there for a minute. I know that wasn't your intention."

I shake my head. "No, that was my intention. I didn't want you to get away. Your instincts were right."

"But you didn't intend to hurt me."

"You had no way of knowing that." God, am I stupid. I'm arguing with her about all the reasons why she hit me.

"Then my dad shoved your face in the dirt." She looks a little irked by that.

"Hell, princess, if I watched my daughter clock some asshole, I'd immediately assume it was his fault. Your dad did the right thing." I believe that. That's what dads are for. Well, mine wasn't, but I have Paul and the others. They would protect me with their lives. Her dad did nothing less than they would have done for me. "Your dad knows all about the assault?"

She nods, biting her lower lip between her teeth. "Can you forgive me?" she asks.

"Nothing to forgive," I say. She stares at me. "Forgiven," I say instead. "I promise."

She takes a deep breath. "Thanks."

Are we going to discuss the elephant in the room? The reason why she was charging away from me in the first place. "I shouldn't have made you feel like you had to get up and run away from me," I admit. We could have avoided the whole punching-and-rolling-in-the-dirt fiasco if I'd just kept my mouth shut and not talked about my dick and how hard she made me. I get that little stirring in my lap just thinking about it. I groan beneath my breath.

"What?" she asks. "Are you hurting?"

Yep. I'm hurting. But not the way she thinks. "A little," I admit. My wrist hurts.

"I like the way you like me," she says. Her voice is so quiet that I can barely hear her.

"What?" I ask. I lean closer to her, but she leans away.

She grins and shakes her head. "I like the way you like me," she says again, this time a little louder.

A smile tugs at the corners of my lips.

"You make me feel things," she admits. Her face isn't pale anymore. If anything, her cheeks are rosy.

"Right back at you," I say.

"You can stop smirking now," she says, but she's laughing. This is good.

"You tell me you like me and you expect me to stop smirking?" I lay my good hand on my chest. "You have to be kidding me. I might have to do somersaults."

"I don't like men," she says quietly.

"Oh." I don't get a lesbian vibe from her at all. Not a bit. But I've been wrong before. "You like women?"

She buries her face in her hands and lifts her head, laughing. "No!" she barks. "I don't like women." She does that little dance with her eyes again, looking everywhere but at me. "I like men. But you're the only man I've liked for a long time." She closes her eyes and flings her head back, groaning. "Being normal shouldn't be this difficult!" she cries.

"Princess, you are anything but normal," I say, laughter bubbling inside me.

She shrugs, looking a little chagrined. "I don't know how to change."

I laugh. "I wouldn't change you for anything."

Her eyes shoot to meet mine. There's a vulnerability there, and I see something else. Hope? "I feel like I've known you for a really long time," she says.

"Yep." She likes me. She likes me lots. I'm suddenly more full of confidence than I have been in a long time. "If you tell me you want me to stay away from you while I'm camping in your backyard, you just say the word." I wait a pause. She doesn't say anything. "But if you don't tell me to stay away from you, I'm going to keep trying to get to know you. And then when you get back to NYU, I'm going to take you out to dinner."

Her brow furrows. "A date?"

"Yep."

"You're kind of cocky, aren't you?" she asks.

"Yep."

"Why were you in prison?" she blurts out.

This time it's me who freezes. "I thought you knew about all that."

She nods. "I knew you were there, but I don't know why."

"Do you care?"

She shrugs.

I mirror her actions. "What does that mean?"

"My dad was in prison," she admits. "And not many people know that so I'd appreciate it if you didn't spread it around."

"What for?"

"People do stupid things when they're desperate," she says.

Yes, they do. "I made a mistake," I try to explain. But it's difficult to speak about why I did something stupid trying to protect one of my brothers. I can't even begin to explain it.

"You didn't hurt anybody, did you?" she asks. She looks at me out of the corner of her eye.

"No," I admit. "Just me. And my brothers when they put me in jail." I heave a sigh. "I disappointed everyone, including myself."

She smiles and says, "So what did we learn from today?" She looks all bright and sunny and reminds me of my eighth-grade science teacher, who I had a massive crush on.

"I learned never to grab you when you're trying to walk away from me."

She nods. She says very quietly, "I learned that I really like sharing my chocolate milk with you."

My gut twists. "I like talking to you," I admit.

"Me, too," she whispers.

I touch my eye again. "You pack a mean punch. Remind me never to walk up on you in a dark alley." I think about it a minute. "Or a dark barn."

"Or a sunny picnic area," she grumbles playfully.

I laugh. "Wait till my brothers hear that you punched me."

"Will they think it's funny?"

"When my brother Logan met his fiancée, Emily, she punched him in the face."

She covers her mouth with her fingertips. "Oh," she breathes.

"He says if you ever meet a girl who punches you in the face when you deserve it, you should marry her." I laugh. I still love that story. "Logan put the moves on Emily within seconds of meeting her, and she broke his nose." I lift up my injured arm. "You just broke my arm. Not quite the same effect."

"Well, you weren't putting the moves on me," she says with a laugh.

"Oh, I was," I admit. "I'm just not as smooth as Logan."

"Thank God," she breathes. I scrunch my eyebrows together, which makes her rush on to say, "If you were any less subtle, you would probably scare me to death." She grins. "I like it."

"You want me to stop trying to put the moves on you?" I ask. I wait anxiously.

She heaves a sigh. "No."

"Don't sound so excited about it," I grouse.

"I don't know what to do with all these feelings," she admits.

My gut twists. "Me, neither."

"So, what do we do now?" she asks.

I hold up my injured arm by the wrist. "I think I need a doctor."

She rushes to turn the truck back on. "I almost forgot you're injured!"

I didn't forget. And I won't forget to be careful with her from now on. But she likes the way I make her feel. That's a good start.

Reagan

The doctor says his wrist isn't broken, thank goodness. It's just strained. It's not even sprained. He recommends that Pete take an anti-inflammatory and rest it. Pete seems satisfied with that.

The questions about Pete's quickly blackening eye were a little unsettling.

"You're sure you don't want me to call the police so they can arrest the person who assaulted you?" the nurse asks. She's been flirting with him ever since we walked in the door.

"I'm sure. It wasn't intentional." His eyes meet mine over her head as she wraps his wrist. Her hands linger a little too long on his, and I see his eyes lower to look down her top. She makes a twittering noise when she catches him.

"You're new in town?" she asks. "I don't think I've seen you around before." She looks him in the eye and smiles. "I'm certain I would remember you if I had."

Pete smiles at me and rolls his eyes. "I'm from the city," he says. He plays with his piercing, and I can't draw my eyes from his lips, watching him as he toys with the hoop with the tip of his tongue.

"Well, if you ever want a tour of our little town, you just let me know."

"I don't think we'll need that," I blurt out.

Pete raises his brow at me, but his eyes are twinkling so brightly that I can tell he's amused.

I rush to continue. I drop my voice down to what I hope is a sultry purr. "I really don't plan to let him out of bed long enough to see the sights." I laugh. It was close to a twitter.

She freezes. "Oh, I didn't realize..." she says.

"I can tell," I toss back. I glare at her, and she has the decency to flush.

"I'll be right back," she mutters as she runs from the room.

A noise bubbles up from within Pete. It might be laughter. But if it is, I think he's going to die from it. He laughs, his shoulders shaking until he falls back to lie on the exam table, his belly rocking as he guffaws out loud. I stand up, walk to his side, and look down at him. "And just what do you find so amusing?" I ask.

He wipes the tears from beneath his eyes with his knuckles. "You had to save me from the nurse," he cackles. "That's some funny shit right there," he says. He's still wiping his eyes, the laughter starting to die back. "Why did you do that?" he asks. "She was harmless."

I look toward the door, remembering her beautiful smile; long, dark hair; and please-touch-me personality. I could never compete, at least not with the last part of it. "She was about as harmless as a piranha in a tank full of goldfish."

He laughs again, big achingly beautiful belly laughs. When it dies down, I realize how close I'm standing to him. He lifts his hand and reaches to place it on my hip. But an inch before it settles there, he says, "I'm going to touch you," very softly. My heart leaps. "I'm warning you so you won't hit me."

"Where?" I whisper. His hand is really close to my hip, but I want to be sure. My pulse thrums.

"Don't hit me anywhere," he whispers back playfully.

I roll my eyes at him, but my insides are flipping over themselves.

His hand lands on my hip, warm and strong. It's not intrusive at all. But I close my eyes because the sensuality of his touch combined with the heat in his eyes makes me want to run far, far away. I don't, though. I let him touch my hip.

"That's not so bad, is it?" he asks quietly.

I shake my head. "It's all right, I suppose," I say softly. I can barely take a breath, much less talk. He sits up and very gently leads me to stand between his legs with gentle pressure at my waist.

"Do you want to hit me?" he asks.

I shake my head and finally let my gaze meet his. "No," I say quietly.

"If you did, it would be worth it," he says softly. His nose touches mine, his lips a mere breath away. I lay my hand on his stomach, and I feel the muscles contract. I jerk my hand back, but he puts his over mine and presses it gently against him. "I like it when you touch me," he says. "You can do it any time you want."

He brushes his nose gently against mine in little eskimo kisses. His lips hover over mine, but they never meet, and I feel like I might pass out from the fear that comes with wanting him to kiss me so badly. "Kiss me," I say.

He freezes, and his hand tightens on my hip. "Nope." He shakes his head.

I pull my head back and look into his eyes. "It's all right," I say. "I want to try it."

He sets me back from him. "Nope," he says again. He shakes his head even more vehemently.

"Why not?" I can't believe I'm begging this man to kiss me. Is this what I've been reduced to?

He heaves a sigh. "I'm not going to kiss you because I can't tell if you want to kiss *me* or if you want to kiss someone you don't think is a threat for practice."

"What if it's a little bit of both?" I ask.

He shakes his head, and I think he might be a little bit pissed. "When you feel an overwhelming desire to kiss me—" He stops and pats his chest. "—When you want to kiss Pete," he says. "I'll kiss you. If you want to practice, you can find someone else to help you out."

I don't understand. "It's just a kiss."

He takes my chin in a gentle grip and forces me to look into his eyes. "When I finally kiss you, it's going to be because you want to kiss me, Pete, the man, the one who looks at you with wonder in his eyes, the one who is so fucking scared of these brand-new feelings for you that he sometimes can't breathe, the one who is dying to taste you. I have thought about you almost every day since I met you, princess, and I don't want to get you off my mind." He kisses the tip of my nose quickly and pulls back. "But when I kiss you, it's going to be because you have a thing for me that's as big as the thing I have for you."

I can't help it. I look toward his lap. He chuckles.

"Yeah, that too," he says with a laugh.

"So what do we do now?" I ask. I can't believe it. The first time I have wanted to kiss someone since the assault and he's too much of a gentleman to take me up on it.

"Let's go shopping," he says. He nods, as though he's thinking it over. "Do we have to be in a hurry to get back to camp?"

I shrug. We probably should. "Dad will light up my phone if I'm not back in an hour or two."

He nods and looks down at his watch. "It's almost lunchtime." He grins. "I think it's time for our third date."

I roll my eyes and follow him out of the exam room. My knees are still wobbly from our near kiss. If he ever really kisses me, I'll probably turn into a puddle on the floor.

Pete

I want to kiss her. I really, really want to kiss her. But I'm not even going to go there. Not until she's ready. And it's not because I'm afraid she'll Cujo my ass. It's because I really care about her. I have for a long time, and these past two days with her have only made me want to get to know her even more.

I remember when Logan brought Emily home for the first time. We laughed at him because she spent the night, and he'd had plenty of women in his bed, but he'd never, ever had one sleep over. He didn't even have sex with her, not until weeks later, and she slept in his bed every single night. He fell head over heels in love with her. Immediately. Looking back on it, I remember trying to figure out what the fuck he was thinking. Now I get it. There are some girls you sleep with. And then there are other girls you want to sleep with so badly that you hurt, but you don't because they're special.

We get out of the truck at the drugstore, and I walk around and take her hand in mine as we walk toward the sliding door at the entrance. She jerks her hand back, but I don't let it go. I hold on tightly but gently. She startles, and I'm afraid for a second that she's going to punch me again. But she takes a deep breath, steadies herself, and her grip relaxes in mine.

"What are we shopping for?" she asks. She looks up, her green eyes meeting mine. They're wary, though.

"Condoms," I say, deadpan. Her mouth falls open. I lean close to her face and whisper loudly, "I'm kidding." I hold up my wrist, the hand that's not holding hers, and say, "I need some kind of anti-inflammatory."

"Oh," she says as she begins to deflate. But then she grins and shakes her head.

"Something wrong?" I ask. I already know that she's unsure how to respond to me. But I'm hoping I can shock her into just being herself. I want her to be just her. Not the her that was created by the trauma of her assault. I just want to see *her*.

She shakes her head and draws her lower lip between her teeth.

"You got to stop doing that, princess," I say. "You're killing me here."

She tenses up. "Doing what?"

I reach out and touch her lower lip with the pad of my thumb. I halfway expect her to jerk back. Or clock me. But she does neither. She smiles and ducks her head, her hair falling in her face. I very slowly brush it back and tuck it behind her ear. She smiles shyly and looks everywhere but at me. "What kind of pain reliever do you want?" she asks. She starts to walk toward the aisle, but I don't let her hand go. I would follow her just about anywhere right now, so I let her lead me in the right direction.

I flex my hand. "I doubt anything is going to make a difference." It'll be all better by tomorrow, but she's already perusing the shelf, looking for the right one. I step up close to her and put an arm around her waist. She looks up at me, her cheeks growing rosy. "I love that I can do that to you," I say quietly.

She nods and bites her lower lip again. "Me, too," she says.

I let her go for a minute and walk over to the other aisle to catch my breath. Tic Tac seriously needs some breath mints. I have to figure out that boy's name, too, because I can't keep calling him Tic Tac in my head. I pick up some breath mints for the kid and walk back toward where I left Reagan. Only she's not alone when I return.

Reagan

I want to go back to the quiet, quaking silence I had with Pete, but he's one aisle over when Chase spots me poring over the pain relievers from the end of the aisle. He calls my name and starts in my direction.

"Reagan," Chase says, like he didn't just see me yesterday. "I was just thinking about you."

He's always full of platitudes. I can't tell if he's sincere or not, which is one of the things I don't like about him. "Hi, Chase," I croak out. I look left and right and don't see Pete. "What's up?"

"I was just about to call you. My dad got tickets for tomorrow night to the dance at the country club. Do you want to go with me?"

"She's busy tomorrow," someone calls from the end of the aisle. Pete comes toward us, his gait slow and ambling. His body is loose and relaxed, yet I know it's not. Not really.

"Who's he?" Chase asks.

Pete holds out his hand to shake. Chase looks at it like it's dirty. Pete pulls his hand back and reaches for mine. I pull mine back and cross my arms beneath my breasts. "Chase, this is Pete." I lean my head toward Chase. "Pete, this is Chase."

"Nice to meet you," Pete says.

"Chase and I go to school together," I rush to say.

Pete smiles. "Lucky bastard," he says.

Chase's eyebrows draw together. He looks at me. "So, you're busy tomorrow night?" he asks. He ignores Pete, which pisses me off. Pete's been nothing but nice until now.

But there's steel in Pete's voice when he replies. "I told you she's busy."

Chase flexes his hand, balling it up into a fist. Pete still appears relaxed. But he's not. He doesn't need to posture to seem fierce the way that Chase does. He just is. And he's so much more. "I'd like to hear that from her."

"I'm—" I start to say.

But Pete puts his arm around me and says, "I'm taking the liberty of speaking for her."

I look up at him. "Don't speak for me," I say. I lift his arm from around my shoulders. "Did you get everything you need?" I ask.

"Not yet," he says slowly. His eyes dance across my face. "Why don't I go finish my shopping?" he asks. He raises an eyebrow at me in question. I nod. He tucks a lock of hair behind my ear before he leaves.

"Who the hell is that?" Chase barks. He watches Pete's prideful swagger all the way down the aisle until he disappears from sight. Chase looks down at me.

I shrug. "He's a friend."

"Since when do you have friends like that?" he asks. He steps toward me, and I step back, until my back is against the shelves behind me. I don't like to be cornered, but Chase has no way of knowing that. I skitter to the side so that I'm not hemmed in.

"Friends like what?" I ask. I know he's referring to the tattoos. Pete walks by the end of the aisle and waves at us, and then he winks at me. A grin tugs at my lips. I shrug again. "He's really very nice."

"Where did you meet him?"

I can tell the truth or I can lie. But then I hear Pete one aisle over as he starts to sing the lyrics to Elvis Presley's "Jailhouse Rock." I grin. I can't help it. "He's helping out at the camp this week," I say instead of the truth. Well, it's sort of the truth.

"Where's he from?" Chase asks.

"New York City," I say.

Pete's song changes from Elvis to AC/DC's "Jailbreak." I laugh out loud this time. I can't help it.

"Your dad's all right with you hanging out with him?"

My dad is covered in tattoos, too, but most of his are hidden by his clothing. "He likes Pete," I say. "I do, too." Chase puts one arm on the shelf behind me and leans toward my body. I dodge him again, and he looks crossly at me. "Don't box me in," I warn.

He holds up both hands like he's surrendering to the cops. But he still looks curious. "So, about tomorrow," he says.

"I can't," I blurt out.

I think I hear a quickly hissed, "Yes!" from the other side of the aisle, but I can't be sure.

Chase touches my elbow, and it makes my skin crawl. I pull my elbow back. "Don't touch me," I say.

Suddenly, Pete's striding down the aisle toward us. His expression is thunderous, and I step in front of him so that he has to run into me instead of pummeling Chase like I'm guessing he wants to do. I lay a hand on his chest. "You ready to go?" I ask.

He looks down at me, his eyes asking if I'm all right. His hand lands on my waist and slides around my back, pulling me flush against him. He's testing me. And I don't want to fight him. I admit it. Chase makes my skin crawl, and Pete makes my skin tingle. It's not an altogether pleasant sensation, but only because I can't control it. He holds me close, one hand on the center of my back, and the other full of breath mints and assorted sundries. He steps toward Chase, and Pete and I are so close together that I have to step backward when he steps forward.

I repeat my question. "You get everything?"

He finally looks down at me. "I got everything I need," he says. His tone is polite but clear and soft as butter.

I clear my throat and turn Pete toward the front of the store so we can pay for the items he's collected. "I'll see you, Chase," I call back. He waves at me. I feel bad because Chase seems confused. He's pulling out his phone as we walk away, and I'm already expecting for my dad to hear from his dad. I don't care. If my dad had a problem with Pete, he certainly wouldn't have sent me out with him.

Pete steps up to the counter and lays his items beside the register. He pulls his wallet from his back pocket and opens it up. I see a couple of foil wrappers in with his cash. Heat creeps up my face. He pays, then closes his wallet and shoves it back into his back pocket. He takes the bag from the clerk and thanks her.

As we walk out the front door, he twines his fingers with mine. I look up at him, blinking away the brightness of the sun. "You really need to learn to behave yourself," I say. But I can't bite back a laugh. I just can't. "'Jailhouse Rock'? Seriously?"

He shrugs, but he's grinning too. "It seemed appropriate."

I bark out a laugh so loud that I cover my mouth in embarrassment. "It was so inappropriate," I say.

He sobers and looks at me after we get in the truck. "Who's that guy to you?" he asks.

"He's a friend," I say with a shrug. "That's all."

"Why didn't you tell him where I'm from?" he asks. He's waiting with bated breath, I think.

"I did."

He shakes his head. "You know what I mean."

"He asked where you're from. I said New York City. What more did you want me to tell him?"

"The truth would be a good start," he mumbles.

"Jail is a place you stayed for a while, Pete. It's not where you're from."

He snorts.

"That would be like the boys saying they live at Cast-A-Way Farms after staying for a week."

"That's not entirely accurate." He rocks his head back and forth as if he's weighing my words. Then his eyes narrow. "You didn't let him touch you."

"I know," I say quietly. "I don't let many people touch me." I had better tell him the truth. "We went on a date once or twice," I say.

"You've been on dates with him and you still don't let him touch you?" He lifts his brow at me.

I nod, unsettled by his question.

"Good," he says. He grins.

I start the truck and lay my right hand on the console between us, driving with my left. His injured arm comes up to settle beside mine and his pinkie crosses over mine, wrapping around it. It's comfortable. It's kind. It's unsettling in a settling sort of way, and I don't know what to do with it.

"Quit overthinking it," he says, smiling out the window. He's not even looking at me.

"Okay," I say quietly. I settle back in my seat and scoot my hand closer to his.

My nerves are a mess by the time we get back to camp. Pete looks over at me and smiles. "Honey, we're home," he sings, grinning. But then he quickly sobers. He lowers his head, arching his neck, so he can look into my face. "You're still overthinking it, aren't you?" he asks softly.

I nod. I blink furiously to push back the tears. He's so kind and he's so sweet, but I've labored over this the whole way home. "I'm afraid I can't be what you need for me to be," I say quietly. "I just can't." I'll never be normal. Never.

"You just met me," he says. "How in the world could you know what I need?"

He lets go of my hand. I feel suddenly more alone than ever. I look into his eyes. "I really, really want to kiss you," I say.

He grins. "Good."

"But what if I can never do that?" Never do it without seeing *his* face in my mind instead of Pete's?

Pete tangles his fingers with mine. "Does this feel all right?" he asks.

It wouldn't have felt all right yesterday, but it's suddenly all right today. "No."

He jerks his hand back like I just scalded him.

"Wait." I need to explain. "It doesn't feel all right. It feels fabulous."

His posture relaxes. "You scared me for a second."

I reach for his hand and hold it tightly. "For me, this might be as close as I'll ever get to having sex or that kiss I think I want from you."

"Okay," he says, grinning. I roll my eyes at him. His face softens. "I happen to like holding hands with you, dummy," he says. "I like it a lot." He scrubs a hand down his face. "Probably more than I should." He squeezes my hand. "So, if that's all you're ready for, I'm happy to do it. And just that." He bends again, looking into my face. "I just met you yesterday. Do most men you meet want to get in your pants within twenty-four hours?"

I heave a sigh. He met me long before that, but, technically, he's right.

"If so, you've been hanging out with the wrong types of men." He lets my hand go and turns to open the truck door.

"Pete," I call.

He looks over his shoulder at me, smiling. "Reagan," he says, his tone mimicking mine. But he holds up a hand. "I know you want to sleep with me already, Reagan," he says grinning. "But for God's sake, I just met you yesterday. Give me some time to get to know you, will you?" He adjusts his clothing like I've undressed him with my eyes. "I'm more than a piece of meat."

He's still grinning, and I know he's joking, but it suddenly hits me how silly I'm being. I'm letting my attraction to this man dictate my actions, and I'm putting up walls, tearing them down, and then building them up stronger. By the time the week is over, I'm going to be a damn fortress. But one thing's for sure. If anyone can get past my walls and make me want him to be there, it's Pete. Because I'm already halfway there.

Pete

Mr. Caster meets us at the truck when we get out, and he takes in my wrapped wrist with a solemn expression. But he regards the way Reagan looks at me with an even more solemn expression. "Everything go okay?" he asks, his gaze skittering between the two of us.

"Just a strain," I say, holding up my arm so I can flex my fingers. I look around. The camp is devoid of kids. "Where is everyone?" he asks.

He jerks a thumb toward the pool. "Half the kids are at the pool. The other half is at the stable."

"Is Link still cursing?" Reagan asks, wincing inside, I can tell.

"Your mother saved you when she dropped the f-bomb in front of him." He smiles. He's not angry at all.

Reagan laughs. "So glad I can count on her to save the day."

"You can always count on your mother to curse more than you." He looks at me. "Where are you stationed today? With Gonzo?"

I have no idea where I'm supposed to be. "Wherever you want me." I hold out my hands waiting for his answer.

He nods his head toward the counselors' cabins, which is where I'm staying. "Check in with Phil. I think he might be having group with some of the youth, and he might need a solid adult presence to help him out." I nod my head. I have never considered myself a solid adult, but my head swells at the thought that he does.

I look at Reagan and cock my head to the side. I hope I look like an inquisitive puppy. Probably not, though. "Will I see you later?" I ask.

Her dad's brow arches, and he looks almost...amused?

She nods at me, blushing a little as she looks at her dad from beneath lowered lashes.

I start off toward the ring of chairs in the middle of the counselors' cabins. Phil stands up and gets a chair for me, putting me across from him on the other side of the ring. "How's the wrist?" he asks as I settle down and lean forward, dangling my hands between my knees.

"Just strained," I say. I don't like that all the attention is suddenly on me.

He grins and winks at me. "Since you just got punched in the face by a girl—" He lets his gaze rake over the group. "—we were just talking about how many of the young men in the program come from homes where domestic violence is the norm."

"Okay…" I say slowly. I don't know what he wants me to contribute.

"Would you like to know how many?" he asks. He smiles at me in encouragement.

"I'd love to know," I reply, because I assume it's what he wants to hear.

Phil commands the group, "Please raise your hand if you experienced domestic violence in your home." Six out of ten hands go up. "That might include violence against your mother, your father, your siblings. Or even your grandparents or foster parents."

Another hand goes up. These boys didn't have families like mine. Far from it. I was steeped in love and compassion, and they were baked in turmoil and anger. "Wow," I say. "That's more than I expected." I don't know what Phil wants me to do. So, I just ask questions. "Do your friends know about your situations? Or do you keep them away from your house?"

One of the boys blows out a breath. "I wouldn't let my friends within a hundred yards of my apartment."

"Do you go to their houses instead?" I ask.

He nods. "Some. There are others who have families like mine, so we hang out at the park a lot."

"You do have friends with normal families, right?" I ask.

Tic Tac scoffs. "Fighting is normal," he says. "If I went to a house and there was no fighting, I'd probably run away scared."

The boys laugh at him, but I can tell by the way they avoid my gaze that this is true. The problems are their "normal."

"How many of you want to be different when you grow up?" Four of them raise their hands. "How about when you have kids of your own?" I ask. "Would you want to provide a better life for your kids?" This time, an additional four hands go up.

Phil asks, "So you think that your kids deserve better than you got?" He takes in the group. "What can you do to make sure that happens?"

"Don't get a bitch pregnant so you have to marry her," one of them throws out.

"That's a word you use to describe women?" I ask. I glare at him. I shouldn't. But he has to know this is not all right.

He shrugs. "That's what they are."

"Your mother is a bitch?"

He shrugs again and avoids my eyes.

"Your daughter is going to be a bitch?"

He sits up this time. He's getting defensive, I can tell. I hold up my hand to stop him.

"Every woman is someone's daughter. Someone at home loves her. And you devalue her and every other female by referring to women as bitches and hos." I'm from the neighborhood. I could spout off a lot coarser words than they could probably imagine. But they get the idea.

"The girl you're with is someone's daughter. You have to remember that when you treat a woman poorly."

The same boy shakes his head. "Some b—" He stops and corrects himself. "Some *women* don't want to be treated like somebody's daughter," he says. "If their dads ain't so good, they don't know no better."

I nod my head. "When a woman grows up, she accepts the love she thinks she deserves. Do you think that's fair? Is that what you want for your own daughters?" I look around.

One of the boys leans forward. I have his attention, I think. He looks me directly in the eye as he says, "I will treat my daughter like a princess. Because if I don't, she'll latch on to the first man who does, even if he's no good. My grandma told me that." He reaches into his back pocket and pulls out a picture. "That's my girl," he says. He beams with pride.

I lean close so I can smile at his picture. Then I reach out and shake his hand. "Your daughter thanks you. And so will the man she marries someday."

"You got a girlfriend?" one of them asks. I am suddenly the center of their attention.

I shake my head. "No. I just got out of prison a couple of days ago."

"He ain't had time to go hit dat, yet," one boy says, and another high-fives him.

"I've done my share of hitting that." I draw air quotes around the last two words. "*Hitting that*'s not enough for me. I want a relationship. I want somebody to share my life. I want someone to take care of me and who will let me take care of her. But even before all that, I want to better myself so that I'm worthy of her."

"Shit," one of them grunts. "You don't even know who she is and you're already trying to change yourself for her. Fuck that." He throws his hands down like he wants to brush away my thoughts.

I shake my head. "I want to be better for me. But I have no doubt that whoever I end up marrying will be better for it." I start to tick items off on my fingers. "I want to go to college. I want to get a good job. I want a house. It may be a humble home, but it will be mine." I pat my chest. "I want kids to run up and down the hallways. I want to go to soccer practice and coach Little League and I want to hold a little girl's hand while she dances on her toes in a tutu. I want to watch my kids make it to college and watch them do better than me." I look at Phil. "Those are my plans."

He smiles at me and nods. "How many of you have solid plans for when you get out?" he asks.

The boys look toward one another.

"How many of you plan to graduate?" he asks.

Only half of them raise their hands.

"How many of you plan to work?"

All of them raise their hands.

"How many of you plan to have children that you'll take care of?"

Only the boy with the picture in his pocket raises his hand.

"How many of you use condoms when you're hitting that?" Phil asks.

The boys laugh.

Phil chuckles. "Then a lot more of you are planning to have kids than I thought."

Phil picks up a stack of notebooks and passes them around the circle. He gives me one, too, and a pen. "For group tomorrow, I want you to write down one solid plan for when you go home."

"You mean like college and straight As and shit?" one boy asks.

Phil shakes his head. "College, buy a goldfish, get married, get a job, go to the state fair… Write about something you can accomplish. And tell me in one page or less what you plan to do to get there."

"Do we have to share it with the group?" someone asks.

Phil shrugs. "Only if you want to."

The boys all take their notebooks and put them away in their cabins, and Phil breaks up group, sending the young men off to do chores. He stops me, though, with a hand on my shoulder. "You did really well talking to them."

I shrug. "I have a lot of brothers. It's what we do."

"Some of these boys have never had a male presence who will actually listen to them."

I nod. "I can tell." I look at the group as they spread out around me, going about their chores. "I might learn as much from them as I can teach them, though."

He squeezes my shoulder. "No doubt."

"Where do you want me to go now?" I ask.

"Check in on Karl. I think he's at the pool." He looks up at me.

I lift up the leg of my jeans and look down at my tracking bracelet. "Can I get this thing wet?"

He nods. "That model can be submerged, yes. So, feel free to jump in any time." He grins at me. "Hey Pete," he says. I turn back. "Tonight, we're going to let the youth boys use the pool. I'd like for you to be there in case any of them want to talk. After dinner, try to get free of whatever you're doing?"

"Yes, sir," I say.

I start for the pool. But at the last minute, I turn back and change into a swimsuit. I can't help but look around for Reagan on my way. But she's not there. Then I find her. Wearing a bathing suit and sitting in a lifeguard chair with a whistle between her lips.

I can't take my eyes off her. She's watching the pool with the trained eye of a professional. Then she sees me, and her face colors.

God, she's pretty. I'm a guy, so I take in the very serviceable bathing suit she's wearing. It's red, and it covers all the parts of her that should be covered and then some. But she might as well be fucking naked as far as my nerves are concerned. And my dick, for that matter. I did mention that I'm a guy, right?

She has her legs crossed, and she has a big funky straw hat on her head, goofy white glasses and her nose is creamed with white paste. She's fucking adorable. She blows her whistle and one of the boys running on the side of the pool slows down, looking up at her sheepishly.

Something hard bumps into the backs of my legs, making my right knee buckle. I look back to find Gonzo grinning at me. *You look like you were on the wrong side of a gang fight*, he signs, and then he points to my eye.

I shrug. *That's what happens you grab a girl the wrong way. Take note: Some of them can kick your ass.*

I thought the other kids were lying, he says. Then he laughs. *She really hit you?* He looks toward Reagan and grins. *That's what you get for putting the moves on my girl. Don't say I didn't warn you.* He points a finger at me in warning.

"Why aren't you swimming?" I ask, using my voice.

He points to the piece of plastic. *Kind of hard to breathe when it's full of water.*

"You can't swim with that thing? Really?"

His face falls. I should have left it alone.

"Then what are you doing here?" I ask. "You could be riding horses or doing something fun."

He looks toward Reagan. *And miss seeing her legs? Absolutely not. I'll stay right here.*

I chuckle and shake my head. The boy's funny. I'll give him that. I pull a chair up close to him and sit down. "Just so you know," I say. "I've called dibs on that one. So you can stop dreaming."

Dude, she punched you in the face. He laughs.

I pat my chest. "I can be charming when I want to."

When will that start? He grins.

I punch his shoulder. "Do you have any siblings?" I ask.

He shakes his head. *You want to apply for the position?*

This kid is a lot wittier than I would have guessed. "I already have four brothers, thank you very much. I don't particularly want any more."

What's it like having that many people in one house? Must be a big house.

I shake my head. "No, it's actually a really small apartment." I shrug. "But it works for us."

Do you miss them?

I nod. Particularly Sam. "I do miss them. I only got to spend one night with them before I got drafted to be your mouthpiece."

At least I put brilliant words in your mouth. He pats his chest. *I could be boring. Where would you be then?*

"My life could be worse. I'm sitting by a huge pool looking at a beautiful girl with a boy who's pretty smart."

Careful or my head's going to start to swell. He looks toward Reagan. Is that longing in his eyes?

"Stop scamming on my girl," I warn.

He doesn't take his gaze from her, but it looks less lascivious and more…needy. *Do you think…* His hands stop moving.

"What? Spit it out already," I prompt.

Never mind.

"What were you about to say?" I ask, turning to face him completely. "Ask it. I won't be able to sleep tonight unless I get to hear what's going in that head of yours," I tease.

I was just wondering... He looks toward Reagan again. *Do you think there will ever be a girl that looks at me like she looks at you?*

I glance toward the lifeguard stand. "How does she look at me?" I ask.

Like she wants to jump your bones. He laughs. But I can tell this is serious to him. More serious than he wants me to know.

I tap his leg with my foot to get his attention. "That's not the question you should be asking yourself, doofus."

I'm in a chair, Mr. Mentor Man. You think it's a good idea to call me a doofus? You might affect my self-esteem.

I roll my eyes. "If you had any ego problems, I'd already know it."

Forget I asked, he says. He looks everywhere but at me.

"There's a lid for every pot, Karl. Some fit better than others, but there's one made just for you. You should be asking yourself if she's good enough for you. Every single time. Don't ask yourself if you're good enough for her because when you find the right fit, you won't doubt it."

He grins. I think he likes that answer. And I mean it.

So you think she exists?

I nod. "I think she's just waiting to find you. So don't fuck it up by being a smart-ass."

He points to himself. *Me? Never!*

Karl's mom approaches from the other side of the pool. She just happens to have a bucket full of water in her hand and she's tiptoeing, so I try not to smile. But I can't help it when she dumps the water down his back. He leans forward, wincing, but he's also laughing.

"That's what you get for being a shit this morning," she says with a smirk. So this is where he gets it from. I like her even more now. She pulls a water gun out from behind her back. She hands it to Gonzo. "Reagan looks like she could use some cooling off, don't you think?" She winks at me.

Gonzo is suddenly a man on a mission. He hides the gun down by his leg and rolls around to where Reagan is sitting. He stops below her and claps his hands together. She looks down at him, smiles, and says something, but I can't hear what she's saying. He grins, pulls out the squirt gun and proceeds to soak her. He doesn't hit her in the face, but he gets the rest of her pretty well. She puts her hands up to shield herself, and it's really pretty amusing. Suddenly, his pistol runs out of water, and she climbs down the ladder of her chair. She has a wet towel in her hand, which she proceeds to flick at him until it cracks against his knee.

"Ouch!" I whisper to myself, wincing. But he fucking loves it. He grins and throws his gun to someone in the pool to fill up. The whole time, she's chasing him around the edge of the pool with the towel, until her dad has to come and send her back to the stand. Mr. Caster points his finger, and she pretends to pout. Then she flicks him on the ass with the towel too. He turns around, picks her up, and tosses her into the water. She floats to the surface and sputters. Her big, floppy straw hat floats there beside her. And her glasses have sunk to the bottom.

That shit's funny. I can't stop laughing. I laugh until my sides ache from it. She looks in my direction and narrows her eyes. She swims over to where I'm still sitting, completely dry. "You're looking a little too amused, there, Pete," she says. She fills her mouth with pool water and spits it from between her teeth at my foot. Damn, that's hot. But, again, I'm a guy. We tend to get a little orally fixated. She could spit a goober and I'd still probably find it sexy.

"What are you going to do about it?" I ask, sitting forward with my elbows on my knees. She looks startled for a second. Then I realize she's plotting. I can almost smell the gears in her mind burning, they're working that hard. Gonzo rolls up next to me. They must have warned everyone about Gonzo's tracheostomy tube because no one tries to get him wet and he's careful about the edge of the pool. Next thing I know, he's beside me, and he doesn't take the same care with me that he took with Reagan. A blast of water hits me in the face.

I put my hands up to block him, but dammit, he's having so much fun with it that I don't want to stop him. Instead, I let him squirt until the gun's empty. Then I blow water from my lips and open my eyes. She's grinning like hell, and Gonzo's almost as happy as she is.

"You so deserved that," she says.

I stand up and point to her. "I'm coming for you, Reagan," I warn. She squeals and backs away. She looks a little panicky, but then I realize she's having fun and she's panicking because I'm going to dunk her rather than because I'm going to touch her.

This shit is like foreplay. The really good kind. I go in the shallow end and stalk her all the way to the rope that sections off the middle of the pool. I want to touch her so badly I can taste it. "Come here, little girl," I taunt. "Let me show you what happens when you mess with a real man."

She laughs and ducks under the rope. She comes up smiling, though. I go under and reach for her, and she almost slides right by me, but I grab her at the last second. I slowly and gently pull her against me. We're so close together that I can feel her heart beating against my chest. She stares into my eyes, and then her gaze drops to my lips and moves back up. "Pete," she warns. She kicks her feet to stay afloat.

"Reagan," I mock.

"It wasn't my fault," she says, but she's a little breathless. "It was Gonzo. He planned the whole thing."

"Liar," I whisper. Her face flushes. I tread water with one hand and hold her against me with the other. This feels so good that I don't want to let go.

"Reagan," her father barks.

She looks up at him, as if she's being dragged from a trance. I let her go, but she doesn't move away from me. Her arm touches mine. "I want to kiss you," I say impulsively, right beside her ear. She shivers lightly.

"You better do it soon," she warns. "Or I'm going to have to replace you with someone more willing." She kicks off from me and goes to the side of the pool, where she pulls herself up and climbs back into her chair. She crosses her long, tan legs, and her foot waves in the air as she fidgets. Then she looks at me and says loudly. "It better be epic, Pete. That's all I'm saying." She points to a place beside me. "And throw me my hat."

I pick up her wet hat and set it on the side of the pool. I dive down and get her funky glasses and lay those beside her. I'm glad I have something to do because I don't trust myself to get out of the pool just yet.

Our first kiss will be the kiss that ends all first kisses for me. I'm sure of it. I just hope she feels the same way.

Reagan

Dad's mad at me, I can tell. He has been glaring at me all afternoon. Pete stares at me, too, but in a completely different way. He shed his shirt about two hours ago, and he walked over to me carrying a bottle of sunscreen Gonzo's mom gave him. Dad intercepted him, though, and spun him around to rub sunscreen on his shoulders himself. Pete let him. It was the funniest thing I have seen in a long time. When Dad finished, he slapped Pete's naked shoulder really hard and pointed him back toward the group of hearing-impaired kids who had just arrived at the pool.

Pete has organized water volleyball and water basketball, and I watch the boys play. My mouth goes dry as he slices out of the water to hit the ball, jumping high as he volleys it back to the other side of the net with his uninjured arm. His body is amazing, and I finally get to see all of his tattoos. I want to trace them with my fingertips and see how far they go beneath his swim trunks. His suit hangs low on his hips, and he has those ridges and a patch of hair leading down his belly that would make any bright girl become stupid. Like now. I can't take my eyes of it. I want to follow the path like it's the yellow brick road. My dad is the cowardly lion because I think he's a lot more afraid of my feelings for Pete than I am. I...I am the wicked witch.

Pete swims over to the side of the pool in front of me. "Come swim with me," he says, splashing water toward my legs.

"I'm on duty," I say, and I blow my whistle at one of the boys.

He jerks a thumb over his shoulder toward the group and says, "They're deaf, you know?" He laughs. "Your whistle is pretty ineffectual."

"Then let's hope they can all swim."

"They're confined to the shallow end." He grins at me.

I look at the boys. They're watching Pete from where they're still hitting the ball back and forth. "They like you," I say. Of course they do. Everyone likes Pete. Even my dad likes him, though I'm not sure he likes the burgeoning relationship between us.

"They like you more," he says. "I told them I was going to come and put the moves on the pretty lifeguard."

A grin tugs at my lips. He thinks I'm pretty. "You did not."

"Oh, yes, I did." He smiles, and my heart trips over. "Prepare to be moved, pretty lifeguard." He hoists himself out of the pool, careful of his injured wrist as he goes up the ladder, and stalks toward me, water sluicing from his body. When he gets close to me, he stops and lays his crossed arms over my lap, and looks up at me. "You don't mind me touching you, do you?" he asks.

My heart's beating so fast I can't take a deep breath, but it's not because I'm afraid of him. He makes me feel things I've never felt before. "Apparently, my inner goddess is a slut. Yeah, I read *Fifty Orgasms*."

He lays his forehead on his folded arms and laughs into the space, his shoulders shaking. I thump him on the top of his closely shaved head.

He covers his head with his hand and looks up, scowling at me. "What was that for?"

"You laughed at me."

He snorts. "You were talking about *Fifty Orgasms*. Of course I laughed."

I narrow my eyes at him. "Do you even know what book I'm talking about?"

"Anastasia and what's his name," he says with a breezy wave. "I read it."

My mouth falls open.

"The last one was the best." He grins. "His surrender was kind of sweet."

"He didn't surrender."

"What do you call it then?" He laughs. "He totally changed for her. And he loved every second of it."

I lay back heavily against the chair I'm in and glare at him. "You skipped around and just read the good parts, didn't you?"

He looks offended. "Just because I'm pretty doesn't mean I'm not smart." He chuckles. He lifts my hand with his so he can thread his fingers though my mine.

Pete jumps when my dad slams through the pool gate. Dad glares at him, but he doesn't move his hand from mine.

"Reagan," Dad barks.

I blow out a quick breath and say very nicely, "Yes, Dad."

"Chase Gerald's father just called." He looks at where my hand is tangled with Pete's, and if death rays that shoot from the eyes existed, then Pete would be a puddle of ashes on the ground.

"Is that the guy from the drugstore?" Pete whispers.

I nod, slicing my eyes toward Pete for a second. "What did he want?" I can already guess, and my heart sinks at the very thought of it.

"He said Chase came home talking about you being at the drugstore with some thug." He glares at Pete, and Pete stiffens, his hand tightening on mine.

"Did you explain who Pete is?" I ask. I don't want to leave anyone with a misconception about Pete.

"I told him that he's someone my daughter is crushing on, but that I wasn't worried about it because she's a smart girl with her head on straight." His voice rises on the last words, and his glare at Pete grows even fiercer.

"I'm not crushing," I protest. But I *so* am.

Dad faces me. "Then what would you call it?"

I don't know what to call it because I don't know what it is. I shrug. Pete stiffens more when I do that than he has since Dad came through the gate.

"Chase wanted to know if you might want to go to the party at the country club tomorrow."

"I already told him no," I say. But I can already see the look on my dad's face. That's not going to work.

"I told him you'd love to." He opens the gate and stops, looking at me from over his shoulder. "He's picking you up at six."

I growl under my breath. Mainly because there's not much more I can do since Dad is gone. The gate slams shut behind him. I pull my hand from Pete's.

"Where are you going?" Pete asks.

"To catch my dad so I can tell him I'm not going."

"Do you want to go?" he asks. He watches me closely, his blue eyes blinking slowly.

"If I wanted to go, I wouldn't have told him no." I heave a sigh.

He steps back from me and takes all the warmth I was basking in a minute ago with him. "I think you should go," he says quietly.

"Why?" I ask softly. Something is really, really wrong. He doesn't usually distance himself like this.

"Your dad wants you to go," he says with a shrug. "You don't want to piss him off."

He starts to walk down the length of the pool. He signs to the boys, and they all start to put away the balls and the floats and they line up by the door.

"I'll see you later," he calls quietly. Then he leads the boys from the pool area back toward their cabins.

What did I do wrong? I seriously have no idea.

I see Dad going through the back door of the house, and I run to follow him. I don't know why he just did that, but what he said made Pete mad at me, so he needs to go apologize.

"Dad!" I call to his retreating back. He doesn't turn around to talk to me. He keeps going.

He's ignoring me now? What the hell?

I follow him into the kitchen and see him glaring at my mother, who looks a little bemused. "How could you do that?" I ask. My heart is thumping like crazy, and I can barely catch my breath.

"What did you do?" my mother asks.

Dad shrugs and washes his hands at the sink. He ignores me completely. Mom raises her brow at me in question.

"He called Pete a thug, and then he told me I have to go on a date with Chase just because his father called and snapped his fingers." I snap mine for good measure.

Mom's inquisitive grin turns into a scowl. "What?" she asks. She grabs my father's shoulder and turns him to face her. "You of all people called Pete a thug?"

"To his face!" I shout. "Then Pete left. And I don't even know what he's thinking."

"I know what he's thinking," Dad murmurs. Mom frowns.

"He's thinking you don't like him!"

Dad makes a noncommittal hum. That's it? A hum?

Mom's face softens. She can read Dad like a book. I just wish I could.

"What?" I ask. I look back and forth between them.

"Your dad is afraid Pete's trying to get in your pants," Mom says. She lifts her brow at Dad. Dad just glares at her. He won't even look at me.

I throw up my hands. "That's just it!" I cry. "He's not trying to get in my pants. He won't even kiss me!"

"Oh," Mom breathes.

Dad murmurs something, and Mom rubs his shoulder, her eyes soft as she looks at him.

"What?" I ask again.

"Your dad's afraid you'll get your heart broken," she says quietly. She looks sympathetically toward my dad.

I take a deep breath and steel myself. "Most girls get to have their hearts broken when they're eighteen or so. Maybe sixteen or whenever they find their first boyfriend." I jab a finger toward my chest. "I've never even had a boyfriend, Dad," I say. My eyes fill with tears, but I blink them back. How messed up is this? "I like Pete, and he's someone you can like, too. So, what's the problem? We haven't even been on a date!"

"I saw him watching you at the pool." Dad heaves a sigh. "He looks at you like I look at your mother." He tips her chin up so that her eyes meet his. "I saw her and I knew she was completely out of my league, but I wanted her more than I ever wanted anything." He looks at me. "And that's how Pete looks at you. That's what scares me, Reagan. Not that he's a thug or that he's poor or that he's been in prison. He looks at you like he never wants to stop looking at you. I'd probably like him more if he was just trying to get in your pants, because that's something you can get over. But a man loving you, that's completely different. You're not ready for it." He shrugs his shoulders. "You're just not."

He may as well have stuck a knife in my chest. "How do you know what I'm ready for?" I ask.

"I saw what that asshole did to you, Reagan," he says. He slams his fist down on the kitchen counter, making the dishes jump. And me, too. "I saw you walking around here, jumping at shadows, wrapping yourself in a protective bubble so no one else could hurt you. You learned how to protect your body, but no one ever taught you to protect your heart." He pounds his fist against his chest. "You're unprepared for what Pete wants. Completely unprepared."

"What do you want me to do?" I ask. I can barely hear myself, but Dad hears me.

"Stop it before it's too late," he spits out. "Just stop it."

"Okay," I breathe. "You win." I turn and walk out of the room.

I just met him two days ago. Why do I even feel like my soul already knows him intimately? I don't understand it, either. Maybe Dad's right.

Pete

I try not to look at her all through dinner. She sits with her brother and her mother, and her dad isn't here. Her mother motions with her hand for me to come and join them, but I shake my head and focus on my meal.

"Why aren't you with Reagan?" Tic Tac asks as he sits down beside me.

I shrug my shoulders. I don't even have the right words to describe it. "What's your name, man?" I ask.

He smiles. "Edward."

"People call you Eddie?" I ask.

He shakes his head. "Only one man ever called me Eddie, and I shot him when I caught him raping my little sister." He avoids my gaze. "So I wouldn't advise calling me that." He grins. "Call me shithead or whatever else you want, but don't call me Eddie."

"Was he your dad?" I ask.

He shakes his head. "Just some man my mom married." He looks off into the distance, as though he's seeing something in his mind instead of what's all around us. "I shot him," he says. He makes that little *pffftt* sound with his mouth like he did on the bus when he first spoke to me.

Wow. I don't even know how to respond to that. "How's your sister doing?" I ask. I think about Reagan and how I found her. And I don't even want to know about his sister.

"She was only eleven," he whispers. "Eleven fucking years old."

I shouldn't have judged this kid when I met him. "I'm so sorry," I say.

"It pisses me off because he stole what she could have been, you know?"

I nod, but no, I don't know.

"Does she live with your mom, now?" I ask.

"No," he replies. "She's in the system. My mom got arrested, too. Drugs, I think, right after it happened." He shrugs. "She's better off with a nice family." His eyes get bright. "They said I can visit her when I get out. It's only for an hour a time and I can't be alone with her, but that's all right. I just need to be sure she's okay."

I nod. "I don't have any sisters."

"Your girl, Reagan," he says. He smiles. "She looks like she can take care of herself."

"She can kick my ass." It's true.

"You think she'd teach me some of those karate moves?" he asks.

I grin. "You could ask her."

"I wish somebody had taught my sister how to do some of that stuff." He gets that faraway look again.

I'm not sure that would have changed her situation, but I nod anyway.

Edward gets up to throw his plate away and turns back to me. "When I get out, do you think I could come hang out with you and your brothers? Phil was telling me how you live close to me."

I nod. "I don't see why not." I don't know this kid, but I know he's had a rough time of it, and it was no fault of his own. "We could shoot some hoops."

He grins. "Okay." He goes to change into a swimsuit. The youth boys all get the night off. They're going to use the pool and just play around and be boys for the rest of the evening.

I concentrate on my dinner. Now that Edward's not here, it's easier to swallow. I don't have any sisters, but I have a niece named Hayley, and I'm not the only Reed boy who would kill anyone who tried to hurt her.

She's five, and I haven't seen her in a long time. Hell, she probably doesn't even remember me. But I could walk out of here today and give my life for hers with no regrets.

The dining area starts to clear out, and I realize I must have been lamenting over Edward's situation a little too long. Mr. Caster sits down across from me and rests his elbows on the table. He blows out a breath. "My daughter's no longer talking to me."

I don't respond and shovel a spoonful of spaghetti into my mouth so I'll have an excuse not to.

"Apparently, she likes you a lot."

I take a bite of bread. I still don't speak. The food is hard to swallow.

"Her mom's not speaking to me, either," he says. He grins a sideways smile. "I kind of like having sex with my wife, so I figured I better come over and clear the air."

I choke on my spaghetti. I look up at him as I try to catch my breath, coughing into my closed fist.

"Women have ways of getting what they want, Pete," he says. "And my wife wants Reagan to make her own choices." He inhales and exhales deeply. "I guess you're her choice." He jabs a finger at me. "But if you hurt her, so help you God, I will hunt you down and do things to you that can't even imagine."

"Yes, sir," I squeak out. I clear my throat. "I just met her," I remind him.

He shakes his head. "She's known you in her head for two and a half years, son. You didn't just meet her. You became her hero the night you took care of her. Now, how much of that is in her head and her head alone remains to be seen. But she feels a connection to you, and you're the only one she's ever let in. So, you're in, with my blessing."

I grin. "Thank you, sir."

I look over to where Reagan's sitting, but she's not looking at me. She's looking at the table. I take the last bite of my food and get ready to go to her. But by the time I get there, she's already getting up and walking away. "Reagan," I call to her.

She heaves a sigh and turns toward me. She kicks at a rock with the toe of her flip-flop. "Can I see you later?" I ask.

"Why?" she asks. She doesn't look me in the eye.

"Oh, good grief," I mutter.

Her gaze shoots up to meet mine. "Beg your pardon?" she asks.

Her back pocket rings, and she pulls her phone out, looking down at the screen. I see the name *Chase* before she lifts it to her ear and says hello. She holds up a finger to tell me to wait.

I grit my teeth and wait. "I'll see you tomorrow, Chase," she finally says. She's quiet, but I hear her.

She's going out with him? Seriously? I know I told her to, but... God. I fucked up.

"What did you need?" she asks as she sticks her phone back into her back pocket.

I feel like she just punched me in the gut. I shouldn't feel that way, but I do. "You're going out with that asshole?" I ask.

She inhales deeply with her eyes closed, as if she's fortifying herself before she speaks. "You told me to go out with him, Pete," she says.

I nod. "I did." She's right. I'm an idiot. "Do you plan to listen to everything I say?"

She rolls her eyes at me. I've never seen anyone roll her eyes and look quite so damn adorable. I grin. I can't help it.

"What's so amusing?" she asks, punching her fists into her hips as she glares at me.

"This is so fucked up," I mutter, more to myself than to her.

But she hears me, and she's hurt. I can see it on her face.

"I didn't mean you," I say.

She cocks her head to the side, her eyes narrowing at me. "Then what did you mean, Pete?"

"I meant this situation." I gesture from me to her and back again. "This whole thing exists on awful timing."

She goes to throw her plate in the trash, and I follow her. She stops and spins toward me really quickly and bumps into my chest. She steps back when I reach out to steady her. She smiles and shakes her head. "This really is fucked up," she says. She lets out a little laugh.

"So, Chase is the man, huh?" I say. I'm a dummy. I know.

"He's some guy I have to go on a date with," she says. She blows her bangs back from her forehead with an upturned breath.

"Can you get out of it?" I ask. Hope blooms inside me.

She shakes her head. "I tried to get out of it, but you told me not to," she reminds me.

"I was angry. I'm sorry." If there's one thing I can do well, it's apologize. "Your father was pretty much telling you I'm not good enough for you, and for a minute there, I agreed with him." This time, it's me who plays with a rock with my toe. I'm afraid of what I'll see if I look at her.

"I want to try something with you," she says quietly. She steps close, so close I can feel her breath against my shirt. It's warm and moist. My heart starts to thud. "Can I touch you?" she asks. She lays a hand on my stomach.

"Yes, please," I croak. I clear my throat, and she laughs.

Her other hand comes up to lie beside the first, and then one hand goes east while the other goes west, until her hands wrap around my back. She locks her hands behind me and lays her face against my shirt. She nuzzles her cheek into my left pectoral muscle. "Hug me back," she says quietly.

I wrap my arms around her, careful to squeeze her soft and slow, calmly and carefully. She exhales heavily, and I rest my chin on top of her head. In that second, I know my heart is hers. I tell myself she's only taking a little piece, but that's a fucking lie. She'll have the whole thing by the time I go back to New York. She undoes me with her simple affection. And I don't know how to behave, so I just hold her. I hold her and let her breathe while I drink in the feel of her. I want to tip her face up and press my lips to hers, but I'm not sure that would be any more fulfilling than this pregnant silence is. It's full of possibility. For me, it's full of longing, and something entirely different for her, probably. I open my eyes and look up. Her mother is standing there with her mouth hanging open. She slams it shut and smiles at me, giving me a thumbs-up. I grin. I can't help it.

I lay my hand on the back of Reagan's head and stroke down the length of her hair. "You have no idea how long I've wanted to touch you," I say quietly.

"You have no idea how long I've wanted to be touched," she says. I can feel the words against my chest, ripe with longing.

She inhales deeply and loosens her clutch on my midsection. Cool air wafts in where her warmth was, and I want to pull her back to me. "I'll see you later, Pete," she says.

"You all right?" I ask.

"Honestly, I'm a little overwhelmed, and I have some things to think about." She looks up at me, but her eyes are clouded by something I don't understand. "I need some time to myself."

I nod. I don't know why. "Can I do anything for you?" I ask. I tuck her hair behind her ear.

She shakes her head. "I don't think so. I'm going to take a break."

She pats my chest with a quick good-bye tap, and then she walks away. She goes inside the house, and she doesn't come back out. She doesn't come back out to lifeguard for the youth group at the pool. She doesn't come back out to roast marshmallows. She doesn't come back out to check on her horse. She doesn't come out the next morning to start events with the campers. She doesn't come outside again at all until the next night, when a neon-yellow Mustang pulls into the drive. Chase Gerald gets out and goes to get my girl. Then she finally comes out. On his fucking arm.

Reagan

I needed some time to get my head on straight. It's still a little crooked, but it feels a little better than it did. I slide my jeweled sandals onto my feet and tug at the length of my dress. I don't usually wear dresses, but this night is fancy. It's a country club dinner; it's not black tie, but it's really dressy. I'm wearing a sheath dress that wraps and ties at my hip. It's kind of clingy but not in a bad way. I turn and look at my butt in the mirror. I look all right. I arrange my hair in an updo, so that it's wrapped up and off my neck with little tendrils hanging down. I line my eyes with light eyeliner and mascara and apply some blush. I've been in the sun all summer, so I'm sure I don't need foundation.

A knock sounds at my door, and my mom sticks her head in. She's wiping her hands on a kitchen towel as she comes through the door. She whistles at me. "Don't you look nice," she says, nodding in appreciation. She walks over to my jewelry box and flips it open. "You want to wear Grandma's pendant with that?" she asks. I hadn't even thought about jewelry.

I turn around, and she puts the necklace around my neck. I lean over and let it dangle. I slide on some clanky bracelets and push them up my arm. They'll fall in a second, but they look nice.

I hold my hands out to the side. "Do I look like a normal girl?" I ask.

Her face softens. "Honey, you are a normal girl," she says softly. She narrows her eyes at me. "Why are you going on this date?" she asks.

"Because I couldn't get out of it," I admit. "And now I don't want to let Chase down."

She shakes her head. "He's not the one for you, is he?" she asks.

I shrug. "I don't know. I've never given him enough of a chance to find out."

She doesn't say anything. My mom is good like that. She's quiet when the situation calls for quiet, and she has a lot to say when the situation calls for that, too. "Your dad shouldn't have pushed this date."

I shake my head. "What if he's right? What if Chase is the one for me? I won't know until I find out." I heave a sigh.

"The heart wants what the heart wants, Reagan," she says.

I laugh, but there's no humor in the sound. "What does that mean, exactly?"

"I think you already know what it means." She sits on the edge of my bed. "This Pete," she says. "You trust him, right?"

"About as much as I can trust anyone I met three days ago," I say flippantly. But Pete's more than that, and I know it.

"Your heart has known him for a very long time," she says.

"My heart doesn't work like everyone else's heart," I bite out. "I can't trust it to lead me *anywhere*."

"Oh, Reagan," she breathes softly. "I fucking hate that man for doing this to you. It's been over two years and you still don't trust yourself to move on with your life. It's like you're stuck in that moment when he hurt you."

"You don't know what it feels like, Mom," I say quietly in warning. She can't talk about this. She hasn't experienced it.

"Did you know that one in five college-age girls will be raped during her college career?" she asks. "One in five, Reagan!" she cries.

"And?" I say. "Life goes on, is that what you're saying?" I ask. My life didn't go on. I got stuck in that moment. Until Pete. "Pete makes me want things that scare me," I admit.

"That's what love is about, Reagan. It's thrilling and scary as hell and it makes your heart pound and it makes your insides ache." She stops and glares at me. "Those feelings are normal. What's not normal is what happened to you and how you closed yourself off to protect your heart."

"Well, my heart is officially in danger," I say drolly.

"So is his," she reminds me.

Not once in all of this have I stopped to consider Pete's feelings about our burgeoning relationship. I've considered my fears. I've considered my feelings. I've considered my needs and wants. But I haven't really considered his. What if he hasn't kissed me because he's afraid I'll damage him? What if he doesn't want me the same way? What if he does want me but he's afraid to touch me because I'll go crazy on him? What if? What if? What if? "Pete's heart is good and kind," I say. "That's all I know about it."

She smiles. "That's a start."

My dad yells for me from the bottom of the steps. "Reagan!" he calls. "Chase is here!"

Mom stands up. "Trust your heart, Reagan," she says. She kisses me on the forehead and walks down in front of me. At the bottom of the stairs, I see Chase looking up at me. His green eyes aren't the ones I want to see, but I need to try, right? I need to give this a shot.

"Hi, Chase," I chirp.

"Reagan," he says. He's all smiles. He swivels his hips. "You ready for some dancing?"

"Of course," I say with a smile. "Sounds like fun."

I take his arm as we walk out. He opens the door of his obnoxious yellow car, and I slide inside. His gaze roams up my thigh where my dress shifts, and I pull it down. He grins and closes the door. Then he slides into the driver's seat and peels out of the driveway, slinging rocks in our wake.

Pete

I glance at my watch again and look toward the driveway. Reagan still isn't home and it has been four hours. That's plenty of time for dinner and dancing, isn't it? Why isn't she home yet?

I hear the rumble of that loud-ass Mustang engine, and my body tenses. I get up from where I was sitting chatting with some of the youth boys and begin to pace. It's dark outside, and the lights are on at the front of the house. I can see the drive but not very clearly.

"I'll be right back," I say quietly. The boys smirk, and one shakes his head. "What?" I ask.

"Nothing," he says, grinning. "You're one pussy-whipped motherfucker, you know that?"

Yeah. I know it. And I don't mind it. I walk slowly toward the front of the house. I stop by the bushes, hiding in the shadows. The car stops, but it's not the douchebag that gets out of the driver's seat. It's Reagan. Her hair is a mess, hanging down her back in tangled waves. When she left, it was a chic knot on top of her head. Her dress is hanging off her shoulder, and she reaches to adjust it before she goes in the house. She stops to fix her hair, too. She's carrying her shoes in her fingertips by the straps.

What the fuck?

Suddenly, a second car pulls up behind the first, and Reagan turns. She shades her eyes and looks toward the lights. She stomps her foot, and then I see Chase get out of the passenger side of the other car. Reagan doesn't even stop to talk to him. She goes inside her house and slams the door. The noise of it reverberates around the yard.

Chase limps over to his car. By this point, darkness is crowding the corners of my vision and I can barely think, much less see. He did something to her, or she wouldn't be so angry. I advance on him and scare the ever-loving shit out of him when I throw him up against the side of the car and get in his face. "What the fuck did you do to her?" I ask, my face an inch from his. He reaches up to wipe my spit from his cheek.

"I didn't do anything to her," he protests.

"You did something or she wouldn't be so angry." I hold him against the car. If I don't, I'll have to hit him, and I really want to hear his story before I hit him. I want to hear him say he's sorry before I kill him.

"I didn't do anything," he swears, holding his hands out like he's surrendering. That's when I notice he has a splotch of blood under his nose. I turn him toward the light. His nose was definitely bleeding because there are gushes of it on his shirt. My heart thrills at the thought of it.

"You have until I count to three," I say. But before I can even start counting down, he blurts out the truth. "We were dancing, and I was touching her..."

"Touching her where?" I growl. I swear to fucking God, I'm going to kill him.

"Just holding her while we danced," he says. But he won't look into my eyes.

"And?" I prompt.

"And," he says slowly. "And I might have grazed her boob once or twice. Then the next thing I knew, she punched me in the face. Then she kneed me in the nuts, and when I bent over to grab for my gonads, she hit me in the jaw with her knee." He mimics her motions, and I can imagine exactly what she did to him. Laughter bubbles within me. But he's not done yet. "Then she pressed the heel of her shoe on my nuts while I was lying on the ground and pressed down hard until I gave her my car keys. Then she stole my car." He points down the road to the other car that dumped him and left. "I had to get my buddy to drive me here."

She stole his fucking car after she beat him up. I laugh. I can't help it. I laugh in his face. I don't need to do anything to him. She did enough. She completely emasculated him. "Are you sure all you did was touch her boob?" I ask.

"That's all. I swear it." The asshole is still grabbing for his nuts and slightly hunches over when I let him go. "That shit hurt, man."

I chuckle. I can't help it. "I'm sure it did."

"That bitch is crazy," he says, looking toward the house.

"I'll tell her you said so." I laugh. I can't even scold him for calling her a bitch, not with everything she did to him.

"Please don't," he begs. "My dad will kill me if her father is mad at me."

"Too late," a voice calls from the front door. Her father steps into the light. "Hi, Pete," he says. He smiles at me.

"Hi, Mr. Caster," I say, waving at him joyfully.

"Hi, Chase," he says.

Chase is smart enough to press his lips together and not say a word.

"You may go now, Chase," Mr. Caster instructs, and Chase scrambles to get into his car. He fires it up and sprays our feet with gravel when he pulls away.

Mr. Caster smiles at me. "I couldn't even hit the poor bastard after what she did to him," he admits with a chuckle.

"Me, either," I say. It wouldn't have been fair. "Is Reagan all right?" I ask. I really want to see her.

"She's pissed as hell," he says. He jerks a thumb toward the barn. "She went out the back door toward the barn."

I look longingly toward the area where he pointed.

"What are you waiting for, son?" he asks. "Go!"

I smile and reach for his hand. He shakes with me and grins. "Thank you, Mr. Caster," I say, and I run for the barn.

I open the door and find her standing in the middle of the lit hallway between stalls. She's still wearing her pretty dress from the party, but she has replaced her strappy sandals with muck boots and her hair is down around her shoulders. Her dog growls when she sees me, posturing so I don't get any closer, so she calls her to her and Maggie goes and lies down at her feet. "What do you want?" Reagan barks at me.

"Did you kiss him?" I ask. I wait, unable to breathe until I hear her answer.

She stares at me for a moment and then she shakes her head, and that's all the prompting I need.

Reagan

I'm so pissed off that I can barely see straight. And Pete wants to know if I kissed Chase Gerald? Seriously?

He rushes toward me and grabs me in his arms, yanking me against him. He looks down into my face. "I'm going to kiss you," he warns.

I shove him back, but it's like pushing a brick wall. "Stop it, Pete," I say. "You're being ridiculous."

He holds on tightly, though, and hitches his hands beneath my bottom, lifting me against him. Then he pushes me back against the wall of the stall. He slides a knee between my legs to hold me up, his foot resting on the side of a bag of feed, and takes my face in his hands. His breath smells like mints and Pete, and his exhale tickles my lips. "Reagan," he breathes softly. It's no more than a murmur, but he may as well have shouted it. My heart beats so loudly I can hear it in my ears, and I know he can feel it.

"Pete," I say. His hands thread into the hair at my temples, and his thumbs tilt my face up so that his lips are almost touching mine. "Please kiss me," I breathe.

His lips finally graze mine, gently at first. His mouth is closed, and he waits, his eyes open and staring into mine as he tests my mouth tentatively. He's tender and soft, but I don't want tender and soft. I lick across the seam of his lips, and he opens for me. His tongue invades my mouth and tangles with mine. His hands hold my face still as he takes over the kiss, growling low in his throat as he plays me. Oh, good God, does he play me. He licks into me, inside me, his tongue sliding against mine, thrusting in and out of my mouth. I match him, breathing so hard I can't catch my breath. I hitch myself higher on his leg, pressing my panty-clad girl parts against him. My clit is thumping like mad, and I can't even think about anything but relieving this most delicious ache he's stirring inside me. His tongue pulls back from my mouth, but I don't want him to go.

A whimper that doesn't even sound human leaves my throat, and I pull him back to me by sucking his lower lip into my mouth. I tongue his piercing, and he growls low in his throat. I rock against his thigh, and he takes his hands from my face and puts them on my bottom so he can tug me forward on his knee. He presses just the right spot, and I lift my face to gasp, trying to find enough breath to keep my runaway heart thumping, my head falling back against the stall door. He's taking all of my weight now because my legs would never support me even if he did let me go. His lips tickle across my chin and down the side of my neck, and he looks into my eyes as he tugs the tie at my hip and parts my dress. His hands are hot and hard as they encircle my waist, squeezing gently, not asking for my permission, but he has it. There's no doubt about it.

He looks into my face as he raises his hand and cups my bra, his thumb tracking across my nipple. I take his hand in mine and press it harder against my breast. He growls into the side of my throat and freezes. He stops, inhaling and exhaling. I take his face in my hands and pull him back to me, but he backs his face away. "Just a second," he pleads. "I need just a second." He's breathing as hard as I am.

But I don't want to give him a second. I tug the cup of my bra down and bare my breast for him. Pete bends his head and takes my nipple into his mouth. He hums as he gives it a tug, his lips insistent as he suckles, his tongue flicking against the turgid flesh. I can't think. I can't stop the whimpers that escape my throat. "Pete," I cry. He grabs my bottom and pulls me further forward, then pushes my belly until I lie back against the stall door. He looks down at my panties, and I can see the wet spot on the pink fabric. I close my eyes.

He takes my chin in his left hand and makes me look at him. "Open your eyes," he says.

I shake my head.

He withdraws from me. "Don't!" I cry. I need him. I don't know what to do with this need. "I'm scared," I say quietly. I'm not scared of Pete. I'm scared of myself. Because I'd do just about anything he asked me to do right now.

His thumb brushes the front of my panties, and my mouth falls open at the sensation. No one has ever touched me like this before. Never with such soft, sinful, sweet hands. His thumb presses my panties into my crease, and he rubs against my clit, the abrasion of the fabric not nearly enough. He kisses me, and I breathe against his lips.

"Can I put my hand inside your panties?" he asks. He nips my ear when he does it, and I cry out. I nod into his neck, moving as close to him as I can get. His hand slides between my panties and my skin, and I press my bottom closer to him, giving him more access. "So wet," he says. I squeeze my eyes shut. His fingers trail through my wetness, and then they find that little button of pleasure that has been thumping since his lips first touched mine.

He presses the pad of his middle finger against me, his touch gentle but insistent. "Pete," I cry.

"Reagan," he breathes. He kisses me again, but it's broken by my breaths, which stutter past my lips. I can't think. I can't talk. I can only take the pleasure he gives me. "Come for me, Reagan," he breathes against my lips.

Then I break. I nip his lower lip when I come, and he growls, thrusting his tongue into my mouth as he absorbs my every shudder, my every gasp, my every quiver. I rock against his hand, pressing against him as he plies me. I tuck my head into his shoulder, my arms around his neck, as he wrings every last bit of pleasure from my body until I'm spent and heavy against him, still quivering, still shaking, still…in love with him. I mewl into his neck, and he hums. When my body stills, he pulls his hand from my panties, lifts me so that my legs wrap around his hips, and he stands up. Then he sits down on a bale of hay with me straddling his lap.

He holds me tightly against him as I fall back to earth. When I can lift my head, I sit up and look into his blue eyes. "What the fuck was that?" I breathe. I laugh. I can't help it, but I never even thought I would feel this free. Ever.

He pulls me to him and wraps me in a tight hug. "That, my dearest Reagan, was one hell of a first kiss."

"Epic," I breathe. Then I giggle. I laugh. Just because I can.

Pete

Jesus fucking Christ that was the hottest thing I've ever seen, done, or even imagined. I've been with a lot of girls, but I have never had one come undone like Reagan just did. I pull her against me, her skin against my shirt. She's warm and soft and feels so damn good on top of me that I'm in danger of coming in my pants. I hold her against me, but then she sits up, looks into my face, and says, "What the fuck was that?"

That was an orgasm. A really, really good one if her cries were any indication. If the way she trembled in my arms was any indication. If the way she said my name over and over and over was any indication. "That, my dearest Reagan," I say, trying to remain flippant, but I'm moved. Moved unlike I have ever been moved before. "Was one hell of a first kiss."

Her body shakes and I worry that she's crying, but she's not. She's laughing. Giggling, actually. "Epic!" she screams. Then she laughs again. She throws her head back, her hair falling down to reach my hands, which are just over her ass. I look down at her boob, which is still uncovered, her nipple pert and perky and…bare. God, her tits are beautiful. I look into her face because I can't look at her boob anymore. I want her. I want her so badly. But she's not ready for what I want. I'm sure of it. She's just not. I slide my finger into the edge of her bra and lift it to cover her. She looks down and flushes. She just came on my fucking hand and now she wants to be shy about it?

"You okay?" I ask, brushing her sweaty hair back from her forehead.

She nods, biting her lower lip between her teeth. I can't help it. I'm a guy. And I'm so hard I could pound nails with my dick. "I'm so much better than okay," she says quietly. A tear forms in the corner of her eye, but she blinks it back. "Pete," she says. "Can I ask you something?"

"Anything," I murmur. I pull her down to lie on my chest and stroke the length of her hair.

"Will you go on a date with me when we get back to the city?" she asks.

Laughter bubbles within me. She just came sitting on my leg with my hand in her panties and she wants to know if I'll take her on a date. "Of course," I say. "I wouldn't like anything more." Well, I'd kind of like to come, too, but I can wait. I can wait for when she's ready.

"Was that an orgasm?" she whispers. I imagine she's smiling against my chest because I can hear it in her voice. She turns her head and hides her face in my shirt.

"A big one," I say with a laugh. "Fucking huge." *I am the man. Yes, I am.*

She laughs, her shoulders rocking with it, her bottom wiggling against my dick. Shit. I wish she'd stop that. "Thought so," she whispers.

I pat her butt. "We need to get you dressed," I say, encouraging her with a squeeze to climb off me.

She stands up, and I help her fix her clothes. Her horse makes a noise, and she looks over the stall door. She heaves a sigh. "It'll be a few hours yet," she says. She makes a twittery, nervous sound that might be laughter and avoids my gaze. Is she suddenly feeling self-conscious?

I scrub a hand across the back of my head and force myself not to think about the way she felt in my arms. I'm already feeling the loss of her and she's just standing a few feet away from me. "For what?" I ask.

"Tequila is going to foal tonight."

She's speaking a language I don't know.

"She's going to have her baby," she clarifies.

"Oh." I don't know what to say to that. "Do you need to call a vet?"

"No, I'll sleep here with her." She points to a stack of blankets in the corner. "She does most of the work. I'm just here for moral support and to help if something goes wrong."

I scratch my head, not sure what to do with myself. "Should I go?"

She worries her lower lip between her teeth. "Want to stay with me?" she asks quietly.

God, I want nothing more. I want to sleep with her and hold her against me. Yeah, I want to have sex with her, too, but that's the least of my desires. I nod.

She spreads out blankets on top of the hay bales where we were sitting. She motions for me to lie down and then crawls into my arms. I let out a contented sigh. "What time is it?" she asks.

I look at my watch and yawn. "Eleven thirty."

"Late," she whispers.

She lays her head on my chest and wraps her arm around my middle. "Let me hold you," I say, and I press my lips to her forehead.

Her exhales tickle the hair at the neckline of my shirt, and I'm instantly hard again. I pull her leg across my lap, and she snuggles even closer to me.

"Hey, Pete," she whispers.

"Yeah?" I whisper back.

"I want to kiss you again tomorrow," she says quietly. She giggles, and it shakes my chest. That's the most beautiful sound I have ever heard.

I want to kiss her again tomorrow, too. A lot.

###

In my dream, I'm running toward the sound of Reagan's voice. I can hear her clearly, but I can't see her. I know it's a dream, and dreams can be fucked up, so I'm not panicking. But she is. She's clearly upset, and I look for her everywhere in the mist. I can't find her. Suddenly, I'm jerked from my dream and find myself lying beside Reagan in the barn where we fell asleep. She's making choked little cries from the back of her throat. I look down at her. She's the one dreaming. Her eyes are squeezed shut and she has curled herself into a ball. When we fell asleep, she was draped across me. When did she scoot away?

"Reagan," I coo softly. She flinches and bats at my hand. She's still dreaming, and I don't know how to pull her out of it. "Reagan," I say with more force. Her eyes blink open as she slowly wakes. She bats her lashes at me as I look down into her face. She's breathing hard, but she quickly calms.

"I was dreaming," she says. She looks around and settles back against the blanket, her body softening.

"Bad dream?" I ask.

She nods. I roll onto my side and rest my head in my hand so I can look down at her. She scoots closer to me, and I drape my arm around her waist. "Sorry," she murmurs.

I tug her waist, pulling her to me. "Don't be," I say.

"I used to take medication to help with the dreams, but they made my head foggy so I stopped them." She looks up at me, her green eyes blinking slowly. "Sometimes I don't sleep well."

I brush her hair back from her face. "You dream about what happened that night?" I ask.

"Sometimes." She looks away and avoids my gaze. She doesn't want to talk about it, apparently.

I want to ask questions, but I don't want to bring it all back up for her if she has pushed it from the forefront of her mind. "Do you relive it in your dreams?" I ask.

She shakes her head. "Not the rape, specifically," she says. She says it like it's such a common word. My gut clenches. "I dream more about the feelings. Regret, mainly."

"What do you regret?" I ask.

She looks up at me, almost like she's seeking a connection with me, and I like it. I fucking love it. "I regret going to that party," she says. "I should have been in my dorm studying."

"Did you know him?" I ask. "Or was he a stranger?"

"I had never met him. That's why I feel so stupid over it. I never should have been alone with him in the bathroom. Alone with a man I didn't know." She heaves a sigh. "One minute he's kissing me, and then I'm calling out to stop because it just doesn't feel right. But he wouldn't."

She shivers, and I want to draw her inside me and protect her. A tear slips from the corner of her eye and tracks down her temple.

She sniffs. "Sorry, I didn't mean to cry on you." She chuckles, but it's a watery sound.

"You came while riding my knee, princess," I say quietly. "I think you can cry on me, too."

Her face colors, but she smiles. She whispers, "I've never done that before."

"No one has ever made you come?" I ask. I know the answer to this, but I want to hear her say it. I don't know why. I just need it. I slide my leg across her thighs and put some of my weight on her, but she doesn't seem to mind. I really want to open her dress so I can lay my hand on her belly. But I settle for this moment, instead.

She shakes her head.

I run my finger down her nose. "You never did that yourself?" I ask.

She shakes her head. "No." She looks into my eyes. "Thank you," she says.

"Anytime, princess," I say with a laugh. "I am at your disposal."

"You're such a giver," she taunts, shoving my shoulder.

"I aim to serve." I laugh. God, she makes me feel so light and free. "I think I could have some very real feelings for you," I blurt out. I want to bite the words back as soon as I say them.

"Good," she says, and she smiles as she rolls into my chest and wraps her arm around me. She buries her face in my shirt. I think she might be embarrassed.

"I pour my heart out and all you can say is *good?*" I jostle her in my arms.

"Mmm hmm," she hums. I feel her lips against my shirt, her breath warming the fabric. She laughs. "You can't really call that pouring your heart out, Pete." She mocks my tone, making her voice deep. "I think I might have some very real feelings for you." She laughs, and damn it all, it's such a pretty sound that she can't annoy me with it.

She lifts the tail of my shirt, and her fingers slide up my stomach. I cover her hand with mine to stop her exploration. I'm too turned on. I don't think my erection ever eased from before, and it's pressing hard against my zipper now.

"Why can't I touch you?" she whispers.

"Because I'm too turned on right now," I whisper back.

She sits back so she can look up at my face. "What does that even mean?"

I press my lips to her forehead, lingering there. "It means I'm a guy. And the wind is blowing."

Her eyebrows draw together. "What?"

I laugh. "Nothing." But now I can't stop chuckling. She slaps my chest.

"It's not funny unless more than one person is laughing." She gets quiet for a minute, and then she says, "How many women have you slept with?"

I close my eyes and wince. "I stopped counting them a long time ago. When I ran out of fingers."

"More than ten?" Her voice is small.

"Yeah," I grunt. I don't like my own answers so I can't expect her to like them.

"More than your fingers and toes?" she asks.

"Probably," I breathe out. "Hell, I don't know."

"Do you know their names?" She sits up in front of me and crosses her legs criss-cross-applesauce style. She tugs her dress down to cover her knees.

I sit up, too, so I can face her. I lay my hand on her knee and draw circles on it with my thumb. "Some of them." I hold up one finger when she starts to ask me something else. "But there hasn't been anyone in a really long time. Since before I got locked up." I squint at her. "Does that count for anything?"

Her face softens, and she blows out a breath. "I wasn't judging you, Pete. Just trying to get to get to know you."

I nod, unable to look her in the eye. "Have you ever been in love?" she asks. She's smiling at me, though, and this question seems more benign than the last.

Not until now. But I don't say that, because if I do, I'll scare her with the depth of my feelings. "Maybe," I hedge.

"What does that mean?" she asks. "Maybe?" She narrows her eyes.

"I don't know," I say. I feel things for her that I have never felt for anyone. Is it love? I just don't know. It's too new to tell. I need some time to explore it before I have to explain it. "What about you?" I ask. "Have you ever been in love?"

She shakes her head. "No." She grins.

"What?" I ask. I scrub at my nose. "Do I have a booger?"

She laughs. "No," and she brushes my hand down. "I have never been in love." Her green eyes dart around for a second and then land on me. "Would you know love if you found it?" she asks.

I tilt my head from side to side as if I'm weighing the heaviness of her words. "I think I would."

She smiles. "Can I keep asking questions or am I getting on your nerves?" she asks.

"Ask me anything." Honestly, I've been locked up for a really long time. Being in jail is lonely, and I need a connection. I want that connection with her. And only her. "But I get to ask you questions, too."

"That's fair," she says. She's thinking hard about her next question. "Our first kiss," she whispers. "It was epic."

"Yeah, it was," I agree.

"Is it always that epic? With every girl you have been with?"

I scratch the back of my head. "Most girls don't have an orgasm when I kiss them." I laugh. "Is that what you want to know?"

She shakes her head. "No. I mean…" Her face colors. "I know it wasn't epic for you, but it was pretty damn epic for me."

I lean close and press my lips to hers because I just have to. "I know. I almost came in my pants just watching you." I kiss her again, and she hums against my mouth. It's a happy sound. But then she covers her face when I look her in the eye.

"You talk about it like it's nothing." She's embarrassed.

I tip her chin up. "What I've done in the past with other girls was nothing. What we did tonight? That was far from nothing." I tweak her nose because I'm about to rock my own world, and I want to ease the blow if she rejects me. "I have real feelings for you, Reagan," I say quietly. "I can't explain them. And I don't want to. But don't try to push what happened between us tonight off as common. Because it wasn't. It was big. And I want to keep doing it. I want to learn all about you and have you learn all about me. I want you to meet my family. I want to go on a date with you." I look around. "This place is nice, but...seriously?"

She laughs. "You want me to meet your family?" she asks.

"If you think you can stand it. There are five of us. All men."

"I'm not afraid of men in general," she explains.

"Just the ones that touch you." I run my crooked finger along her cheekbone, and she turns into my hand to kiss my palm.

"Your brothers look like you," she says.

"How do you know that?" I ask.

"I saw them when you got out of prison," she says quietly.

"You were there?"

She nods. "My dad made me sit in the truck while he talked to you about camp." She draws her lower lip between her teeth and bites down like she's anxious about my response. "Sorry. I should have told you sooner." She groans. "I kind of asked for you to be here. So I could see you."

"I'm glad you did." Never been happier about anything.

"Your brothers all have tattoos, too," she says. She looks at the tattoo on my arm that's for my mom. She picks up my hand and traces the tats that go up my forearm to my sleeve. "I want to look at all of them so I can find out what makes you tick." She draws a circle around the American flag.

"That one's for my buddy who died in Afghanistan."

Her silky fingertips slide up the dragon on my inner arm. "And this one?" she asks softly.

"That one was a little too much courage one night," I say with a laugh.

Her hand slips beneath the edge of my sleeve. "I guess I can't go much farther," she says.

I reach behind my neck and pull the shirt over my head the way guys do. She grins and gets an evil glint in her eye. But I move, lean back against the stall door, and pull her across my lap. "If you get to explore me, I get to explore you," I warn. I tickle my fingers up the side of her leg.

But then her lips press against the words that line my collarbone. She suckles my skin gently. I groan quietly and move my hand to her inner thigh. Her skin is soft and silky, and I know I'm going to have to call a halt to this soon. I can only take so much in one night. She tilts her head to read the words she just tongued across my chest. "*All for one, one for all,*" she reads quietly. "That one is about your brothers?"

I nod. "I live for them. When I thought Matt was dying, I wanted to die with him."

"Your brother was dying?" she asks. Her hands stop exploring, and she looks into my face.

"Matt had cancer. It was really expensive, and Logan had to come home from college. We were broke, and we were all afraid he was going to die." I look into her face. "Do you want to hear about this?" I ask.

She nods and settles in my arms. "I want to hear everything."

"Sam and I took side jobs with this guy in our neighborhood to make some extra money. It wasn't really illegal." I stop and growl. I can't lie to her. "We knew it was illegal, but we needed money for Matt. That's how

I got arrested." I'm not proud of it, but I can't undo my past. That would be like putting toothpaste back in the tube.

"Desperation can make a person do things they wouldn't normally do," she says softly. "How's Matt now?"

I smile. "He's in remission."

"Oh, good," she breathes. "Tell me about the others."

"Paul's the oldest. He has a daughter named Hayley, and she lives with us half the time. And Logan is the one I told you about who goes to NYU."

She counts on her fingers. "There's one more, right?"

I nod. "Yeah."

"Where's he?"

"He's away at college on a football scholarship." He's living the dream. My dream. Sam just wants to bake cakes. But Paul says we all have to finish college, so he went.

"Are you close?" she asks.

"Not as close as we used to be."

"Can you remedy that?"

Can I? "I'm going to try." And I will. As soon as I go home.

She tucks herself closer under my arm and settles there. After a few minutes, her breaths even out and she gets soft in my arms. I look down my nose at her. She's asleep in my arms, and I don't ever want to put her down. So, I pull the blanket over the both of us and hold her close to me, as close as I can get her.

Reagan

I wake up to a tinny, clanking sound. I sit up, sticky where I slept against Pete's shoulder. We must have sweated together, our skin pressed close. And I might have drooled on him a little bit, too. Yuck. I wipe the side of my mouth and sit up. Pete stirs under me and then freezes. He lifts his head and looks around. He groans and falls back against the blanket. "Shit, I'm fucked," he grunts.

"You better not have been," my dad calls out. He clanks the lid of the feed bucket as he scoops out sweet feed for the horses. Link helps him, and Dad's making a lot more noise than Link is.

I close my eyes. Dad's mad. I just slept in the barn with Pete. And he knows it. "Oh shit," I say.

"Oh shit," Link parrots.

Pete closes his eyes as he grins. "You better stop while you're ahead," he whispers with a laugh.

"Good morning, Pete," Dad says, faking joviality as he walks by us carrying buckets. I start to sit up, but as I pull the blanket from Pete, I realize he still doesn't have a shirt on. He took it off last night so I could explore his ink. This looks really bad.

"Where's your shirt?" I whisper. I look around in the lump of blankets and don't see it.

"Oh shit," Link says again. He pops his head up beside mine and holds up Pete's blue T-shirt.

"Oh, blue shirt," Pete says.

"Oh, blue shirt," Link parrots.

Pete takes it and pulls it over his head. He reaches out to ruffle Link's hair, but Link steps to the side. "At least he's not saying shit anymore," Pete says.

"Shit," Link says.

I groan and run a hand through my hair.

"Lincoln!" Dad barks. "Bring me that bucket."

"Bring me the bucket," Link says. He scampers off to get Dad's bucket.

"Good morning," Pete says quietly. He turns to drop his feet to the floor and stands up, stretching tall. He shows a small strip of his abs, and I want to lean forward and lick him. God, where did that come from?

"Morning," I mutter. I lick my lips.

"Stop looking at me like that," Pete whispers.

"Like what?" I whisper back. But a grin tugs at the corners of my lips. I can't help it.

"Like you want lick me like a lollipop," he says. He adjusts the front of his pants, and I can't help but notice the bulge there. "Stop looking at it," he hisses.

I look for my dad, but he's gone outside the barn. "I don't even know what I'm looking at!" I complain. Pete takes my hand and presses my fingertips against the bulge of his erection. He gasps in a breath as my fingertips explore the ridges of him. "Reagan," he groans. He turns his hip and puts up a knee to block me. "Would you stop it? I'd like to walk out of here sometime today."

"Licking it like it's a lollipop?" I ask, unable to get the idea out of my head. "You can do that?"

He grins and scratches the back of his head. "Well, I can't. But you could." His voice is gravely and kind of nasally since he just woke up.

"Never mind," he says. He pulls me to my feet and presses a quick kiss to my lips.

"Uh," I say, brushing him away. "Morning breath."

"I don't care," he says, leaning to kiss me quickly. I give him my cheek. "Give it to me," he says. I pucker my lips and touch his quickly, careful not to breathe on him. "That's better," he croons. "Should I go talk to your dad?" he asks.

It's really sweet that he would even think of that. "I doubt that's a good idea."

I hear a horse blow, and I remember the whole reason why we slept in the barn in the first place. I step onto a bale of hay and look down at Tequila. She's on her feet and apparently, I was wrong. False alarm on the foaling.

Pete drops an arm around my shoulders and pulls me close to him. Dad bursts back into the barn with the slam of a door. I jump. Pete doesn't let me go.

"Pete, don't you have somewhere to be?" Dad asks. "Like in your own cabin in your own bed?"

Pete nods his head. "Yes, sir," he says. He turns to me. "I'll see you later?"

I nod. My belly does a little flippy-floppy thing, and he touches his lips to mine.

"See you later, Mr. Caster," he calls.

"Not if I see you first," Dad calls back.

Dad slams around the barn for a few more minutes while I feed Tequila a carrot.

"Have a nice night?" Dad barks. He doesn't look up from whatever he's doing.

I smile. My belly drops down toward my toes at the thought of it. "I did, actually."

"Reagan," Dad breathes.

"Yes, Dad?" I say sweetly. He's mad, but I can't make him un-mad. And I probably deserve it for spending the whole night in the barn with Pete.

"Don't make me have to kill that boy," Dad warns.

"Yes, sir," I say, dipping my head so he won't see my smile. "You should know that we didn't do anything wrong, though. He was a perfect gentleman. He just…" I square my shoulders. "He just held me."

Dad draws in a quick breath. I don't let anyone touch me, and Dad knows it. So in this situation, I might as well have said, "he just fucked me all night long." The level of intimacy is about the same in my dad's mind. I'm sure of it. "All right," he mutters. He throws hay to the horses, one flake at a time.

"Dad," I call out. He stops and looks up at me. "Is it okay that I might be falling in love with him?"

Dad's eyes open wide, and he blows out a breath. "Reagan," he says quietly. "You should go and talk to your mother about this."

"Okay…" I say.

"If you want to talk about the best way to knee him in the nuts," he says, pointing to his chest, "then I'm your guy. But if you want to talk about feelings and emotions and birth control and stuff, go talk to your mother."

"How did you just jump from feelings to birth control?" I have to ask.

"Because that's what happens, Reagan. You jump from strong feelings to birth control. It's the natural order of things for men." He takes off his cap and runs a hand through is hair. "I was a twenty-one-year-old man once myself."

"That's when you met Mom," I say, and I start to smile. He looks uncomfortable. So I have to press it. "So you and Mom went from strong feelings to birth control?" I ask. I snap my fingers. "Like that?"

"Nope," he says, stopping to stare into my eyes. "How do you think we got you?" He grins this time. He nods his head toward the house. "Go talk to your mother."

"TMI, Dad," I sing. "TMI!" I turn to walk toward the house.

"Reagan!" Dad calls. I turn to face him. "Pete's a good guy," he says. "But he's still a guy."

"We're taking things slow, Dad," I say. Heat floods my face.

"Mmm hmm," he hums. He goes back to work.

"Take it slow," Link says.

"I love you, Link," I call.

"I love you, too," he calls back.

I walk into the back door and find my mom pouring a cup of coffee. "Pete still alive?" she asks me as she goes to sit down at the table.

"For now." I sigh. "We fell asleep. Nothing happened, I swear." Well, not nothing. But we didn't do anything, really. Nothing that didn't rock my world as I know it.

"That's why you're glowing?" she asks. "Because nothing happened?" She pats the table next to her. "Come sit," she says.

"Mom," I grouse, sounding like a child, I know.

"Sit," she says more forcefully. I drop into a chair.

"Was he kind?" she asks.

I nod.

"Was he considerate?"

I nod and draw my lower lip between my teeth as I fight a smile.

"Was he careful?" She arches her brow at the last question.

"God, Mom," I complain. "We didn't do anything. He just kissed me."

"I'll make an appointment with my gynecologist if you want birth control," she says. She looks at me.

I find myself nodding my head, and Mom smiles and pats my hand. "Good girl," she says on a sigh.

Pete

I'm with the group of hearing-impaired boys, and they're taking turns riding the horses around the ring. The deaf kids tend to make a group of themselves, and they haven't been interacting with some of the other kids at the camp. I'll have to see what I can do about that. Since my brother is deaf, there's one thing I do know, and it's that deaf kids don't see themselves as handicapped. They have a culture all their own, and they can function in society with little or no intervention. But they do tend to clique up since sign language is something they all have in common.

I've never spent much time around horses. Or any, if I have to tell the truth. They're great, big, heavy beasts, and the one I'm leading around the ring keeps nudging me with her nose against my shoulder. "Would you cut it out?" I ask, but she just makes a breathy noise and nuzzles the back of my head. She knocks off my baseball cap, and I bend over to pick it up. But when I do, she bumps me in the ass, and I fall onto my hands in the dirt.

I dust off my hands and look around. Edward, who I can no longer call Tic Tac since I heard his story, is leading one of the other horses. He snorts at me. "Dude, I think you just got bitch slapped. Again." He chuckles, so I flip him the bird. Edward looks over my shoulder and whistles low, and I turn around to find Reagan walking toward us. She must have gone and taken a shower because her hair's still damp and she's plaited it into two braids that hang over her shoulders. She's wearing a T-shirt and a pair of cut-off jeans, and some brown leather boots that come up mid-calf. Damn, she's pretty.

She pats the horse I'm leading as she comes closer. "Is Juliette giving you a hard time?" she asks. She leans close to the horse's ear and whispers to her. The hair on my arms stands up, and it's not even my ear she's whispering into. Juliette shakes her head, and Reagan laughs. Damn, that's a pretty sound.

She walks by me carrying a bucket. "Where are you going?" I yell to her.

She turns back, smiling over her shoulder. "Gotta go get Romeo for Juliette," she says. "That's why she's being so ornery. Her boyfriend is hanging out with the cows." She nods toward the pasture. "Want to help me?" she asks.

She has Link with her, and he's following her almost as closely as Maggie, her dog. I doubt that dog ever leaves her side. Hell, I want to be a puppy and follow her, too. I toss the lead rope of the horse I'm holding to one of the boys from the prison program. He grins and shakes his head. He's the one who called me pussy whipped last night. Yep. I suppose I am. And it doesn't bother me in the least.

I run after Reagan, who laughs as I catch up with her. "You look really pretty today," I say. I want to kiss her so badly I can taste it.

She blushes. "Thank you," she says, looking down toward her feet.

"I missed you," I say.

She grins. "You just saw me an hour ago," she reminds me. Like I need it. All I can think about is the way she felt in my arms. She fit perfectly against my chest.

"Was your dad mad?" I ask. It matters. It really does. I want her parents to like me, but I'm afraid I'm going about it all wrong. I've never met a girl's parents before. Never had any need to. But with Reagan... Everything is different.

She shrugs. "A little." She laughs. "We had a talk about how to knee you in the nuts, the fact that men only want one thing, and then he gave me way TMI about birth control."

I stop walking. Wow. That's a lot to take in. "You talk with your dad about that stuff?"

She shrugs. "Some of it. He sent me to my mom for the rest of it."

"The rest of what?"

Her cheeks get even rosier. "The talk about birth control and all that stuff."

"Oh," I say. I sound like an idiot. But she just threw me for a loop. She walks toward a fence and bends to duck between the rails. I follow her, and Link does, too. He's in his own world, and I think he's singing a song. But it's so soft, I can't tell. "So, you're…um…thinking about that kind of stuff, huh?"

She bites her lower lip and nods. "Yep."

"I…ah…don't know what to say about that." I take my cap off and scratch the back of my head.

"You don't have to say anything," she says with a shrug. "I just wanted you to know I'm thinking about it."

Oh, Jesus Christ. My heart trips in my chest like crazy. Shit just got real.

She narrows her eyes at me, but that may be the sun in her eyes. "You can tell me if you don't have any romantic interest in me, Pete." She heaves a sigh. "I'll be all right with it."

She turns and puts two fingers to her lips. A shrill whistle bursts through the air. Link covers his ears and grins. Suddenly, a horse gallops up, barreling toward us like a streak of black-and-white lightning. Reagan shrieks when I thrust her behind me, but she's laughing too. The horse stops a step from my feet and snorts in my face. "Motherfucker," I breathe.

"Motherfucker," Link parrots.

Oh, hell. That's bad. I've got to learn to watch my mouth around the kid. "Pretty horse," I say, and I watch Link.

"Pretty horse," he repeats.

"That's better," I say quietly. Link nods, and he holds the bucket up so the horse can stick his nose in it.

"This is Romeo," Reagan says as she slips a halter over his head. She pats his sides. "He escapes all the time and goes to hang with the cows. Then Juliette gets upset and takes it out on everyone else." She pats him but all he wants is to stick his head in the bucket. She starts to walk back toward the barn.

I follow, careful where I step, as we walk together. She's quiet. Hell, maybe she's thinking about birth control. I don't know. I'm prepared. I'm always prepared, but she's not ready for what I want. Not even close.

When we get to the barn, Reagan tosses the lead rope to Link and says, "Would you take him to Juliette, Link?" He nods and takes the horse, and Reagan motions for me to follow her. We walk behind the barn, and I can't help but think of all the ways her dad would try to emasculate me if he caught us back here.

She narrows her eyes at me and a corner of her lip kicks up. "You remember last night when you said you could have some real feelings for me?" she asks quietly.

I nod.

She clears her throat and her discomfort is so damn cute that I want to kiss her immediately. "Well, I want you to know that I *know* I have some very real feelings for you, Pete. There's no doubt about it. So, yeah, I'm scared. I'm scared of these feelings, and my mom was being a mom and my dad was being a dad and their first thought was keeping me from getting pregnant."

Damn, I want to sleep with this girl, but I want so much more than just to sleep with her. "Reagan," I say. I reach for her, and for the first time ever, she doesn't flinch. She lets me cover her hips with my hands and pull her against me. "I'm the guy," I say, trying not to grin. "I'll take care of all that birth control stuff when the time is right."

She nods. "I know you will." She lays her forehead against my chest, and I can feel her breath against my skin, hot and warm. "You just asked about what my mom and dad had to say. And that's what they had to say." She shrugs. "So I told you." She steps up onto her tiptoes and presses her lips to against my cheek, lingering long enough for me to smell her minty toothpaste. "Don't worry, Pete. I promise not to defile you." She grins. But with what happened to her, that's not the least little bit amusing.

I groan and lay my head back, closing my eyes while I think. I can't think while she's looking at me.

"What's wrong?" she asks. She steps back, and I feel the loss of her immediately. "The idea of having sex with me turns you off completely?" she whispers. "Doesn't it?" She shakes her head. "I should have known."

"No," I start, but I don't know what to say. She steps away, and I reach for her fingertips. She turns, and I grab her shirt. She spins around, but this time she doesn't clock me. She looks at my hand and smiles. But it's a sad smile. It's not what I want to see on my girl's face. "I want you."

"It's okay, Pete," she says quietly. "Maybe I read this all wrong." She motions from me to her and back again. "I thought we were at the same place."

"I'm further gone than you are," I blurt out.

She stops walking and looks me in the eye. "Gone?" Her green eyes blink slowly.

"Gone. Done. Head over heels. Can't stop thinking about you. Want to be with you all the time. Can feel you against my skin even when you're not with me. Gone."

Her breaths quicken. "Oh," she says. Her hands lay flat on my chest.

"But I think I might be further gone than you are." I lean down to look into her eyes. "Are you going to break my heart, Reagan?" I ask. "You're already thinking about birth control, and it scares the fuck out of me, the very thought of getting to be inside you. Because I want you, Reagan. I want every piece of you."

"Even the shattered pieces?" she asks.

I bracket her face with my hands and pull her face up to mine. "I'll be the glue that puts you back together," I breathe. "I've been locked up a long time, Reagan," I say.

"I've been locked up even longer than you have, Pete," she says, her voice heavy with emotion. She swallows.

"Don't give me hope unless you're sure," I plead.

"I've never been more sure of anything," she says. She wraps her hands around my neck and pulls my head down to hers and kisses me. Her lips are soft and warm and insistent, and when her tongue touches mine, I almost come in my pants. I break away from her because I can't take much more. She looks into my eyes. "I'm not ready for sex yet, Pete," she says. "But I'm closer than I was. I feel like you've unlocked the door to my future. Now I just need for you to walk through it with me. So, quit being so fucking scared you're going to hurt me, Pete. And just like me. And then someday, maybe you'll love me."

I laugh. I can't help it. I chuckle quietly. "I'm glad you had the birth control talk with your mom," I say. "My brother Paul shoved condoms at me as I was going out the door to come here. I don't know who he thought I'd screw at a camp for boys."

Her face goes rosy red.

"I mean, not screw. Well, if it wasn't you, it would be screwing." Shit. I'm fucking this all up. With her, it's going to be so much more than screwing. "That's what scares me, princess. I've never done what I want to do with you."

"You've done it lots of times," she says with a breezy wave.

I shake my head. "No, I haven't." I look her in the eye. "Now you think about what that means and be sure you're ready for it."

I turn and go back to Juliette and take her lead rope. My fucking legs are shaking, and I can barely breathe. If this is what love feels like, I'm glad it waited until I was old enough to understand it.

Reagan

Maggie's not feeling well again, and I hear her wretch from across the room. "Mags," I say. But it's too late. She tosses her kibble all over my bedroom floor. I rub her head. She's still pretty spry for her age, but she's been throwing up for the past few weeks. I'm going to have to take her to the vet to see what's up. I clean her mess, and hunker down with a wet cloth to scrub the carpet. But there's a knock on my door. "Come in," I call absently.

The door opens, and my heart leaps into my throat when I see Pete standing there. It's late. "Pete," I say, as I look up from the puke spot. "I was just…" Are you supposed to talk about puking with a man? Probably not. "Maggie got sick," I finally say.

"Need some help?" he asks. He walks toward me and drops down.

"I think I've done just about all I can do with the floor." I look down at my pajamas and cross my arms in front of my chest. I don't even have on a bra.

Pete grins and looks away like a gentleman. I'm wearing a tank top and tiny shorts that my dad would freak out if he saw. I'm not even allowed to leave my room when I'm wearing them. I go into the bathroom and wash my hands really quick. I walk back out and find Pete looking around my room. He touches a music box on my dresser. He opens the top, and a ballet dancer stands up and twirls around to the tune of a song. He smiles and looks over his shoulder at me. "It's pretty," he says. "Kind of like you." His eyes roam down my body, and he licks his lips.

"What are you doing here?" I ask.

He startles for a second. "I wanted to see you. Your mom said I could come up."

That makes me smile. "Does my dad know you're here?"

He shakes his head. "He wasn't downstairs."

I have a feeling that Dad wouldn't like Pete being in my room. Particularly with the way I'm dressed. "If I'd known it was you, I would have dressed," I try to explain. My gaze skitters to the bed, where a hoodie lies balled up. I usually sleep in it, and I pull it over my head and down past my hips.

Pete's eyes narrow at me. "That sweatshirt looks familiar," he says. His eyes grow wide. "Is that the one I gave you that night?" he asks.

I nod. "Yeah." I kept it. And I love it. "Do you want it back?"

He grins. "If it means you're going to take it off, then hell yeah, I want it back."

Heat creeps up my face. I reach to pull it over my head, and I close my eyes to do it, but suddenly, Pete stops my motion with his hands.

"I was just kidding," he says. "Keep it."

I nod and tug it back down over my hips.

"I'm surprised you still want it, considering how you ended up with it." His brow furrows.

"You're the only good thing that happened to me that night, Pete," I say.

He opens his mouth to say something but shuts it quickly.

"I sleep in it." I lift the neckline to my nose. "It used to smell like you, until my mom made me wash it." I have a small futon in my room, and I motion toward it. "Do you want to sit down?" I ask.

He nods, but he has gone back to assessing my room. He drags his fingertips down the winning horseback-riding ribbons that line my mirror. I sit down and cross my feet under me. I stick a pillow into the space and rest my elbows on it. Pete wanders toward my bathroom and sticks his head inside. "I think your room is bigger than our whole apartment," he says.

I don't know what to say to that, so I say nothing.

"When you go back to school, will you be in the dorm?" He sits down on the other end of the futon. He turns to face me, and his knee brushes mine. I like it, so I inch closer.

"I have an apartment across from campus," I say. "Dad didn't want me in the dorm, and I wanted to take Maggie back and forth with me after what happened." Maggie hears her name and wanders toward me, slipping her nose beneath my hand. I absently rub her head. "I don't like to be alone at night."

Pete makes a kissy noise with his mouth, and Maggie wanders toward him. She's wary, but she's not afraid. He lets her sniff his hand and touches the top of her head gingerly. She pushes herself into his path, and he scratches behind her ears.

"You trying to win over my dog?" I ask. But secretly, I love that Maggie trusts him. She has good instincts, much better than mine.

"Trying?" he scoffs. "Succeeding," he says with a grin. Maggie hops up on her back legs to put herself in his lap. He leans back and pats his leg, and she hops up to sit on him, between us. He pets her head. "You look pretty in my hoodie," he says to me.

My face is probably scarlet, with the way that he's making my face flush. "Thank you," I breathe.

"I like the idea that my hoodie has been all over your body while you sleep," he says. His voice is suddenly gravelly and thick. His gaze lingers on my legs, but he doesn't reach for me or try to get me to come closer. He just keeps petting my dog, who is all but upside down as she tries to give him her belly.

I swallow hard, my heartbeat thick and heavy. I clear my throat, and he just looks at me from behind hooded lashes.

"So, what do you want to do?" he asks.

Honestly, I want to kiss him. "Is this a date?" I ask.

He shakes his head. "This is me coming to visit you for a few minutes because I wanted to see you and inviting myself to stay for a while." Maggie flips over, and Pete laughs. "You're a pushover," he says to my dog.

"She's a dangerous beast," I say with a laugh.

"As long as she protects you, she can be as beastly as she likes."

"Fine job she's doing of that right now," I grumble.

"Dogs like me. Because I'm a good person." His lids lower, though, and he licks his lips again.

I tug the hoodie lower over my hips. "Stop looking at me like that," I whisper, my voice cracking.

"I would, if I thought you really wanted me to," he says. He jerks his head. "Come here," he says quietly.

I shake my head, but a grin tugs at my lips. "Nope," I say.

He jerks his head. "Come here," he says again. "Please?"

I smile at him. I can't help it. "What do I get if I come over there?" I ask.

"Come here and find out," he says.

My heart thuds. What should I do? Should I stay? Should I go? I feel like there's an invisible tether between us, and he gives it a tug when he lifts his hand and crooks his finger at me, beckoning me forward.

I give Maggie a gentle shove to get her off his lap. Because I suddenly want to be there. I want to snuggle against him and wrap myself in his warmth. Maggie hits the floor and blows out a breath as she flops at his feet. And I crawl toward him on my hands and knees.

Pete

One minute, the dog is in my lap, and the next Reagan is heading toward it. She's so fucking pretty as she crawls across the couch that she takes my breath away. One palm lands on my knee and the other on my thigh. She bites her lower lip between her teeth as she looks up at me. I brush her hair back from her forehead and look at her. I really look at her. She's trembling. Her hand shakes against my knee, so I cover it with mine. Her eyes meet mine. "I'm all right," she whispers.

"I know you are," I say, and I slowly and gently pick her up and flip her over so that her bottom is in my lap, and her legs lie toward the empty end of her futon. I try not to move too fast because this is all so new to her and I know it. "I think I'm the one who's scared," I admit, my voice quavering. I clear my throat.

Her brow furrows. "Why?" she whispers. She lays her forearm on my shoulder, and her fingers absently tickle the hair at the back of my neck. I can't even think when she touches me.

"I didn't think you'd come," I say.

Her face flushes, and I can tell she took that the wrong way. A laugh bursts from my throat. "I meant come across the couch toward me, doofy," I say, and I reach up to tweak her nose. I lean toward her and kiss her quickly on the cheek. "Although," I say. I have to stop and clear my throat again. I drop my voice down to a whisper. "When you came with my hand in your panties, that surprised me, too."

Her breaths aren't falling naturally now. They're a little more hurried, and her cheeks are all rosy. I run my hand up the outside of her thigh, all the way up her leg because she's wearing those crazy-tiny little shorty-shorts. "How do you think I felt?" she asks. She laughs, and it's the prettiest sound I've ever heard. I can feel her words against my cheek, she's that close to me. They're hot and humid and all Reagan.

I jostle her in my lap with a bump of my knee. "Tell me how you felt," I prompt. I want to know everything.

Her brow arches. "You mean, when we were doing *that*?" she asks.

I nod and slide my hand around the top of her thigh, tracing the line of those shorts, which really means that I'm tracing the crease of her inner thigh. Her legs part ever so slightly, and my heart thrills at the way she responds to me.

She hesitates for no more than second. Then she starts to talk. "I was angry," she says. "Chase was an ass all night long, and then he touched me and I actually thought about walking away from him, but he was so damn smug. It wasn't completely a knee-jerk reaction when I hit him. It was me being pissed off and hitting him just because I could. Just because he deserved it. Then I stole his car and came home, and he showed up. But then you were there. I knew you were there in the bushes. And I knew you'd seen me come home with my clothes all messed up, and I was afraid you'd think the worst."

"The worst?" I ask. Her legs part a little farther, and her mouth opens on a heavy sigh as I trace her inner thigh. I want to pull her shorts off and drag her panties down her legs. Then I want to touch my mouth to all of her wet girly parts and lick her until she comes on my face. But her parents are downstairs.

"You were afraid I'd kissed him?" she asks.

I don't respond because I'm too busy sliding my fingers beneath her shorts to trace the line of her panties. "Uh huh," I mutter.

"I thought about it," she says. "I kind of wanted to get it over and done with."

I look up. Did she really just say that? "Over and done with?" I ask.

She winces. "You make me feel these...feelings, Pete. And I don't know what to do with them all or where they came from. And that scares the crap out of me, that I can be like this with you without even having to calm myself down or work to push my feelings into the corner of my mind. So, I kind of wanted to test it with Chase. But when he touched me, I didn't feel anything."

"Did he scare you?"

She shakes her head. "Not really. He was an ass. And I knew it before I went out with him. But then he grazed my boob, and my skin began to crawl. It wasn't like when you touch me at all. So it made me think. It made me want to come back here to you. But I figured I should probably finish out the night. But then he touched my boob again and laughed about it, and I hit him. It wasn't a knee-jerk reaction. I meant to hit him." She winces again. "I feel kind of bad about that."

I just realized I stopped tracing her panties when she started to talk about this, and I look into her eyes. "So you didn't freak out. You hit him on purpose?" She has no idea how fucking happy this makes me.

"Yeah," she admits. But she's not smiling. She's laboring over this a little. "But then you came into the barn and asked me if I kissed him. I couldn't lie to you." She turns my face to hers and looks into my eyes. "You're the only one I want to kiss, Pete. You're the only one I want to be with. You're the only one I want to hold me and touch me." She waves a hand in front of her face like a fan. "God, it's getting hot in here," she says.

I pick Reagan up again, and her eyes go wide when I lay her down on the futon. I part her knees ever so slowly and run my hands up the inside of her thighs, one on each side, spreading her open so that I can lie down on top of her.

When I settle into the warmth of her, I realize she's trembling again. "This okay?" I ask as I brace myself on my elbows, my head just below her chin.

"Yeah," she breathes. She wraps her arms around my neck and pulls me down to her chest, where I lay my head on her boobs. I turn my face and nuzzle into her and realize the crest of her breast has to be directly beside my mouth. Her hands sift through the short hair on my head, her fingertips playful and light. "So, last night," she says. She waits. I lift my head so I can look into her face. She has her lower lip caught tightly between her teeth, and then she rushes to say on an exhale, "I really liked what we did last night."

I chuckle. "I could tell." God, I feel so light and so heavy at the same time. I rock my hips against her and her bottom lifts, pushing her soft, warm, probably pink and pretty parts toward my dick. Shit. "I did, too."

She tugs my hair until I look into her face again. "Is this too fast?" she whispers.

I look down toward where my dick is only separated from her warmth by my jeans and those tiny little things she calls shorts. "I still have my pants on. I promise."

She groans. "I'm not talking about that." She gestures from me to her and back. "Me and you. Is this going too fast?" she asks.

My breath hitches. "I don't know," I say. "Is it too fast for you?"

She shakes her head. "We just met a few days ago." Like she has to remind me.

Then why does it feel like my heart has been waiting for her forever? "Mmm hmm," I hum, as I scooch myself up a little so my lips can touch hers. She kisses me back, her mouth soft and insistent against mine. I pull back, and she grins. "What?" I ask, her smile contagious as I feel my own tug at the corners of my lips.

"That kiss wasn't quite as epic as the last one," she says.

I take her lips again, soft and slow, my tongue sliding into her mouth, my heart rejoicing when hers rasps against mine, all velvet and heat. "We'll have to work on that," I reply when I finally lift my head.

She nods. Her mouth is close to my ear when she says, "I want it to be as epic for you as it was for me." A shiver runs up my spine, and I rock my hips, pushing against her heat. I can't help myself. Shit. "Would you let me do that for you?" she asks.

She looks so unsure of herself that I can tell this is hard for her. She doesn't like asking. And she wouldn't be asking if it wasn't important to her. "Not with your parents downstairs," I murmur.

"I don't mean now," she says with a blow of her breath.

"Oh." Wishful thinking and all that.

She laughs. "Another time?" she asks. "When my parents aren't within thirty feet of us?"

I nod. Shit. What did I just get myself into?

I hear a door slam nearby, and I lift myself off her. She closes her legs and sits up, pulling my sweatshirt down around her hips. But all I can think about is how soft her skin feels under my fingertips and how much I want to touch her. But there are footsteps coming up the stairs. I call the dog, and she hops up into my lap. Thank God.

The whisper of footsteps against the carpet is the only warning before her dad stops in her doorway. "What are you doing?" he barks. His eyes land on me, and then on the dog, and then he meets my gaze. I smile at him. But I have to break eye contact after a moment. I was just on top of his daughter, after all.

"Talking," Reagan chirps. She scratches the back of her head. "Did you need something?"

"Your mom and I are going to rent a movie. Do you want to watch it?"

"Can Pete come?" she asks. He glares at me, and I focus all my attention on the dog.

He nods. "If he must," he says drolly. I have to admit it—if I had a dad, I'd want him to act just like Mr. Caster. I'd want him to try to protect me over all else and care about me more than anything. I don't have that, at least not from a dad. I have it from my brothers. But it's not the same.

"Do you want to watch a movie?" Reagan asks quietly. But she's smiling. I notice she doesn't get up.

I nod. "Sure."

She looks at her dad. "Ten minutes?" she asks.

He nods, glares at me for a second longer, and then leaves. "Your dad is pretty awesome, you know that?" I tell her.

She rolls her eyes.

"If I had a dad, I would want him to act just like that." I avoid her gaze this time. Because I don't want her to see too much. She already sees enough.

"Your brother, the one you don't talk to," she starts. "Does he have a phone in his dorm?"

I nod. He has a cell phone that Paul got for him since he was going away. Paul got one, too. I know Sam's number by heart, even though I've never called it. I have dialed it a million times, and then I hang up the phone because I'm a chickenshit. She holds her phone out to me. "It's time to call him, Pete," she says. Then she picks up a pair of jeans, pulls them up her legs while I watch. It's so fucking hot watching her dress that I get all turned on again. She bends over and kisses me really quickly. "I'm going to make popcorn. Come downstairs when you're ready."

She leaves me and closes the door behind her. I look down at the phone. When I stopped talking to Sam, I felt like I lost a piece of myself. Maybe it's time to find it. I dial the number and lift the phone to my ear and my heart is beating even faster now than it did when I was on top of Reagan.

Ring.

Ring.

Ring.

Ring.

His voicemail picks up. "This is Sam. I'm busy, so leave a message and I'll call you back if I feel like it." The beep sounds, and I hesitate. I can't help it. Then I clear my throat. This is the time for new beginnings. And I can't find out if he wants one or not unless he'll talk to me.

"Sam, it's Pete." I stop and think, burying my forehead in my hand. "I just wanted to talk to you and be sure you're doing all right. I miss you, Sam. That's all. I just miss you." I heave a sigh. Because I don't know what else to say. "Sam, do you think you could come home this weekend? I want to see you. I'm on a friend's phone so you can't call me back, but I wish you could… I really, really wish you could. I love you, Sam. Just wanted to say that."

I press the "end" button and stare at the phone. I pretty much bungled that. But I feel lighter now. I'm glad I called him. I miss him. Like crazy.

I tuck Reagan's phone in my pocket and go downstairs. I find her in the kitchen pouring popcorn into a bowl. She throws a piece at me when I get close, and I catch it in my mouth. She laughs and hitches her hip against the counter. "Did you make your call?" she asks.

Her phone buzzes in my pocket. "I think you're getting a text," I say as I pass it back to her. I want to be nosy and look down at it. She glances at it and grins.

"I think it's for you," she says. "Is that the number you called?" She shows me the screen. It's Sam's number, and he just wrote:

I love you better.

I grin. "Yeah. That's Sam."

"Sam?" she asks. Her brow furrows. She points to the back of her neck. "The Sam on your neck? That's for your brother?"

"Yeah. Our dad put the tattoos on us because he never could tell us apart."

She frowns. "Then why does yours say Sam?"

I grin and shrug. "He couldn't tell us apart, so when he sat Sam down for his tattoo, he said he was Pete, and I said I was Sam. So, we have each other's names on our necks."

"He couldn't tell you guys apart?" She's not laughing anymore, and she looks kind of sad.

I shake my head. "We're twins. Identical."

"Wow," she says.

"Our mom was so mad," I say with a laugh.

"Could she tell you two apart?" she asks.

I shrug. "Anyone who knows us can." That doesn't speak very well of our dad, but it is what it is.

I pull her to me by the belt loops on her jeans, and she falls into me. Her arms lift to wrap around my neck. I kiss her quickly.

But her dad yells out, "Pete, when you're done having sex with my daughter in the kitchen, the movie's ready!"

Reagan laughs.

"Even I'm not that quick," I whisper to her. She blushes again. I kiss her forehead. "Thanks for letting me use your phone," I say.

She nods and takes me by the hand, her other holding the popcorn. I sit down on the edge of the sofa, and she settles down next to me, close but not touching. Her dad glares at us from where her mom is draped against his side on the opposite couch. "Nice to see you, Pete," he says.

"You too, Mr. Caster," I say. "Thanks for inviting me."

I spread my thighs a little so Reagan's leg is touching mine, and she squeezes my hand as the movie starts. Damn, that feels good. Tomorrow is Friday, and tomorrow night is when I go home. I don't want to go. I want to stay by her side forever. Just like this.

Reagan

Today's the day that Pete goes home. I stayed up most of the night last night thinking about it. I don't want him to leave. My gut clenches at the thought of it, and I stare across the table at my mom.

"Something on your mind?" she asks.

I shake my head.

"Not something you want to talk about, huh?" she asks. Her voice is soft, but she's not prying. She's just being my mom.

"Pete's leaving today," I say quietly.

"Hmm," she hums.

"So, I was thinking…" I start slowly.

She smiles and tips her head at me like a curious puppy. "What were you thinking?"

"I was actually thinking I might go back to the city a week early," I say, my voice hesitant and quiet. My classes don't start until next week.

She lifts her coffee cup to her lips and regards me over the rim of it while she takes a sip. "Does this have anything to do with Pete?" she asks.

I can't lie to my mom. I'd be really bad at it if I tried. "Only everything." I grin at her expression. She's grinning, too, and it's almost contagious. "I want to go back and spend some time with him." I shrug. "See where things go."

"He's the one, huh?" she asks.

I nod my head. "Yeah, I think so." My voice is quiet, but I feel lighter than I have in a long time.

"Do you want me to call to see if I can get you in to visit the doctor today?" she asks. Doctor? Why do I need a doctor? "There's a tiny little matter of birth control," she says.

"Oh." I completely forgot about that. Heat creeps up my cheeks. "Do you think you could?" I ask. I wince inward. This is so awkward. But who can you talk to about this stuff if you can't talk to your mom?

She picks up her phone. "I'll see what I can do."

"I'm going to go upstairs and pack," I say. I am almost giddy. This is a big decision. I just hope that when we get back to the city, things are the same between Pete and me. What if we go back and real life intrudes? What if the magic is gone? What if he doesn't like me as much as I like him?

I can't find my flip-flops, so I go to the top of the stairs to call down to my mom. But she's talking to my dad. I can hear their voices, soft and hesitant. Then my dad says, "What the fuck are you thinking, encouraging this?"

I freeze. I shouldn't even listen in but I can't help it.

"I'm encouraging her to grow up, honey," she says. "That's all."

"She's not going back to the city. Not yet. Absolutely not." I hear some dishes slam, and I wince with every one of them.

"She's going. She's packing now." Mom is quiet but firm.

"Why doesn't this bother you? She needs her family around her more than she needs some boy."

My mom steps into my line of vision, and I can see her lay a calming hand on my dad's chest. "She doesn't need us for this stage of her life, honey," she says. "She needs him."

"Why him?" Dad growls.

"Pete's a good man," she says. "You know it."

Dad growls again, and mom laughs. "I'm not going to like any man who wants to get in my daughter's pants," he grumbles.

"Can you see how she's woken up since he got here, Bob?" she asks. Her voice is firm. "She's not jumping at shadows, and she's letting people touch her. She's laughing. She's thinking about more than just hiding in her room. She's living again, Bob. So, knock it off. This is a good thing." She points her finger at him in warning. "And don't you say a thing to her about it."

I go back to my room and finish packing. I feel bad for Dad, but I suddenly am living a hopeful existence. And I like it. I don't want to change it. I want to chase it all the way to New York so it won't get away from me. It's not just Pete I'm chasing after. It's the promise of a future. That'll happen with or without him, but I'm hopeful for the first time in a very long time.

Pete

It's time to start packing up and loading the bus, even though the campers aren't done with their activities yet. But we have to pull out around dark so we can be back to the city by midnight. I look around and hate to even think about leaving. When I go back to the city, I'll go back to house arrest and I'll be back with my brothers. I've enjoyed the freedom I've had here, though, and now I know what I want to work toward. I don't know what Reagan's schedule looks like, but I hope she'll still want to see me when she comes back to the city.

Gonzo rolls up and stops in front of me, cutting me off on the walkway toward the barn. I'd hoped to be able to find Reagan there. I want to talk to her before we pull out. I really don't want to leave her, but I don't see how it can be avoided. Gonzo doesn't grin at me for the first time since I met him. He looks almost as morose as I feel. "What's up?" I ask.

The sky, he says, pointing toward the heavens.

"Ha ha, very funny," I say. But he's not laughing along. "Something bothering you?" I ask.

Just you, he says.

"Me? What did I do to bother you?" I go back to stacking chairs because it's what we're supposed to do before we leave. He follows me. Then I have to help all the youth boys load their bags into the bus.

You were going to leave without saying good-bye? He glares at me.

"We still have a few hours left before we leave," I remind him, glancing at my watch. "Were you hoping I wouldn't forget to kiss you good-bye?" I walk over to him, wrap his head up gently with my arm, and give him a noogie. He shoves my arm away. Is he really angry? "You're serious, aren't you? You think I would leave without saying good-bye to you?" I squat down and look him in the eye. He's serious. Much too serious.

I thought we were pals, but you kind of disappeared for the past few days, he says.

I look toward the house. I have spent quite a bit of time with Reagan, but I haven't left Gonzo out. I've made sure he had boys to talk to and hang out with. "Did you get to make some friends while you were here?" I ask. I reach into my pocket and pull out a folded piece of paper. "I was going to give this to you later, but I guess I can do it now," I say. I hand it to him. "It's just my phone number and my address. I hope you'll stay in touch."

He grins. *You do love me*, he signs.

Hell yeah, I love the little shit. He's hard not to like. "*Love* is a pretty strong word," I say. "*Tolerate* would be a better word."

He grins. *I tolerate you, too*, he signs. He draws air quotes around the word *tolerate*. *If that's how you tell people you love them*. He looks me in the eye. *Thanks for everything this week. I appreciate it. And appreciate you.*

"I appreciate you, too, kid," I say. "I want you to contact me if you need me. For anything, all right?"

His eyes get all shimmery, and he signs the word *yes*. His mom calls his name from their cabin where she's packing, and he turns to go help her. "Hey, Gonzo," I call.

He looks back at me.

"You're a good kid, and I'm glad I met you," I say.

Yeah, yeah, he signs back. *You're going to make me think you have a crush on me*. He looks past my shoulder. *Speaking of crushes*, he signs. Then he points and winks. *See you later.*

"Not if I see you first," I shout to his retreating back. He just flips me off rather than looking back at me.

I laugh and turn around to see what he was pointing at. But it's not Reagan. It's her dad, and he's bearing down on me carrying that fucking hatchet. I cross my hands in front of my lap and step to the side. "Pete," he says. He's a little out of breath, and I feel like he ran here to find me.

"Mr. Caster," I say. I look at the hatchet, and he raises it up, appraising it greedily, like he's enjoying all my discomfort. "Everything all right?" I ask.

"Fuck no, everything is not all right," he says. He scrubs a hand down his face. He points a finger in my face. "I've messed around with you all week long, and now I'm done playing."

"I didn't realize we were playing, sir," I start.

He holds up a hand to stop me. "My daughter likes you a lot, and that's the only reason I tolerated you this week."

"Um," I start. But he shuts me up again with a hushed breath.

He raises the hatchet, and I step to the side. "But I swear to God that if you do anything to hurt my daughter, I will chop off your head right after I chop off your nuts."

"I wouldn't hurt her, sir," I say.

But he shushes me again. "When you get back to the city and there's no dad with a hatchet waiting to emasculate you, you remember that I am just a phone call away. Do you understand?"

"Clearly," I say.

"That's all I wanted to say." He heaves a deep breath and blows it out. "It was nice to meet you, Pete. Hope you have a good life if I never see you again."

He walks away, swinging his hatchet. Shit. I wasn't expecting that.

Phil whistles as he walks out from behind a tree. "Thought he had you there for a minute," he breathes. He grins and shakes his head.

"Do you know what that was about?" I ask, jerking my thumb toward Mr. Caster.

"Hmm," he hums. "Maybe."

"Care to share?" I ask.

"He's a dad and you're a young man who likes his daughter. He knows it, and it smarts when a dad has to share his daughter's affection. He has been her protector his whole life, and now she'll start to look toward someone else to fill that role. Maybe even you." He narrows his eyes at me. "How would you feel if it was you?" he asks. He pretends to be busy stacking chairs just like I am, but he's astute and I know it.

"I'd be fucking ecstatic," I say.

"Are you going to see her when you go back to the city?" he asks. I lift my pant leg and remind him of the ankle bracelet I'm wearing. He grins. "I have a feeling that's not going to stop her."

"I hope not." I take a deep breath. "I like her, Phil," I admit. "I might even be falling in love with her."

He stops and looks me dead in the eyes. "That scares you?" he asks.

I laugh. "Quite the opposite actually," I admit. I feel hopeful. And it's been a long time since I've felt this way.

"What's your plan when you get back, Pete?" he asks.

I pull a piece of paper out of my pocket. He told me to write my plans down. To make them real. So, I did. I start to read. "One—work things out with Sam. Two—decide what my future will be. Will it be college? Will I get a job? Will I decide what I want to be when I grow up?" I close the paper and put it back in my pocket.

"Nice," he says, nodding his head.

"Do you think I could do what you do?" I ask. "You get to help a lot of boys."

He nods. "I think you'd be really good at what I do."

"I might be able to keep some boys from ending up in my situation."

He nods. "That's a pretty good goal to have. I'd be happy to help you decide if you want that. You could even come to work with me for a few days and see if it interests you." He looks around camp. "Most of my work isn't quite this glamorous, unfortunately. It's a lot of work at the prison and the youth detention center."

I nod. I might like that.

"You know how to reach me when you get home."

I do. And I will. I go back to stacking chairs until I see Reagan striding in my direction. She's smiling, and her hair is loose and blowing around her face in the wind. She brushes it back with her hand and grins at me. "Hi, Pete," she says. She shuffles her feet and looks down nervously. "Did I just see my dad come talk to you?" she asks. "With a hatchet?"

I squeeze my lips together and try not to grin, but she's so pretty it's hard not to. "Your dad scares the shit out of me," I admit.

She giggles. "I think that's how he wants it." She narrows her eyes at me. "Did he talk to you about me?" she asks.

I nod. "He volunteered to gleefully chop off certain parts of my anatomy."

She looks uncomfortable. "No, I mean did he talk to you about plans for New York City?"

I shake my head. "What plans?" I stop stacking chairs and turn to face her.

She threads her fingers together and looks everywhere but at me. She looks so uncomfortable that I immediately feel bad for her. I walk closer and tip her face up to mine.

"What plans?" I ask again.

She lays her palms on my chest and looks into my eyes. "Pete," she starts. But she stops and shakes her head, then buries her face in my shirt and groans. "I feel so stupid," she says against my chest. I can barely hear her. I pull her against me and hold her close, lacing my fingers behind her back. I lift the tail of her shirt and lay my hands against her skin. And she lets me. This part still amazes me and makes me melt every single time I get to touch her. Finally she looks up at me. "So you're going back to the city today."

I nod and squeeze my eyes closed. I don't even want to think about leaving her. But I guess there's no way around it. "Yeah," I say on a sigh.

"So," she says hesitantly, tipping her face up to look into mine. Her green eyes blink at me slowly. "I was thinking about going back to the city today, too."

My heart leaps in my chest. I grab her shoulders and set her back a little so I can look at her. "Are you fucking serious?" I ask. I can barely breathe.

Her face falls. "You don't want me to go," she says quietly.

I laugh. I jerk her against me and then wrap my arms tightly around her and pick her up, spinning her around so quickly that she has to grab for my shoulders. "Of course I want you to go! Are you kidding? I've been so fucking worried that I would never get to see you again or if we didn't see one another for a few weeks, that we would lose what we have."

"What do we have, Pete?" she asks, but she's smiling.

"You don't know?" I ask.

She shakes her head. "I'm not always good at reading people, Pete," she admits, blushing.

I tweak her nose and steel myself. "I think I'm falling in love with you, Reagan," I say. I swallow hard because there's suddenly a lump on my throat. I don't know where it came from, and no matter how hard I swallow, it won't go away. I wait. She has to say something, right?

"Good," she finally says.

Good? That's it?

"Thanks for telling me." She grins and spins to walk in the other direction.

I grab her arm and pull her back to me, and my heart swells because she doesn't punch me and drop-kick me or knee me in the chin when I jerk her to me and back her up against a tree. "That's all I get?" I ask. My heart is thudding like crazy. Maybe I misread her. Maybe I'm way off base. Maybe I'm an idiot.

"What do you want?" she whispers.

I palm the side of her face and stare at her. She's so fucking beautiful that I can barely think when I'm this close to her. "I want you to love me back," I admit.

"Done," she says. A blush creeps up her cheeks, and I thought she couldn't look any prettier than she did a minute ago. But I was wrong.

"Done?" I parrot. God, now I sound like Link.

She heaves a sigh. "Done. Gone. Don't want to be away from you. Can't breathe when I think about you leaving. Want to be with you all the time, gone. Done." She blinks, and then she says, "You're inside me, Pete. And I want to keep you there."

Fuck. That's the best fucking thing I've ever heard in my life. And I can't even put two thoughts together to tell her.

Suddenly, I hear boots stomping in my direction, and I spring back from on top of Reagan when I see her father striding toward us with that hatchet. He stops and glares at me. "Pete, can you do me a favor?" he asks. He doesn't look very happy, but then he never does when he's around me.

"What do you need, sir?" I ask.

"Reagan is determined to drive back to the city tonight, and it'll be late when she gets there." He jerks a thumb toward where Phil is standing. "So I asked Phil if you could ride with her instead of on the bus, in case she breaks down or something."

Reagan grins, and I want to, too, but I force myself not to. "Phil said it's okay?" I ask. I look toward where Phil is standing, and he walks over.

"You'd have to be in your apartment by midnight tonight," Phil says. "I'll know if you're not." He motions toward my tracking bracelet.

"I'll take him straight home," Reagan chirps. She's grinning, and I want to grin with her.

"What about the youth boys?" I ask.

"You can see them the next day at group. At eleven, if you want to be there." He arches his brow at me.

"I'll be there," I say. I want to see those boys. If I can help even one of them, I'll feel better about my own past.

"Thanks, Pete," her dad says. He claps me on the shoulder and squeezes a little too hard. I take it as a warning, which I think is how he meant it. He walks away, leaving me with Reagan.

"It's going to be really late when you drop me off," I say.

She nods. "I know."

"I don't want you to go home to an empty apartment all by yourself. I'll send one of my brothers with you when you drop me off." I wish I could go with her and walk her to her door and do all the gentlemanly stuff I've never wanted to do before.

"I'll have Maggie with me," she reminds me.

"Still," I say. I brush her hair back from her ear. "Want to have a sleepover at my house?" I ask.

Her eyes widen, and she licks her lips. She's interested. I can tell.

"I'll sleep on the couch," I say. It'll fucking kill me, but I'll do it.

She shakes her head. "I'm not going to stay if you're going to sleep on the couch."

My hear trips in my chest.

"I'm not going to run you out of your own bed," she says, laughing nervously. Her eyes search mine, and I hope she doesn't look too deeply because I'm not sure what she'll find. "I'll stay if you'll sleep there with me," she says. Her voice quivers.

"Okay," I say quietly. But my gut is doing somersaults. She steps onto her tiptoes and kisses me quickly.

"I have to go take care of a few things," she whispers. She kisses me again, a little slower this time. We're going to have a sleepover. Her and her dog.

"Maggie can stay, too," I say. I'm an idiot, but I can't even think right now.

"I'll tell her," she whispers playfully. "She's going to be so excited."

Not nearly as excited as I am.

Reagan

Pete's kind of quiet on the way home. He fiddles with the radio and pets Maggie. Sometimes his hand reaches for mine, and he squeezes it to reassure me.

"Are you sure your family is going to be all right with me staying with you guys tonight?" I ask.

He nods. "I'm sure. Sam's at school and Logan lives with Emily at her apartment, although I don't know why. They're at our apartment a lot more than hers, according to Matt. Sam and I share a room, and since he's not there, you can sleep in my bed, and I'll sleep in his."

Well, damn. I was kind of hoping we could sleep together.

"Or we could sleep in Logan's room, since there's a double in there. I just didn't want to presume that you'd want to sleep with me." He pays a lot of attention to Maggie's ears instead of looking at me when he says it.

"I like option two," I say quietly. I pretend to mess with the windshield washer, even though it doesn't need washing.

"Oh yeah?" he says quietly. He grins. "I was hoping you'd say that." He winces a little. "I do have to warn you that our apartment is nothing like your house. It's not in that great an area of town. And it's kind of small."

"None of that matters to me, Pete," I say. I'm telling the truth. I just want to be with him. He could live in a cardboard box, and he'd still make it amazing. I jerk my thumb toward Maggie. "Maggie can be a bit of a snob, though. So you might have to give her lots of dog treats to keep her happy."

"Maggie's a pushover," he says. She got sick in the car, and we had to stop long enough to clean it up. Pete was pretty good about it, though. "I think she loves me."

He's easy to love. He grins at me.

"So, do you sleep naked?" he asks. His eyes twinkle.

Heat creeps up my face. "No!" I cry. "Of course not."

He leans his head against the seat, tilting his head like an inquisitive puppy. "So, do you think I could talk you into it?" He laughs at what must be a hilarious look on my face.

"Maybe," I say quietly.

He sucks in a breath. He's surprised. "I'm not sure if I can keep my hands off you all night," he warns, his voice quiet but strong. His voice is deeper and rougher than it was a minute ago.

"Who said I want you to?"

He lays his head back and groans. He flattens a hand on his chest and breathes harder. "Is my virtue in jeopardy, Miss Caster?" he asks.

"If you had any to be in jeopardy, I would say yes," I grumble. But he's so funny I can't keep the grin from my face.

"We're here," he says. He points me toward a parking spot on the side of the street. I pull into it and take a deep breath. I don't know what to do with myself now that we're here.

"You're sure you want me to stay?" I ask.

He nods. "You better text your dad and tell him you've arrived in the city." He snaps a leash on Maggie and helps her from the car. "You do that and I'll walk Maggie really quick. Then I'll get your bags."

I nod and start to text my dad. Pete makes kissy noises at Maggie until she follows him.

Me: *We're here!*

Dad: *Are you back at your apartment? Everything all right?*

I don't want to lie.

Me: *No, I'm at Pete's. I'm going to hang out with his family for a little while.*

Dad: *It's 11:30 at night, Reagan.*

Me: *Dad, it's fine.*

Dad: *Do I have to drive up there and kill that boy?*

Me: *Not today.*

Dad: *Let me know when I need to.*

I laugh.

Me: *Okay.*

Dad: *Text me tomorrow to tell me you're alive.*

Me: *Love you!*

Dad: *Love you too.*

Pete opens my door and leans on his elbows in the doorway. "Hi," he says. "You ready to go upstairs?"

I grin. I can't help it. I move to get out, but Pete blocks me. "You know I don't have any expectations about tonight, right?" he asks.

"I know." I do know. He would never make me do anything I don't want to do. "Can I still stay?"

He pulls me from the car and goes to the trunk to get my bag. But it's a big bag. I was going home, after all.

"Just this one," I say, picking up my cosmetic bag. "I can get the rest when I go home tomorrow. No need to lug it up the elevator."

He chuckles. "You *are* spoiled, aren't you?" he asks.

"What do you mean?" I don't understand.

He puts my bag on his shoulder, along with his backpack, and takes my hand. "We're on the fourth floor. And no elevator."

"Oh. I'm tough. I can take it."

He tugs my fingertips toward his building. "You sure you'll be all right with all my brothers?" he asks. He looks more uncomfortable than I've ever seen him.

"Stop worrying," I say. "I'm not made of glass, Pete."

This place is nothing like where I'm from, and I jump when someone walks by us. He pulls me into his side. "I got you," he says quietly. But he's sure, and I feel completely safe with him. There's graffiti on the wall of his apartment building, and I stop to look at it. "Come on," he says. "I want you to meet my family."

We go up four flights of stairs and step into a long hallway. Pete turns the knob and motions for me to precede him into the room. I do, with Maggie following, and immediately hear the TV. There are men stacked up like cord wood all over the place. Someone hits the "pause" button on the TV, and everyone turns to face us.

"Hi," Pete says. He sets my bag down beside his, and we walk together into the room. The men get up, and the biggest one walks toward us. "I didn't think you were coming back until later," he says. He eyes me up and down but not in a creepy way. "Who's your friend?" he asks. He sticks out a hand to shake, and I take it. "I'm Paul," he says. He's huge, and he has even more tattoos than Pete does.

There's another guy behind him. He's thin and has long, blond hair, and it's held back with a rubber band at the nape of his neck. "Matt," he says as he sticks out his hand to shake.

Then I notice a guy and a girl sitting on the couch. She's the blonde I saw at the prison, and she eyes me with the gaze of an antiques dealer, as if she's looking for all my imperfections. "Emily," she says with a little wave. "Logan," she says, as she pats Logan on the chest. He extends his hand, and I take it.

But there's one more, and my breath catches in my throat when he steps out from behind Logan. He looks so much like Pete. He has to be Sam. I look from Pete to Sam and back. "I'm the pretty one," Sam says. He reaches out like he wants to hug me, but I recoil. I can't help it. I've come a long way, but not that far. "It's nice to meet you," he says with a nod. I extend my hand, and instead of shaking it, he lifts it to his lips. His short little moustache tickles the back of my hand. I twist my fingers out of his grip, and Pete glares at him.

"Keep your fucking hands off my girl," he growls. But then he opens his arms, and Sam falls into them. They hug the way men do, with lots of backslapping and murmured words. "I'm glad you're here," Pete says.

"You called. I came. Like a good big brother."

"Eight minutes," Pete growls playfully. He drops an arm around my shoulders. "He was born eight minutes before me and he thinks he's the shit because he's older."

He coughs into his fist. "Excuse me. I *am* the shit." He grins. He looks so much like Pete that it's almost disturbing.

"I think you're both shits," Paul says as he goes to fridge and gets a beer.

"You want something to drink?" Pete asks me quietly.

I shake my head.

He cups my face with his hand. "You look a little tired. You want to go to bed?"

I nod. "We probably should."

He grins. I think he likes the *we* part.

"Do you think it would be okay if I take a shower first?" I ask. I've been in the car for hours, and I feel kind of grimy. I'd kind of like to be clean when I snuggle naked with Pete for the first time.

He nods and leads me toward the bathroom, where he flips the light on. He takes out towels and lays them on the counter for me. "You need some help taking your clothes off?" he asks. He waggles his eyebrows at me playfully.

"Yeah," I say, and I close the door behind us.

Pete

Shit. She said yes.

She shoves the door closed behind me, and I freeze. I want to reach for her, but my family is about ten feet away from us on the other side of the door. "Do you need some shampoo or something?" I ask again. I reach behind her and shift the shower curtain. There's still girly-smelling stuff in there from when Emily lived with us.

"I like your family," she says, and then her arms wrap around my waist. She lays her head on my chest and nuzzles me with her nose, and my heart melts like it does every time she touches me.

"I'm glad." I hold her close. I was a little worried they would scare her. It's a lot of testosterone in one room. Luckily, Emily was here, too.

Finally, she pulls back from me. "Okay," she breathes. "You can go." She shoos me toward the door with a wave of her hands.

I kiss her, lingering a little too long on her lips, but she doesn't pull away from me. I groan, pull back from her, and adjust my junk. I slip out the door and close it behind me, and then I hear the thumb lock click behind me. I lean my head against the door and breathe for a minute. But then I turn around and see Sam standing there. "Is that who I think it is?" he asks quietly. He has his shoulder hitched against the wall and his feet crossed.

"Who do you think it is?" I ask as I walk to the linen closet and take out clean sheets to put on the double bed in Logan's old room.

"That's the girl from that night," he says quietly. He obviously doesn't want anyone else to hear him. I asked my brothers to keep an eye on her. Of course he knows who she is. Paul or Matt would have told him.

I nod. He follows me into the bedroom and helps me strip the bed, and we start to put the clean sheets on.

"How did you end up with her?" he asks.

"She came looking for me when I got out," I say. I can't explain it any better than that. She's the reason I was at the camp, after all. It's true.

"You like her?" he asks as he tucks in a corner of the sheet.

I nod. "A lot," I admit.

"Uh oh," he breathes. His brow arches. "You're in love with her."

I nod, and a grin steals across my face. "A lot," I say again.

Maggie walks into the room and lies down at my feet. "Cute dog," he says.

"She's a trained killer," I say.

He laughs. "Tell me another one."

"Try to get close to Reagan and see what happens," I warn. I'm not kidding. That dog almost made me piss my pants that one night.

"I'd rather not," he says. "So, you doing okay?" he asks.

"I'm sorry," I blurt out. He looks up, shocked.

"For what?" His brow furrows.

"For ignoring you. For not answering your letters. For being mad at you when I told you to run."

His mouth falls open, like he doesn't know what to say next. "I should have stayed."

"I didn't want you to stay." I heave in a deep breath. "I was jealous," I admit. It hurts like fucking hell, but it's the truth. "You went off to college and started living the dream. And I wasn't there." We'd never, ever been separated before that.

He sits down on the edge of the bed. "We were pretty stupid to work with Bone when we knew it was wrong."

I nod. "Fucking idiots."

"We should have known better," he says.

"Yep." I sit down beside him.

"Do you want to kiss and make up now?" he says, grinning.

I reach over and hug him, knocking him to the bed in the process, and he wraps his arms around me. His grappling quickly becomes wrestling, and he pins me for a minute on the sheets. But we're pretty evenly matched. I wiggle out of his hold and flip him over, and it's my turn to be on top. He makes a noise because he knows I have him, and then he flips me over his head. I live for this shit, but then I hear Maggie. Sam freezes on top of me and looks down.

Shit. Maggie has her teeth bared at him, and she's gnashing them. "You might want to let me up," I warn.

"Is she going to bite me?" he asks.

"Fuck, I don't know." He lifts his hands and moves to the other side of the room. Maggie hops onto the bed, gets between me and him, and growls. "Mags," I say, just like Reagan would. Maggie turns and slides her head under my hand. A laugh bursts from my throat. "Now that shit's funny," I say.

Sam doesn't agree, if his scowl is any indication. "You cheated with a fucking dog," he says. But a grin breaks across his face.

I scratch Maggie behind the ears. She loves me. Already. "He's all right, girl," I tell her. She nuzzles my hand, her eyes going back and forth between Sam and me. "She can tell us apart. Ain't that some shit?" I ask.

Sam backs out of the room, and I follow with Maggie at my heels. I sit down on the couch, and she drops at my feet and lays her head on her paws.

They still have the movie turned off, and I can tell they're waiting to grill me.

"Did you two make up?" Paul asks, as he crosses one foot over his leg. He's trying to be casual about it, but we both know there's nothing casual when he's being serious. And he's serious about this.

"We tried, but then Pete sicced his dog on me," Sam grouses. He sits down on the arm of the couch. Emily's in Logan's lap in the lazy chair, and Matt and Paul are on the other couch.

"Who's the girl?" Paul asks, jerking his thumb toward the bathroom.

I look toward it, and my insides go soft just thinking about her. "Her name is Reagan. You don't care if she spends the night, do you?"

Sam raises his hand like a teacher is calling on him in class. "She can sleep in my room."

I throw a pillow at his head, but he ducks and it sails past him.

"Is that *the* Reagan?" Matt asks. He reaches for a can of nuts on the coffee table and pops a handful into his mouth.

"Yeah," I reply. "But don't mention that to her, will you?" They all know about the rape. "And don't act like you pity her when she's around, all right? She's private about that stuff."

"I don't pity her," Emily says. "I admire the hell out of her." She steals Matt's nuts by crawling into his lap and prying them from his hands. He bats at her fingers, but he's playing. He fucking loves Emily. We all do.

"Well, I think I love the hell out of her, so you guys be nice."

My brothers freeze. All but Sam, and he's busy trying to steal the can of nuts from Emily. She knocks him over the head with it, and he gives up, sulking.

"You love her?" Paul asks quietly.

I can't bite back my grin. "Yeah."

"He's got the coochie disease," Sam says. "You know, the one where you get some and can't stop thinking about getting some more."

I throw another pillow at his head. "We haven't even done that," I say quietly. I look toward the door. I don't want her to hear me.

"You haven't?" Matt asks. He walks over and sits down on top of Emily, who's still in Logan's lap, and steals the nuts back from her. She squirms under him and finally gives up. He holds out a cashew for her, and she opens her mouth like a baby bird so he can pop it in. Then he climbs off her.

"Nope." God, they're nosy. "She has an apartment across town, over near where Emily lives."

"Oh, then we can take her home," Emily chirps. But she's already harassing Matt for the can of nuts again. He pins her down on the couch with his elbow and eats them while refusing to let her up. "Logan!" she whines, but she's laughing.

Logan just smiles. She gets herself into these messes; she can get herself out.

"I want her to stay here," I say, shaking my head at Emily. Matt lets her up, and she leans against him with her head on his shoulder. He likes to cuddle with her. She's like a sister to all of us, and I hope Reagan will fit in as well as Emily does one day. But I really can't imagine her wrestling with them the way Emily does.

"What happened to your eye?" Paul asks. My eye is still a little blue from when she hit me.

"Reagan hit me," I admit. Logan grins.

"Marry her," Logan says. "Marry her right away."

I nod. "I think I might," I say quietly. I watch their faces. They all look at me, and then Logan starts to laugh. He gets up and high-fives me.

"Thank God," he says. "I thought Emily would be the only girl around her forever."

"Emily's not a girl," Matt says, grimacing at the thought of it. She shoots him a heated glance. But she's not a girl. Not to any of us.

"So, you guys will be nice to her, right?" I ask.

"Duh," Sam says drolly as he walks into the kitchen and gets a beer. He brings one to me, but I shake my head. I'm going to have Reagan in my arms for the first time ever tonight, and I want to keep my head straight.

I hear the bathroom door open and get up. Reagan walks to stand beside me and whispers, "Which room is ours?" Her hair is loose and damp, hanging down over her shoulders. Her face is free of makeup, and she smells so damn good that I want to lick her. I adjust my junk, and Matt snickers. I scowl at him, and he nods toward the bedroom. It's a subtle warning, but I take it. "It was nice to meet you, Reagan," he says.

"You too," she calls back, but I'm already ushering her toward our room. I wait for Maggie to walk into the room with us and then close and lock the door. She looks around. "I'm nervous," she says quickly. She puts down her bag, and I notice she's wearing the clothes she had on before.

"Do you need something to sleep in?" I ask.

She shakes her head and smiles shyly at me, avoiding my gaze. "Could you turn around for a second?" she asks.

I grin, and it makes me so fucking happy that she asked. I hear a rustle of clothing and sheets behind me, and I look back to find her sliding between the sheets of the bed we'll share. And she's stark fucking naked. "What are you doing?" I ask.

"Going to bed," she says, looking at me like I've lost my mind. She rolls onto her side and rests her head in the palm of her hand, her elbow pointed toward the head of the bed. She pats the space beside her. "You coming?"

Her voice is shaking, so I know she's not nearly as cool as she wants me to think.

I point toward the lump her body makes under the covers. "Are you naked under there?" I ask. I'm not sure I can stand sleeping next to her naked. I know I asked her to try it. But I'm not sure my nerves can take it.

She lifts the edge of the blanket and looks down. "I still have panties on," she whispers.

Jesus Christ. I run a hand through my hair. "Okay," I say slowly.

I kick off my shoes and sit down on the edge of the bed to pull my socks off. Then I shuck my jeans off quickly and pull my shirt over my head. I slide between the sheets in my boxers, trying to stay turned away from her so she won't see how hard my dick is. The last thing I want to do is scare her.

I feel her fingertips on my arm and heave in a breath. "Jesus," I say.

Her fingers still. "What's wrong?" she asks.

"Nothing," I croak.

She sits up. "You sure?" She clutches the covers to her chest.

"Yeah," I bite out. Her fingers start to trace my tattoos again.

"Do you think you could give me a tattoo?" she asks.

Finally, a safe topic. "What do you want?" I ask. I roll over to face her.

She shrugs. "I don't know."

I roll toward the nightstand and open the drawer. This used to be Logan's room and he's an artist, so there's a drawer full of pens and markers. I pick up a few and lay them on the bed. "Roll over," I say.

"Why?" Her brow furrows.

"Just trust me," I say, and I motion for her to roll over again. She does, looking back at me over her shoulder as she moves to lie on her stomach. The blanket is hitched up nearly to her shoulders. "Can I pull this down a little?" I ask.

She nods and wraps her arm around the pillow, then rests her face on it. She smiles softly. "All right," she says quietly. Her breaths are harsher now, though. And she has goose bumps on her arms and the back of her neck.

I uncap a pen and touch it to her back, drawing a quick little picture of a butterfly. "We can do a butterfly like this one."

She looks back, rolling a little to look at what I drew, and I see the side of her naked breast. Good God. I scrub a hand down my face.

"I like it, but I was thinking more dainty, with vines. Maybe up my side." She pushes the blankets lower, and I can see the indentations on top of her butt and the elastic of her panties.

"You want thorns?" I ask as I start to draw.

She shakes her head, giggling as I move my way up her side. "That tickles," she laughs.

"Whatever you get, we'll have Logan draw it so it'll be spectacular. Then I can ink you." I draw vines all the way up her side, and then put a flower on the side of her breast that I can see. I'm a guy. I can't avoid touching it. It's there. I want it. "Roll over just a little," I say, and I give her a nudge.

"Why?" she asks. But she's already covering her breasts with her hands as she rolls. I rearrange her fingertips over her left boob so I can finish my drawing. I think I catch a flash of her nipple, and I suck in a breath.

"So pretty," I breathe.

"Can I see it?" she asks quietly.

"Not until I'm done." She relaxes as I keep drawing across her stomach. But she's still, so I nudge her again to get her to roll over. "We could give you a tramp stamp," I say.

"What's that?" She giggles.

"A tattoo right over your butt. They used to be really popular." I start to write some words on top of her butt, and the elastic of her undies gets in my way. "Can I pull these down a little?" I ask quietly. I'm getting into dangerous territory, and I know it.

"Yeah," she breathes. It's no more than a puff of air, but it sounds like an air horn.

I fold her panties down so that I can see the tops of her butt cheeks. I smile as I draw. I fucking love that she trusts me this much. "You definitely need a tattoo here," I say. I rock my hips against the mattress, trying to adjust and ease some of the ache in my balls. It doesn't work.

I give her my shirt to cover her boobs because I can't stand to look at them plump around her fingertips when she rolls over. I'm too far gone. I gently turn her and lay the shirt over her boobs so I can see her belly. It's flat, and her hips are curvy. I pull her panties down a little so I can draw down the side of her hip.

"You can take them off," she whispers. Her words are soft but heavy. They fall on my ears like booms of thunder. I'm on my knees between her bent legs, and I look into her face.

"You sure?" I ask.

I can't help but remember the last time I helped her with her panties, but I push those memories away, and I kiss the inside of her thigh before I pull her undies down her legs and toss them to the side. I draw across her hip, but I keep blankets bunched on the area where I'm not working. I kiss her belly button and dip my tongue inside. She squirms and eases out a breath.

"We should pierce you here," I say. "You have the perfect belly for it."

"Where else would you pierce me?" she asks. Her voice is quivering, and I fucking love it. She's so turned on that she rocks her hips up toward my face while I draw over the top of her curly short hairs, the ones that cover her mound. I pull the blankets lower and sift my fingers through her hair and dip into the wet crease. "Here," I say.

"There?" she breathes, but she squirms against my hand, so I push a little harder. I very gently spread her legs and ease down between them, setting my pens to the side. "All done tattooing me?" she asks. She's breathing like she just ran a five-minute mile.

"Can I kiss you?" I ask. I don't want to do anything she doesn't want.

"You'd have to come up here for that," she says.

I strum my thumb across her clit, spreading her open so I can see what I'm doing. "No," I say. "I mean down here."

She hisses out a breath. "Do you want to?" she asks. She adjusts the pillows behind her so that she's sitting up a little more and raises her arms behind her head so she can watch me.

I laugh. "Oh yeah, I want to," I say. Her clit is all swollen, and I push the hood back with my thumb. I lean down and lick across it. I want to slide my finger inside her, but I'm afraid she's not ready for that. I'm afraid of everything when it comes to her because I don't want to mess this up. "I want to lick you until you come on my face," I say.

She groans when my head dips, and I suckle her clit. Her knees raise so she can rock against my mouth. I look up from where I'm working on her, and she draws her lower lip between her teeth as her eyes close.

"Pete," she cries. I nod, and I keep sucking. She's so wet, and I have her spread open and she trusts me and this is the most fucking perfect thing I've ever done before in my life. "Pete," she says again. Her fingers slide into my hair, and she pushes me a little to the left. I let up on my grip on her clit and move over. She cries out when I latch onto her again, and she pushes my head, moving me closer to her. I hum against her clit, and she cries out, her breaths ragged and choppy. "Pete," she says again. "Pete, Pete, Pete, Pete," she chants. Her eyes close and her head falls back, and then she breaks. I hold on and thread my fingers through hers when she tries to push my head away. I gentle my tongue, and she relaxes, her body pulsing as she does it. She comes on my face, and I fucking love everything about it. She quivers and quakes and shakes and those noises she makes drive me wild. She pushes my forehead and whispers, "I can't take anymore. Please, Pete." She's still shuddering though, and I push her all the way through it. When she's finally still, I open her up with my thumbs and lick her from top to bottom, over and over. She's so wet and she tastes so good and she still has these little aftershocks that quiver through her. I wipe my face on her inner thigh and crawl up her body. "Oh my God," she moans. Her body is soft and lax under me. I kiss her, and I hope she can taste how fucking happy she just made me. She lifts her head. "Do you do anything that's not epic?" She laughs. It's a happy sound, and I want to make her do it over and over.

"I'm an overachiever," I say. I kiss her, drawing her lower lip between my teeth. I'm hard against her belly, and I'm afraid it will scare her.

"What about you, Pete?" she says. She reaches down my belly and slips her tentative fingers beneath my waistband, and her eyes open wide as she wraps her fingers around me and grips me tightly.

I bury my face in her neck. I'll just let her touch me for a second. But a second is all it takes. "Oh shit," I groan as my balls crawl up toward my body, and I spill into her hand. Her hand stills for a second, but her eyes close as she makes a happy sound and she grips me tighter. I thrust into her fist, which is now wet with the product of us. She doesn't let go. Her hand is tight and sure. She rolls her thumb around the tip with every thrust of my hips. She's touching me, and I look down between us and see that I made a god-awful mess on her belly. I still and look up into her face. She's laughing. I don't think I've ever seen her look quite so happy. She wraps me up with her clean hand and holds me tight against her. Her other is trapped between us, and she's still holding onto my dick. I pull my hips back, trying to slide out of her grip, and hiss as she squeezes me tighter. I throw the shirt that's over her tits to the side and lay my forehead against her naked skin, trying to catch my breath. "I'm sorry," I say. I didn't mean to do that.

She takes my face in her hands and lifts it so that I look at her. She's grinning. "Are you kidding?" she laughs. "That was amazing."

"Yeah, it kinda was," I say. I kiss her. I can't stop it. I have to. "We're a mess," I warn.

"I don't care." She giggles, and I have never, ever heard a happier sound.

"Are you all right?" I ask. What if she's delirious from the stress of it?

She lays her head back against the pillow, her chest shaking with laughter. "I think I just came on your face," she says. She giggles again.

I laugh, too. I can't help it. It's contagious—her happiness. She's fucking happy. And so am I.

Reagan

I wake up in Pete's arms, our naked limbs tangled together. Pete had taken off his boxers and used them to clean up the mess between us, and then he slid into bed naked, just like me. He'd pulled me against his chest and kissed my forehead, murmuring softly to me about how amazing that was. I don't think it was nearly as amazing for him as it was for me. He had to work to get me off, and all I had to do was touch him really quickly. I smile against my pillow at the thought of it. Perfect. That's what it was. Perfect.

He stirs when I start to move, and his arms reach for me. But now I know what woke me. Maggie is retching beside the bed, and I need to get up. I'm going to have to call the vet. This isn't normal for her. Not at all. I suppose it can wait until the sun comes up. I glance at the clock on the bedside table, and it's not even morning yet. "I'll be right back," I whisper to Pete. He rolls into his pillow, and I'm not even sure he's awake. He makes a low sound, but it's more of a mumble. I pull Pete's shirt over my head and slide into my jeans. Then I stick my feet into Pete's sneakers. He won't mind. I'm not wearing underwear, but I just need to go to the bathroom and find something to clean up Maggie's mess. I pet her head for a second, and she looks up at me like she's sorry. The hallway is dark when I step out, and it takes me a minute to get my bearings.

I go back and clean up the floor and go pee really quickly, but then I see Maggie standing at the front door, scratching at it. She needs to go out. It's the middle of the night, and we're not in a good section of town. "Oh, Mags," I say. "Can't it wait?" I throw my head back and groan. I suppose I could wake Pete up. I really don't want to go down by myself. Then again, I'll have Maggie with me.

Papers rustle at the kitchen table, and I jump. One of the brothers is sitting there, and he closes a book in front of himself. It's the one with the ponytail—Matt? He lays his pen down and says quietly, "Does she need to go out?" He stands up and reaches for his shoes. "I'll take her." He slides his feet into his shoes and walks toward me.

"You don't have to go to any trouble," I say. I take a step back, and Maggie growls at him. He holds out his hands to the side. "Mags," I scold. She buries her head under my hand and runs back to the door, where she scratches. "I'm just going to take her out really quick," I say. I go back to our room, get Maggie's leash, and clip it to her collar. I open the door and step out, but before I can close it behind me, Matt joins me. "You really don't have to go," I say.

He jams his hands in his pockets and walks by me, opening the door to the stairwell. He doesn't say a word. He just walks down with us and out toward the street, where he leads us to an area with some grass and trees. It's small, but it'll do. Maggie immediately squats and comes back to walk circles around my legs. "All done?" he asks. He brushes his hair back because some of it's falling out of the rubber band at the back of his neck. He really does look a lot like Pete, but he's thin and tall. He's not as broad as Pete, but he's wiry and I can tell he's strong. He's not threatening at all, and the fact that he's not surprises me. Men usually scare the hell out of me.

"Yeah," I say, and we start back toward the apartment.

The city is not asleep. I doubt it ever sleeps, and some men walk by us wearing knit caps and football jerseys. I back up and step into Matt. He puts his hands on my shoulders and says, "Careful." He squeezes my shoulders gently, and then he steps back. He holds the door wide, and I slide through without touching him. But in the back of my mind, I'm lamenting over the fact that he didn't make my skin crawl. "You okay?" he asks as we start up the stairs.

I nod. But I have this lump in my throat. I officially have three men in my life now who don't scare me. My dad, Pete, and this man I don't know. And the fact that I don't know him, yet feel okay with him touching me, amazes me. "Thanks for going with me," I say.

"I couldn't let Pete's girl go out in the dark alone. He'd never forgive me." My belly flips at his choice of words. Pete's girl.

"I should have just woken him up. I don't think he'd mind."

He snorts. "You've never seen Pete in the morning, huh?"

I guess I haven't. Not when he gets right out of bed. "No," I admit. But up until tonight, he'd never came in my hand, either, so I guess I'm learning all sorts of things about him, how he looks in the morning being just one of them.

We get halfway up the stairs and I realize Maggie's not with us. I let her leash drop after we came through the door because she always follows so closely. I look down and see her on the second level, lying on the floor panting. "Mags?" I say. I walk toward her, and she lumbers to her feet. But she's unsteady, and she refuses to walk up the stairs.

"Will she let me carry her?" Matt asks.

I doubt it. I can carry her myself, but before I can say so, he walks over to her and lets her sniff his hand. He pets her head and down the length of her back. Then he hoists her into his arms and carries her up the stairs. She doesn't complain, and she doesn't try to bite him.

He lets us into the apartment and sets her down, and then he sits down on the floor and lets her crawl into his lap. "She doesn't usually like people," I say.

He smiles. "They can tell when we're harmless," he says softly. "Do you want me to find a vet tonight?" he asks.

"I think she'll be okay until morning, don't you?" I never know what to do with emergencies. I've never had to deal with one all by myself.

"Probably," he says. He rises to his feet, and I realize how big he really is. He's at least as tall as Pete, and he's covered in tattoos just like Pete is, but he's...different. It's hard to explain. "Want something to drink?" he asks softly as he goes to the fridge.

I'm wide awake, so I may as well. He brings me a bottle of water, and I see him take a carton of ice cream from the fridge. It's Rocky Road, my favorite.

"Want some?" he whispers, and he takes out two bowls. He starts to scoop ice cream into them.

"Did we wake you up?" I ask, and I sit down at the table when he hands me a bowl and a spoon.

"No." He shakes his head. "I don't sleep well sometimes, so I get up and write." He shrugs. "It clears my head."

"What do you write?" I ask.

He shrugs again. "Just journal stuff," he says. "They had me start doing it when they thought I was going to die." He chuckles, but it's a sound with no humor.

I pull the spoon out of my mouth. This really is good ice cream. "You're better now, right?"

"As far as I know," he says. "I have to go back next week for tests."

"Oh." I don't know what to say.

"Can I ask you something?" he says, and he winces as he asks.

"I guess so."

"What you feel for Pete," he says, "is it truly affection? Or is it gratitude?"

I choke on my ice cream. It won't go down. When I finally get through it, I say, "I can't define it that easily."

"Try," he says. "He's my brother. I'm worried."

I point the spoon toward my chest. "About me?"

"Yeah," he grunts. "My little brother is in love," he says. He smiles softly. "I'm happy for him, but I still don't want to see him get hurt."

"I don't want to see that, either." The ice cream churns in my gut. "We're still figuring things out."

He smiles. "Glad to hear it." He clears his throat. "I've seen Pete with a lot of women but never with one he looks at like he looks at you."

Wow. I don't know how to respond.

"Just be careful with him, okay?" he says.

A door closes down the hallway, and I hear the rapid slaps of little feet. A tiny blonde stands in the hallway and looks around the corner at me. She's wearing Tinker Bell pajamas. "Hi," I say. I look toward Matt, but he just chuckles.

"You're not supposed to be up," he says. He motions her forward, and she settles in his lap. "I think she can smell ice cream from a mile away." He laughs and brushes her hair from her face with gentle fingers.

"Is she yours?" I ask.

He laughs. "She's Paul's. She lives here every other week. She was already in bed when you got here." He bumps his knee under her bottom and says, "Can you tell her what your name is?"

"My name is Hayley," she says. She licks her lips and looks into his bowl. He heaves a sigh and passes her his spoon but he's smiling.

"Hayley, this is Reagan. She's Pete's girl."

My heart swells at his words. "It's nice to meet you," I say.

She doesn't look up from the ice cream until the spoon clanks against the empty bowl.

"You better go back to bed before your daddy sees you're missing," he says. He sets her down, and she kisses his cheek quickly. Then she runs back down the hallway and creeps slowly into her room.

"She's adorable," I say.

"Adorable is not the right word for Hayley," he says with a laugh. "She's five going on fifteen."

"Do you have any kids?" I ask.

His blue eyes meet mine, and they're full of sadness. "Kids aren't in the cards for me. I'd love to have some, but after my treatment, there's not a very good chance of that." He brushes his hair back and resecures it with the rubber band. "So, I get to spoil Hayley. Paul would kill me if she knew she was up eating ice cream in the middle of the night."

I take my bowl and his to the sink and rinse them out. "Thanks for the ice cream. And for helping with Maggie," I say.

"There's a lady who was in my chemical trial. She's dying." He looks around like he doesn't know where to settle his eyes. "Her son called today and asked if I wanted to come to see her."

"Are you going?" I ask.

"I'm too fucking scared to look my mortality in the face," he says. "That could be me." He drums his thumb on the table, his palm flat. "I'm a chickenshit. And a terrible friend." He shakes his head, like a dog shaking water from its fur. If only it were that easy.

"Do you want some company when you go?" I ask. "I could go with you."

His gaze leaps to mine.

"I mean, I could wait in the waiting room."

He nods. "Maybe." He smiles. "Thanks for the offer."

He comes forward and grabs my arm, squeezing it gently as he walks by me. And I don't freak out or feel like I need to hit him. Maybe it's just him. He seems like a good guy. One of the best, probably. He's been through a lot.

"Good night," he says quietly.

"'Night," I say.

I cluck my tongue at Maggie, and she follows me into the bedroom, where I close and lock the door. I shrug out of my clothes and slide into bed with Pete. He pulls me to him immediately, and I roll forward, putting my face against the light dusting of hair on this chest. "You're cold," he says.

"Maggie needed to go out," I explain.

He lifts his head. "You didn't go out alone, did you?" he asks.

"Matt went with me." I yawn.

"Oh, okay," he hums. He grabs my leg and pulls it over his hip, and my naked girl parts are right beside his naked boy parts. But I'm not worried, not even when I realize his parts are reaching toward mine. He kisses my forehead and murmurs, "Go back to sleep."

I close my eyes and snuggle into him. He's quiet and still when I say, "I love you, Pete."

"I love you, too," he says, his voice husky from sleep but clear. I smile and find the sweet spot where my head fits best.

Pete

I sit on the couch with Maggie at my feet. She's not well. She hasn't been able to stand up this morning, and so I just sit and pet her and talk to her about Reagan.

"This doesn't look good," Paul says, eyeing Maggie. He's worried since Hayley is here and he doesn't want her to mess with Maggie. It's hard to tell a five-year-old to leave the dog alone.

"I know. I made an appointment for nine a.m.," I say. "I just need to go and wake Reagan up."

"Does she know how bad it is?" he asks. He's making breakfast for Hayley, and he stops every few minutes to dance around the kitchen with her.

"I doubt it," I grunt. "She was walking around just fine yesterday."

"You had better go and wake her up or you're going to be late," Paul warns. Paul's the timekeeper of the family.

Sam starts to put his shoes on. "I'm going with you," he says.

"Do you want me to go, too?" Matt asks.

"Neither of you needs to go," I remind them. "Why don't you stay here and make a cake or something, Sam?" I ask. She might need cheering up when we come back.

He shrugs. "Okay."

But Matt gets ready to with us, and he comes to take my place petting Maggie while I go get Reagan. I step into the room and close the door behind me. She's kicked the covers down so that one of her boobs is exposed. Her skin is pale where her bathing suit covers her, and she has tan lines that I want to trace with my tongue. But not right now.

I sit down on the side of the bed and give her a gentle shake. "Reagan," I say quietly. Her eyes open slowly, and she stretches, her lips spreading into a smile. "Good morning," I say. I'm hard. I admit it. I'm a guy and she's naked and she came on my face last night. So, yeah, I have to adjust my junk. This isn't the time.

"Morning," she says, her voice hoarse from sleep.

"You need to get up," I say. "I made an appointment for Maggie this morning at nine at the vet."

"She still acting tired?" she asks. She sits up on the side of the bed, holding the covers up over her breasts.

It's worse than her being tired. I'm sure of it. "Yeah."

"Okay," she says, covering a yawn. She looks at her clothes lying across the room.

"Do you need clothes out of the car?" I ask.

She shakes her head. "I just need to get dressed and brush my teeth."

"I'll give you a few minutes," I say. But what I really want to do is stay and watch her get dressed. And then undress her and do it all over again.

I walk out and Matt's got Maggie in his lap. She doesn't look that bad, but she's tired. I can tell. This is a big deal. She threw up again and again last night, more than Reagan probably is even aware of. Reagan comes out a few minutes later with her hair pulled into a ponytail. She slips into the bathroom, and I hear her brushing her teeth.

She comes out, and I stand up with Maggie in my arms. "I'll carry her down," I say.

"She can walk, can't she?"

I shake my head, and I see Reagan's features cloud with worry. I start toward the door, and she follows. Matt goes with us. Reagan climbs

into the backseat of her Camry, and I put Maggie in her lap. I toss the keys
to Matt, and he drives so I can sit with Reagan. Reagan coos at her dog,
talking softly to her about how she is going to get some vitamins and then
they would go home. But I doubt that's going to be the case.

We get to the vet's office, and they put us in a room. The vet
comes in and does a quick exam. She takes Maggie to the back for pictures
and tests. She doesn't have Maggie with her when she returns. She has her
vet's face on. "I'm sorry. I don't have good news," she says quietly.

Reagan covers her mouth with her hand, and a sound escapes her
lips. I pull her into my side. I had a feeling this was coming. "Maggie is
fifteen years old. That's pretty old for her breed."

"She was fine yesterday," Reagan protests.

"She wasn't," the vet says, shaking her head. "She has a mass in her
abdomen. It's really big, and it's so big that it has ruptured, so she's
bleeding into her belly. I'm very sorry."

Reagan looks at me, her eyes gleaming with hope. "So, you take the
mass out, right?"

The vet shakes her head. "I'm sorry, but this isn't something that
we can fix. I recommend that you put her to sleep."

"When?" Reagan asks. She thinks Maggie still has time.

"Now," she says. "Making her wait isn't humane."

A strangled noise comes out of Reagan's mouth, and I pull her to
me, but she shoves me away and walks to stand in the corner of the room.
She paces back and forth. Then she stops. "There's nothing you can do?"
she asks, her voice small.

"I'm sorry. There's nothing." The vet is being as sympathetic as
possible. "Do you want me to go to get her so that you can say good-bye?"

Tears roll down Reagan's face, and I catch Matt wiping one of his own. He doesn't even know the fucking dog and Reagan has him crying over her. But that's Matt. "Yes, please," Reagan whispers.

A few minutes later, they bring Maggie back, strapped to a board, and she's lying there quietly. She doesn't look unhappy at all, but looks can be deceiving.

"Can I have a minute with her?" Reagan asks.

We all go into the hallway and wait. After about five minutes of murmuring behind the closed door, Reagan comes out and nods. She's ready.

The vet and an assistant come into the room. "We're going to give her a little sedative, and then we'll give her a shot that will stop her heart."

Reagan's eyes are puffy and red, and her cheeks are wet. She swipes at them, but it doesn't matter. The vet tech gives Maggie the sedative, and Maggie lays her head down. Her eyes are wide open, and her breaths are soft. "Now we'll give her the shot," the vet warns.

Reagan lays a hand on Maggie's side, but she doesn't come closer. She already said her good-byes, I'd wager. Maggie struggles when they stick the needle into her back leg, and Reagan starts to sob. Matt reaches out and covers her hand with his, and I lean down close to Maggie's head. Maggie's fighting it, so I lean forward and whisper into her ear. Maggie's eyes go wide, and then she relaxes. Her breaths slow, and then they stop. I watch her chest, and my gut clenches when I realize it's not moving. Reagan is wrecked, and I stand up, grab Reagan, and pull her to me. She wraps herself up in my arms and lets me absorb her sobs in my shirt. I coo at her and hold her, and I don't know what else I can do. I hear Matt making arrangements for the cremation, and they take Maggie's collar off and hand it to Reagan before they take Maggie from the room.

Reagan sobs as Maggie leaves, and she cries in my arms until it dissolves into soft hiccups. I just hold her. There's nothing else I can do. "Better now?" I ask.

She nods. "I thought we were just going to get some vitamins."

I brush her hair back from her face. It's wet and stuck to her lips. "I'm sorry," I say.

Reagan catches my shirt in her fists and holds me, looking into my eyes. "What did you whisper to her?" she asks.

I cough into my fist because there's a lump the size of an apple in my throat. "It doesn't matter," I say.

"Tell me," she protests.

I take a deep breath and steel myself. I clear my throat. "I thanked her for protecting you all these years and told her how much I appreciate it. But that she could go ahead and leave because I got you from here on out. I told her I'd take over where she leaves off."

Reagan falls against me and cries even more. And Matt passes me a tissue so I can blot my eyes. But he nods subtly and claps a hand on my shoulder. He squeezes my nape tightly, and I absorb it, because this is what my brothers do for me. Every single time. Reagan lets me go and hugs Matt really quickly. He squeezes her, and I think I see him drop a kiss near her hair. Damn. She's part of the family now. No doubt.

Reagan

Pete takes my keys from Matt, who must have pocketed them when we got out at the vet's office. I don't complain. I can barely put one foot in front of the other, much less drive. Pete slides behind the wheel, adjusts the seat and the mirrors, and looks over at me. "You want me to call your dad for you?"

I shake my head. "I can do it." I do need to call my parents. But I know I'll be a sobbing mess if I try to do it now. Pete looks at the clock and swears. "What?" I ask.

"I'm supposed to be at the youth center for group at eleven," he says. He takes my hand and squeezes it. "I'll call and tell them I can't go."

"No," I protest. I don't want him to change his plans. My dog is dead. Him not going to help those boys isn't going to bring her back. "You should go." I turn around and look at Matt. "Do you want to go to the hospital and see your friend this morning?"

He looks into my eyes. "You've had enough sadness today." His eyes start to dart around the car, and I can tell he's upset.

"She's going to die, Matt," I say quietly. "You need to see her."

Pete sits up tall so he can look at Matt in the rearview mirror. He's curious about why I know so much about Matt. I should have told him that we talked last night, but I kind of feel like it was between me and Matt. "Who's dying?" Pete asks.

"Kendra," he says quietly.

"Oh no," Pete breathes. He shakes his head. "You need to go, Matt. We'll go with you."

Matt heaves in a breath and points to me. "She can go. You can't."

Pete's brow furrows. "Why can't I go?" he asks.

"Because you have to go see the boys at the center." He looks into my eyes. "Can we go today?" he asks.

I nod. "I'd love to." It'll be better than sitting around missing Maggie.

We drive across town and drop Pete off at the youth center. He gets out, adjusts his jeans, and pulls me to him. We're standing at the front of the car, and Matt gets into the driver's seat. I brush Pete's shirt off. He has Maggie's hair stuck to him in places. "Are you going to be all right with Matt?" he asks. "I don't have to go to the meeting. I can go with you. I really don't want to leave you today."

"I need something to do." It's true. If I sit at home, I'll think about Maggie all day. And Matt needs to do this. I can feel it in my gut. Besides, Matt doesn't scare me. The look on his face makes me want to hug him and hold him close. He's struggling, and I know what that's like. Pete bangs on the hood of the car, and Matt sticks his head out.

"What the fuck do you want?" Matt grouses. But their banter is playful. I love the way they interact with one another.

"You'll bring her home after, right?"

He shrugs. "If that's where she wants to go."

Pete reaches up and tucks a lock of hair behind my ear. "I want you to sleep in my bed."

Butterflies take flight in my belly. "Okay," I whisper.

"Will you do me a favor?" he asks.

I'd do just about anything for him. "What do you need?"

"Take care of Matt. He's not as strong as he looks."

I disagree because I'd wager he's a lot stronger than he looks, and he looks like a linebacker. "I'll keep an eye on him."

His lips touch mine, and it's not a peck on my mouth. He delves in and let's me know he's there. When I'm breathless, he sets me back from him with a groan, his hands on my shoulders. "Don't forget to call your parents," he says. He walks away from me toward the youth detention center. I watch him walk, admiring his backside. He turns back and cups his hands around his mouth. "I love you," he calls.

I shake my head and mouth the words back at him. Then I get in the car, where Matt is tapping on the wheel with his thumbs singing along with a song on the radio. He acts like he's sticking his fingers down his throat and makes a gagging noise. "You guys will make me puke if you keep that up." He grins, though.

I shove his shoulder. "That's not funny."

"No, it won't be funny at all when I puke. I puked a lot during chemo. I'm good at it." He laughs. He reaches out and squeezes my knee. "Call your dad on the drive. We have about an hour to kill."

I pick up the phone and call my parents, and they put me on the speakerphone. I can't talk about it for long without breaking down. Mom is noticeably upset, and Dad wants to drive to the city to be sure I'm all right.

"I'm fine," I tell them. "I'm hanging out with Pete's family today. So I'm not alone."

Dad grunts.

"Dad," I warn.

"Fine," he says. I can tell he's biting his tongue.

"I miss her already, Dad," I say.

"I know," he says softly. "She's been with you a long time."

I can hear Mom crying softly in the background.

"Who's going to protect you?" he asks. "Maybe you should come home."

"Dad, I'm fine."

Matt grins at me and winks. I have a feeling I have the whole Reed clan to take care of me, if I ask them. I hang up with Dad while he's still protesting, and I settle back against the seat. Matt turns up the radio, and we get all the way to the cancer center without him saying much.

Then he turns off the car and takes in a deep breath. "Now or never," he says.

I get out of the car with him and walk inside. The staff knows him by name and greets him at the desk. "I'm here to see Kendra."

She points over Matt's shoulder, and I see three kids sitting in the waiting area. One is older, maybe sixteen or so, a boy, and he's holding a small child in his arms. She can't be more than three. And there's a young girl about Hayley's age in the chair beside them. He's reading a book to both the girls. "Seth?" Matt asks. The boy looks up, confused. He sets the littlest girl in the floor and gets up. Matt extends his hand, and they talk quietly. I can't quite hear them. I go to the vending machine and get some gum, and then take it back and offer the two little ones a piece. If there's one thing I know, it's how to win over small children. "Don't swallow it," the oldest girl says. She shoves the little one in the shoulder.

The little one grins. "Oops," she says, and she sticks her tongue out so I can see her empty mouth.

"Oops," I repeat, and I go pick up the book they were reading. "Can I read your book?" I ask.

They nod and climb into a chair on each side of me.

"Reagan," Matt says. "Will you be all right here for a few minutes?" I nod and smile.

"Can I go?" the little one chirps.

"Not right now," Seth says. He sits down and heaves a sigh. He sounds much older than he looks.

I watch as Matt walks into a nearby room. He stops in the doorway, startled, and I see his head fall. He walks to the bedside, and as he walks over, the door shuts slowly behind him, leaving a view of him walking to the bedside, where he drops and lays his forehead against the woman's knee. The door snicks shut on its own, and I can't see anymore.

"How are things going?" I ask Seth.

"They're going," he says. He nods toward the little ones, and I see that they're watching us closely. I get it. He doesn't want to talk about his mom right now.

Suddenly, there's a flurry of activity at the door, and a woman walks in. She's wearing a pencil-thin skirt and a jacket, and she's carrying a purse that probably cost more than these kids eat in a year. She runs to the desk on her four-inch Louboutin heels, and they clack against the floor. She stops, shoves her rhinestone-encrusted sunglasses to the top of her head, pushing her blond hair back, and asks for Kendra's room. She runs inside, and the door closes behind her, too.

"Who was that?" I ask.

"Probably our aunt," Seth says with a shrug.

"You don't know?"

He shakes his head. "Never met her."

She doesn't look anything like them. These kids have dark skin and are obviously biracial. She is as white bred as they come with flaxen hair that falls down over her shoulders. The woman I saw in the bed is biracial as well.

"I know," he chuckles. "I don't get it either."

After about a half hour, Matt comes out with the woman. He looks at me. "Reagan," he starts. He brushes a hand down his face and scrubs the back of his head. "I need a favor."

I get up and walk down the hallway with him. "Kendra wants the kids to go home. Or at least the little ones. She wants Seth to stay, if he wants to. But their aunt is going to take the little ones back to their apartment. Do you think you could ride back with her and let me keep your car so I can come home after?"

"You're not coming with us?"

"I'm going to stay," he says. "Until the end. I promised," he whispers. "I need to."

He still has my keys from earlier. I nod. "Should I stay with the kids?"

The lady is down on her knees in front of the two girls, and she's talking softly with them. They all stand up, and she takes them by the hands. "Ready?" she asks.

"I can stay?" Seth asks. He looks from Matt to his aunt and back. His voice is suddenly deep, and I see him clear his throat, coughing into his fist. He wants to stay. He wants to be there for his mom.

"Of course you can stay," his aunt says. She looks at Matt. "You'll bring him home? After?"

Matt nods. He claps a hand on Seth's shoulder, and Seth looks at him, blinking hard.

I walk out with the aunt and the little girls. "My name is Skylar," she says. "People call me Sky."

"Reagan," I say.

She opens the doors with her key fob and says, "I bought a car seat on the way here, but I'm not sure how to use it."

I help her install it, and we settle the kids in the tiny backseat of her sports car. She sighs heavily and starts the car. "If you want to stay, I can take the kids back with me and watch them," I offer.

"I don't want to stay," she says crisply.

"Kendra is your sister?" I ask.

"Half sister," she says, and she makes a noise at the back of her throat. "We've never met until today."

Then what on earth is she doing with the kids?

"Kendra doesn't have anybody else," she explains. "So they called me." She snorts. "I've been taught to hate her my whole life," she says so quietly that the kids can't hear her, but I can. "And now they want me to raise her kids." Her jerks a thumb toward the small one. "I've never changed a diaper in my life."

"I can go with you."

She shakes her head. "I suppose I need to learn."

"You're going to their house?" I ask.

She looks at me. "I think they'll be more comfortable there, don't you? Their own beds. Their toys."

"I can help."

She shakes her head again. "They said it won't be but a few more hours. Then Matt will bring Seth home, and he can help me."

I nod.

"I can make do until then." She looks at the girls in the rearview mirror. "Who wants ice cream?" she cries.

"Me!" both girls squeal.

After ice cream and a quick stop at the store for diapers and kid food, she stops at a stoplight. "Are you sure you don't want me to go with you?" I really wouldn't mind.

She shakes her head and pulls her expensive sunglasses down to hide her eyes. "Thanks, Reagan," she says. "I think I got this."

I don't believe her. Not at all.

Pete

I'm worried about Reagan, so I call her from Reed's, the tattoo shop where I work with my brothers. Since no one was at home, I went to work with the guys. I hang up the phone and take a deep breath. Someone is dropping her off in five minutes at the shop. I have no idea what happened with Matt, but he has Reagan's car and she rode home with a stranger. I don't particularly like that, but Matt wouldn't do anything to hurt her. At least not on purpose.

Finally, she walks in the door. I have my gun resting against someone's back as I draw an outline. She blows out a frustrated breath as she walks through the door. "Everything okay?" I ask. I can't stop what I'm doing. Not right now.

"Fine," she says. "That was so strange."

Emily is perched on top of a desk swinging her feet, sucking on a lollipop. She's so fucking cute in her combat boots and jeans that I want to hug her. "What was strange?" she asks.

"Those kids," Reagan said. "I'm worried about them."

She tells us the story and all about the aunt that had never seen the kids before. "Maybe Matt knows more about it and can fill us in later?" I suggest.

"I'm glad he went," Reagan says. "He would have hated it otherwise."

A woman walks in the front door, and every man in the house stops to look. She's wearing a short, short skirt, and a fitted top with an open back. "What can we do for you?" Friday, the girl who runs the front, asks.

"I'd like to get a piercing," she says, and she bites her lower lip.

"Can one of you do a piercing?" Friday calls. Friday is really pretty in a Katy Perry kind of way. She has tattoos on her shoulders and across her back and up her legs. I know about the ones on her legs because I put them there. She has skulls and cross bones and turtles and some really weird shit. And she dresses all retro, like a pinup girl from the sixties.

"What kind of piercing?" I ask.

Every gaze in the place turns to the woman, and she flushes. "One of *those* piercings!" Friday yells dramatically.

"Pete can do it," Paul says.

Reagan's mouth falls open. She walks over close to me. "You are not doing a private piercing," she hisses. I do them all the time, but I don't even want to do them anymore. She cups her hand around my ear. "The only private places you're touching are mine."

My heart swells. I like this. I like it a lot. "Sorry," I say. "The little lady has spoken." I lift my face, and she bends down to kiss me.

Paul looks at Logan, but Emily signs something to him really quickly and he grins. He shakes his head. "Can't do it," he says.

"Why not?" Paul blows out a heavy breath.

"Because I want to have sex tonight," Logan says. "And tomorrow night. And the night after."

Sam's not here. He's probably baking a cake somewhere. And we all know where Matt is. Paul throws down the pencil on the table where he was drawing a tattoo. "You guys are worthless," he complains. "And pussy whipped."

I'm happy to be pussy whipped. Logan walks over and high-fives me, and Emily grins at Reagan. "Thanks for taking one for the team," I say to Paul.

It won't be hard on him. The girl is gorgeous. "The things I have to do so you guys can have sex." He hitches up his jeans and makes a production of helping her pick out a piercing. He takes Friday with him when he goes behind the curtain because we have learned through the years that you don't do intimate jobs without a girl present. Kind of like a male gynecologist always having a female nurse in the room. He comes out a few minutes later, and the girl is walking funny.

She leaves, and Paul sits down and then starts to laugh. He throws a napkin at my head. "You guys suck," he says.

Friday stands up and says, "Let's go get a hot dog."

"I got a hot dog for you," Paul says.

"Promises, promises," Friday chirps.

He grabs her in a headlock and rubs the top of her head with his knuckles. "I'd hook you up if you liked dick, Friday."

Friday makes a face like she smelled something bad.

Friday isn't a lesbian, but Paul thinks she is. When she first started, he hit on her pretty hard, and she started talking about one of her girlfriends one night. He assumed she's gay. She and I were working late one night, and she admitted to me that she's not. She likes men. It's just easier working around a bunch of them when they think she's a lesbian. I haven't set Paul straight yet. It's too funny watching him with her. She's one of the guys, and I like her that way. I couldn't think of her as a girl if I tried, and that was before I even met Reagan.

Friday takes Emily and Reagan with her around the corner to get a hot dog. They leave, and I can't keep from laughing while Paul watches the sway of Friday's ass. He grins at me and shrugs.

"Dude, you're not getting in her pants," I say.

"I can look," he tosses out, still grinning.

A boy runs in the door carrying a box. This happens a lot in our neighborhood. Kids need to eat, and they take any opportunity they can to make a buck. "Do you want to buy one?" he asks, and he shows me what's in the box.

"How much?" I ask.

"Five dollars," he says.

I give him a ten and reach into the box, pulling my purchase out.

"You are not bringing that thing home with you," Paul warns. "What if it's sick?"

Oh shit. What if it's sick? I stuff it into my hoodie pocket, making sure it can breathe. "I'll take it to the vet."

"You better do that before you give it to her. Her dog just died, dummy."

"Fine. I'll be back in a little while." I turn back to Paul. "Do you have any cash?" I grin at him.

"Fuck, it was cheaper for me when you were in prison," he grouses. But he reaches into his pocket and pulls out his wallet.

"Tell Reagan I'll be back in a few," I say. I walk out, keeping a gentle hand around the bulge in my pocket. The one that's purring. Not the other one.

Reagan

It feels kind of strange going out the door with Emily and Friday, but they're both parts of the Reed family, and I want to be a part of it, too. "I think Paul was checking out your ass again," Emily says to Friday. Friday twitches her hips in the short skirt that flares around her hips. It's very Marilyn Monroe, with the ties that go around her neck and the short, belled skirt.

Friday shakes her head. "Paul thinks of me as one of the guys, no matter what I wear to work."

Emily lifts her V'd fingers up to her lips and licks through the middle of them. "That's because he thinks you do that as much as he does." She laughs, and Friday shoves her in the shoulder.

Emily giggles. She looks at me. "What kind of hot dog do you want?"

"All the way," I say. I wonder if I should take one back for Pete. But I don't even know what he would like. "What does Pete like?" I ask. "Do you know?"

"Onions and mustard," Friday and Emily say at the same time, and Emily makes a gagging noise in her throat.

Friday holds up forty bucks. "Paul gave me cash to get hot dogs for everyone," she says. Someone bumps into her, and she drops a twenty. I bend over to pick it up.

I hear a whistle behind me and immediately tense. But it's just Emily. She lifts the edge of my shirt with delicate fingertips. "Somebody had a really good time playing with markers last night," she says, but she's grinning. Heat creeps up my face. I tug my shirt down. "And somebody doesn't want to talk about it." She laughs. She and Friday lean close together with their shoulders touching. They both narrow their eyes at me. "How high up do you think those markers went?" she asks Friday. But she knows I can hear her.

"I'd rather know how far down they went," Friday says.

They both laugh. A grin tugs at my lips despite the heat that's flooding my face. "Far enough," I say quietly.

Emily's eyes narrow again. "They haven't done it yet," she says. She turns around to order.

"She's right, isn't she?" Friday asks. I nod, and she curses, pulling a five from her pocket. She slides it into Emily's back pocket. "And it won't be tonight because he'll still feel bad about your dog." She puts a hand on my shoulder and rubs it fondly. "I'm really sorry about that," she says.

I hadn't thought about Mags in hours, and now I feel bad for forgetting her. Tears sting my eyes, but I blink them back.

"Oh shit," Emily says. "What did you do?" She glares at Friday.

"I mentioned her dog," Friday says.

"I told you not to do that," Emily hisses. "Pete said not to bring it up."

He did? "It's all right. I don't mind," I say. I want to miss her. I want to remember her. I want to talk about her.

Someone bumps into my shoulder, and I tense again. I don't like this busy street. Not at all. I edge closer to Friday.

She looks at me as the vendor wraps up our hot dogs. "I want to like you, Reagan," Friday says.

"I...want to...like you, too," I say slowly.

"Those boys are like my family," she says.

"Friday," Emily warns.

But she holds up a hand. "Those boys are like my family. When I didn't have anyone, they were there." There's a story here, and I really want to know what it is. "You have a family," she says. "So if you fuck mine up, I will cut you." She wields a plastic fork in my direction, but then she starts to laugh. "I'm just kidding," she says. "Well, sort of."

"I get it," I say.

"She's not even sleeping with him yet," Emily says. "Leave her alone."

Friday snorts. "I didn't leave you alone."

"You told us to spray disinfectant if we have sex at the shop." Emily shakes her head. She grins. "So we bought extra disinfectant."

"Eww," Friday says.

I laugh. I could like these women.

We collect our hot dogs and head back to the tattoo parlor. But Pete's not there when we get back. "Where did he go?" I ask.

"I sent him on an errand," Paul says. He's doing a tattoo and seems a little distracted.

"Is he coming back?" I ask. I'm not too happy to be stuck here, particularly since Matt has my car.

"Eventually," Paul says.

I sit and eat my hot dog, but then the shop fills up. A group of marines walks in the door. There are five of them, and I suddenly feel cornered. I step toward the back of the building, but that doesn't help my growing sense of unease, not in the least. Paul looks up from the tattoo he's running, and his eyes narrow. "You okay, Reagan?" he asks. I'm not. I'm not all right at all. I thought I was past all this. But I'm not. Apparently, I'm only able to move past it when Pete's with me, and that leaves me as disquieted as the men do.

I nod, but I'm seriously not all right.

Paul puts down his tattoo gun and walks to the back of the shop with me. He pulls the curtain around the private area. I heave in a breath, finally able to fill my lungs since those men came in the room. "Better?" he asks.

He sits down at a table and opens a box of pens. He starts to absently draw on a piece of paper.

"Don't just stand there," he says. "Sit." He pats the table in front of him. "People make me nervous when they pace," he says. He doesn't even look up at me. He's just sits and draws quietly.

"Paul," I start. "I think I should go."

He nods, but he still doesn't look up. "Let me know when you're ready so I can pack up my stuff."

"What?" Why would he need to pack?

He finally looks up, and his blue eyes meet mine. "I sent Pete on an errand. And he left knowing I would take care of his girl. So if you leave, I have to leave. Just let me know when you're ready."

"I don't need a babysitter," I bite out. But my eyes are filling with tears already. I blink them back furiously.

"I didn't say you needed a babysitter," he replies, and I can tell he's annoyed. He's still gentle and caring, but there's something roiling beneath the surface, too. "Those guys make you feel uncomfortable, huh?" he asks. He looks down at his paper again. He's not paying me much attention, yet I get the distinct feeling that he is.

I nod and bite off the end of my fingernail, pulling so hard that I tear the cuticle. I wipe the blood on my jeans.

"Shit," Paul says. He goes to a drawer and pulls out a Band-Aid. "If Pete comes back and you're bleeding, I'll never hear the end of it." He tears the bandage open with his teeth and pulls the tabs off it. He holds it out like he wants to wrap it around my finger. I stick my hand out, because I get the feeling he's not going to stop. My hand is shaking, though, and I hate it. He wraps it up, and then he gives me a squeeze.

He sits back down and starts to draw again. I sit across from him, and he passes me the paper, where he's drawn a simple daisy behind prison bars. The daisy is reaching toward a shaft of sunlight. "Shade that in for me," he says.

"I don't draw," I say, but I sit down across from him.

"Everyone knows how to color," he says with a snort. "Just pick some colors and stay between the lines. Or go outside the lines with purpose." He shrugs. "I don't care."

I pick up a marker and start to fill in the lines. And I go outside the lines with purpose. I smile at Paul, and he grins back and winks.

When I'm done, I stare down at it. The daisy is colorful and pretty, but withdrawn with its petals submissively lying down, and it's leaning toward the shaft of sunlight. "This is me, isn't it?" I ask quietly.

"Is it?" he replies, but he doesn't look up at me. He keeps drawing.

"Yeah." It's me. I tap his arm, and he looks at my fingers, his brow arched like he's amused. "Can you put this on me?" I ask. I'm almost breathless, I'm so excited.

"Do you want some time to think about it?" he asks.

"Do you usually ask people that?" I reply.

"Only when I think I need to." He still looks amused but serious at the same time. He heaves a sigh. "Where do you want it?"

"Where do you suggest?" I ask.

"Maybe on your shoulder?" he says. He slides latex gloves over his fingers and snaps them on his wrists. "You don't think Pete will mind if I do this, do you?" he asks. I'm not sure he really cares, but I'm glad he asked.

"Well, if you were going to put it on my inner thigh," I say, "I could see him not liking it." I laugh at the thought.

"Oh, that was going to be next place I suggested." He snaps his latex-covered fingers, but they don't make any noise. I get the idea, though.

A laugh bubbles from my throat. Paul starts pouring colors into tiny little cups. "You're going to have to take that off," he says, and he tugs on the arm of my T-shirt.

Uh oh. I didn't think of that. He pulls a T-shirt from a cabinet and uses a pair of scissors to cut down the back of it. I take it, grateful that he thought of it. He turns his back while I pull my shirt over my head and slide the torn T-shirt on. It hangs open at the back, but I don't care. I leave my bra on. He did say my shoulder, after all.

"Wow," he breathes, when he walks around behind me. "You guys had a lot of fun last night, didn't you?" He chuckles. I look over my shoulder and flush at all the ink that I never did wash off. I haven't been home long enough.

"We were trying out some designs," I stumble to say.

"Umm hmm," he hums. "Sure you were." He laughs, and a grin tugs at my lips. "The tramp stamp is pretty creative."

I haven't even seen that one yet. "What does it say?" I look back over my shoulder.

He points to a mirror behind me, and I go stand in front of it and look over my shoulder. I blush like crazy when I see that he's written, *Pete's girl* in a gothic script with squiggly flowers and vines draping down below the waist of my jeans.

Paul opens the curtain and motions to Logan. He comes to the back and signs something to Paul. Paul shows him the design, and Logan picks up a pencil and starts to add something to it. "Don't worry," Paul says to me. "You'll love it."

"What is it?" I ask.

"Trust me," he says. He turns me around, and I sit down on the tattoo table. "Ready?" he asks.

I nod.

He transfers the outline of the design to my skin. The quiet motor of the tattoo gun starts to run, and I feel it touch my shoulder. It's like an ant bite. It doesn't hurt. And when he starts to move it, the pain goes away completely. I sit quietly, and sometimes Logan speaks to me. I talk to him, careful to look at him when I respond, but he doesn't have any problem talking to me even though I don't know sign language. He's pretty witty, actually. After we start the second hour, Emily sticks her head behind the curtain.

"Are all the marines gone?" Paul asks. He looks down at me to check for my reaction, I assume.

"Yeah, only one of them wanted a tat," she says. She comes around to look at my shoulder. I hear her draw in a breath.

"Shh," Paul says shushing her.

"What?" I ask.

"Nothing," she says, but her voice cracks, and she wipes a tear from her eye.

"Did he put some boobs on me or something?" I ask. Now I'm really worried.

"Did you draw that?" she asks Logan. She goes and wraps her arms around his chest. He nods and kisses her forehead. "You did a really good job," she says.

"Hey, I shaded it," I say.

"All done," Paul says. And he turns the gun off and lays it down. He swipes some lotion across the tattoo and washes it, then pulls me up by my elbows and points me toward the mirror. "What do you think?" he asks.

He watches my face closely. Paul does that a lot. You don't have to speak for him to know how you're feeling.

I turn my back to the mirror, and I see the work of art he's created. He drew the daisy, and he's colored it with my colors. It's reaching toward a shaft of sunlight from behind bars. That part is exactly what I expected. But at the base of the daisy, Maggie lays with her head balanced on the lower petals, just like she used to balance it on my knee. She's perfect in all her black-and-white glory, and the eyes sparkle, just like hers did. A sob builds in my throat. "I love it," I croak out. "It's perfect."

Paul reaches for me slowly, careful not to scare with me with his slow movements, and he pulls me to his chest. I wrap my arms around him, and he closes my open shirt behind me with his fingers and draws me close into him. He strokes a hand down the back of my head. "You're welcome," he says. I see Logan give him a thumbs-up.

"Thank you, Logan," I say. I look in the mirror again. It's truly perfect.

"Next time, we'll do one without bars," Paul says as he sets me back and looks into my eyes.

I nod. "Next time," I say. For the first time since the assault, I feel like my cage is slowly being unlocked.

Paul still has his arms wrapped around me when the curtain opens and Pete sticks his head into the area. He's grinning until he sees me wrapped up in Paul's arms. "You guys should put up a sign so I know there's something intimate going on back here," he says. He looks at me closely and scowls when he sees me wipe my eyes. "What the fuck did you do to her?" he asks.

He walks forward, and Paul lets me go. Pete tips my chin up. "Are you all right?" he asks. He's worried, and I both hate and love that he is.

"I'm fine," I say. Logan, Emily, and Paul leave the area and close the curtain. I turn my back so Pete can see my new tattoo. "See what I got?" I ask. I pull my ponytail to the side so his view is unobstructed.

"Woah," he says. "That's fucking fantastic," he says. His fingertips tickle across my skin, very lightly outlining the area where Maggie has been immortalized. "Logan drew her, didn't he?" he asks.

"Yeah, but I did the shading, and Paul drew the flower and stuff."

"I can tell his work from a mile away," Pete says.

Suddenly, there's a movement down by my belly. I look down. Pete's lap is moving? "Seriously, Pete," I say. "This is not the place." He chuckles and drops onto a sofa. The hand warmer of his hoodie is wiggling, moving up and down.

"Why don't you come and see what I got for you?" he says, waggling his eyebrows.

A laugh escapes my throat, even though I say, "That is so not funny."

"Come on, little girl," he taunts. "Come and see what's in my pocket."

His hoodie is definitely wiggling, and there's something in there. I go sit beside him, and he arches his hips toward me when I reach out and press gently on the lump. "Keep going," he says. His voice is suddenly hoarse.

I reach into the side of the pocket and feel a cold nose sniff my hand. I lift the edge and look down. "What's that?" I ask, but I'm already smiling.

"That's your present," he says. He's still smirking. "I just got back from the vet with her. She got deflead and dewormed and had her ears cleaned and got tested for kitty diseases. She's healthy." He pulls her out, and she's so tiny she fits in the palm of his hand. "I got a litter box and some food and stuff, too," he says. He's watching me, almost like he's waiting for me to shove it at him and start screaming.

She's teeny weenie, and she has orange hair. "What's her name?" I ask.

He shrugs. "That's up to you."

"Ginger," I say. "She's a Ginger." I lift her to my cheek, and she nuzzles me. "Is she really mine?"

"Well," he says, grinning, "If I wanted some pussy of my own, I would just ask for some."

I startle. But then I realize what he said is so freaking ludicrous that I start to laugh. It's a deep belly laugh, and I can barely catch my breath. I lean over and kiss him. "You want some, all you have to do is ask," I say.

He growls low in his throat and pulls me in so he can kiss me.

I pull back when I'm breathless. "Later?" I ask.

His brow arches. He nods, but he avoids my gaze. What is that about?

Pete

Reagan likes the kitten, I can tell. She likes her a lot. She hasn't stopped cooing to her since we came home. She left her with me long enough to take a shower, and now she's lying in my bed, her hair damp and hanging over her shoulders, and she's wrapped around that little no-account kitten. The thing only cost me ten dollars, but I would have paid a lot more than that just to see her smile.

I come out of the bathroom with a towel wrapped around my hips and close the door behind me. She looks up from my bed, and her eyelids drop as her eyes roam around my body. My dick gets hard immediately, and I turn away from her long enough to put on a pair of boxers and run the towel back and forth across my closely cropped hair.

"Thank you for the kitten," she says quietly. Then I hear the bed squeak as she gets up and comes toward me. Her fingertips touch my back. "Do you think one of your brothers might babysit so we can spend some time together?" Her voice is soft and quiet, like her footsteps and the touch of her fingertips. Her voice quivers just like her hands do.

"I can wait," I blurt out. I'm a pussy. I know it. I don't want her to feel like she has to do anything. And in all honesty, I'm afraid it'll change something between us. What if I can't meet her needs? She needs to be loved calmly and carefully. What if I can't do that? What if I get too caught up in the moment and forget about her needs? What if I do it wrong? What if I make her hate me? What if she loathes the idea of having sex with me again after this?

She scoops up the kitten and puts her in my arms. "I don't want to wait," she says. She pulls her shirt over her head, and she's not wearing a bra. My breath leaves my body. All I can see is her perfect rack and her pert, pink nipples, which are tight and pushing toward me. Ginger struggles when I squeeze her too hard. I look down and force myself to unclench my hands.

Reagan hooks her thumbs in the waistband of her sleep shorts and pulls them down, along with her panties. Oh, dear God.

"Be right back," I grunt. I turn and slide out the door, stopping to press my back against it once I'm outside, and take deep breaths until my junk realizes it's not in the room with her anymore.

When I can finally catch my breath, I walk out into the living room and see Paul and Matt sitting there watching a movie. Matt came home about an hour ago, his eyes rimmed in red. He was quiet, but when I went to say something to him, Paul shook his head at me in warning. So, I let it be. I walk over and hit the "pause" button on the TV. They both look up, scowling. But I must look a fright, because they are suddenly concerned. "What's wrong?" Paul asks.

"Nothing," I gasp out. I drop onto the sofa and put Ginger in Matt's lap. He smiles and lets the kitten burrow into his neck. He grins and nuzzles his face into her. I drop my face in my hands.

"She's not ready, is she?" Paul asks. I fucking hate it when he does this. It's like he's psychic. He knows what we're thinking before we even say anything and he always has. We couldn't get away with shit, unless Sam and I worked together to pull off one prank or another. Or get arrested.

"She's ready," I gasp out. "But... But... But... But..." I shut up, because I can't find the right words. I groan and flop back against the couch. "What if I fuck it all up?" I ask.

"How do you think you'd do that?" Matt asks. The kitten has nuzzled into the collar of his shirt and sits there, soaking up his heat. "It's not like you're a fucking virgin, dummy," he says.

I don't even know how to articulate what I'm feeling. Not at all. "I've never loved any of those other girls."

Matt takes a sip of his beer and stares at me. "But you love this one." It's not a question. It's a statement. And it's a fact.

"Yeah."

"You need a lesson on the birds and the bees?" Paul asks. "You put tab A into slot B." He makes a crude gesture with his fingers. "Or tab A into slot C." He grins. "Or Tab A into slot D. But some girls don't like that, so don't start there. You might even save that for a birthday or special occasion. Yours. Not hers."

I pick up a pillow and throw it at his head. He laughs and catches it.

Finally, he says softly. "Stop psyching yourself out."

"She's been through so much," I say. I look toward the closed door.

"You haven't had any problems being what she needs, Pete. She doesn't need much. Just for you to love her. Let her lead this. Let her show you what she wants," Paul says quietly

She's naked in my room. I already know what she wants. "Okay," I say. I look at Matt's, who's rubbing noses with the kitten. "Can you cat sit?"

"I'll keep Ginger Von Stinkybutt with me. No problem," he says. He's so quiet, and I know he had a hard day, but I don't know what to say to him.

I squeeze his knee and walk toward my bedroom. Paul calls my name and jerks a thumb toward the drawer in the kitchen with all the condoms in it. I grin and go get a handful.

"Never could say that boy isn't prepared," Matt says playfully. He gives me a thumbs-up and a stupid grin.

I open the bedroom door, but Reagan has turned off the light. There's a dim glow from the lamp beside my bed, but that's all. Reagan lies on her belly her arms folded under the pillow. Her tattoo is shiny and a little puffy. I still can't believe she got a tattoo. Her dad is going to kill me. And her. Her back is naked, and I know she's in her birthday suit beneath the sheets.

I walk to my side of the bed and lay the condoms on the corner of the bedside table. Then I slide between the sheets and lie on my back, staring up at the ceiling. She doesn't move, and I think she might be asleep already. But when I roll toward her to pull her into my arms, she comes to me, all soft, naked skin and wonderfully full girl parts. Her naked breasts press against my chest, and her nipples jut against my skin. She nuzzles her face in my shoulder.

"Hey, Pete," she says.

"Yeah," I grunt. I can't put two words together. Not right now.

"If you don't want me because of what happened, you should tell me now." She's quiet, but her words are strong. The problem is that I don't know what she's referring to. Is she referring to Maggie? Or to the assault?

The only thing I can do is be honest. "I don't want to take advantage of you," I say. "And I kind of feel like I might be."

She chuckles against my chest. "I'd say that's actually in reverse. I feel like I'm taking advantage of you." She kisses my chest. "Let's just go to sleep."

I brush her hair back from her forehead and place a kiss there. "Okay," I breathe. Thank God. Because I'm a chickenshit. A big, fat, old, worthless chickenshit.

She rolls to her back and stares up at the ceiling. I can see her profile in the dark. I grab her hand tightly in mine. I'm kind of sweating, so I don't pull her back against me.

Her breathing evens out, and I can relax a little. I settle deeper into the pillow. But fifteen minutes later, I'm still lying there staring up into the darkness. Her naked body is less than half an inch from mine.

Her hand moves, and she gently extracts her fingers from mine. I let her because I kind of want her to think I'm asleep.

I hear a tiny exhale from her mouth and cut my eyes toward her without moving my head. She pushes the covers down below her breasts, and I see her fingertips start to play around her chest. She traces circles around her nipples, and then she gently pinches them. I hear her intake of breath, and if I wasn't hard enough from just having her lying next to me, I am now.

Her hand slides down her belly, and I imagine she's reaching into her curls. She's probably all slick and wet and hot and needy. Her knees lift, and she begins to rub herself. Her breath hitches again. I really should tell her I'm not asleep, but I can't. I don't want to mess this up for her.

"Oh, Pete," she breathes.

I can't take anymore. I just can't. "Reagan," I say. My voice sounds like a cannon-shot in the darkness.

She freezes. "Pete," she says. "I didn't mean to wake you." Her hand is still down between her legs. She stops moving it and brings it up to lie on her belly. "How embarrassing," she whispers. And her voice cracks.

"Reagan, come here," I say.

She leans up an elbow and says, "Where?"

"If it's all right with you, I'm going to lie really still and you're going to come over here with me."

She hops up onto her knees and lays a hand on my chest. "Like this?" she says.

I take her hand in mine and lift it to my lips. "Reagan, I'm scared," I admit.

"So am I," she says.

"I want to be inside you so fucking bad it hurts," I admit. I squeeze my eyes shut tightly.

Reagan's fingertips hook in the waistband of my boxers, and I feel her lift them over my dick. I raise my hips so she can slide them down and off. Now I'm as naked as she is. "Can I?" she asks. "Can I try some things?"

"You can try anything you want," I say. I lift my arms up so my palms are behind my head. If I touch her, I'm going to have to roll her over and slide inside her. And I know this needs to be done at her pace.

Her fingers wrap around my dick, and she groans. "I'm not sure this can fit inside me," she warns.

"It'll fit," I say.

Reagan reaches across me, and I realize she's reaching for a condom. I'm not ready for that yet, so I catch her while she's on top of me with my hands around her waist. I lift her so that her breasts are in my face, and I kiss her left nipple until it's tight and reaching for my mouth. She whimpers and lets me, and then I move to the other breast. I give it the same lavish attention, and she quivers in my arms.

"Pete," Reagan cries.

I dip my hand between her legs to see how wet she is. I can't help it. She's fucking soaked. She's nearly dripping. "God, Reagan," I say. I trail my finger across her clit.

I hear a condom wrapper as she tears it, and then I feel it press against the head of my dick. She wants to put it on me. Fuck yeah! But I grab her hand. "Reagan," I warn.

"What?" she breathes.

"I'm just a man."

"What does that mean?" she whispers.

"It means that if you put that on my dick, the next thing that will go on it is you." She freezes for a moment, and I hear her breaths stutter from her.

But she starts to roll the condom down my shaft and when she gets to the base, I tug it a little lower. She's being way too gentle with me.

"Come on," I say quietly. "Come and ride me. Show me how you want it."

She throws a leg over me and straddles my hips, and all her wet girly parts are touching my hard manly parts. She rocks, riding the ridge of me, until my dick is notched in the cleft where her clit hides.

"Reach between us and take me inside," I say. My voice is so rough, I can barely understand it. But she hears me and she does. She places the head of my dick at her opening, and then she stops. "Everything all right?" I ask. I bite my lower lip to keep from screaming.

She doesn't respond, but she starts to sink down on me. Her legs and arms are trembling, and I take her hips to help guide her. She's hot, and she slides onto me like a tight-fitting velvet glove. "Shit," I say. I wish I didn't because she stops moving.

"What's wrong?" she asks.

"Nothing," I say. "You're fucking perfect. Keep going."

She sinks down some more and says, "You're in."

God, yes, I am. "Yep," I say. I grit my teeth to keep from coming.

"You're inside me, Pete," she says.

I feel a wet plop on my chest. "Are you crying?" I ask.

"Maybe," she says. She's very still.

"Are you hurting?" I ask. I run my hands up her naked thighs.

"No," she says. "And I was so worried it would. I just..." She sniffles. "I just don't want it to be over, Pete," she says. "I want to stay like this forever."

I chuckle at that, and my dick moves inside her. "Oh," she says. She adjusts her body. I'm only about halfway in, but I wanted her to do this her own way. My dick pulses, and I lower her on me and arch my hips to push further into her at the same time. She cries out. "Oh!" she says.

I pull her down to me and kiss her so she'll be quiet. My brothers are in the living room. "Shh," I say. I arch my hips and fuck into her, and her tongue slides in my mouth. "Jesus," I say when she lifts her head. Her legs are shaking, and she balances herself on my chest.

"Can you?" she asks.

"Can I what?" Can I stay like this forever? Nope. Because I'm going to come and leave her unsatisfied.

"Can you do it?" she asks, her voice hesitant.

I sit up and wrap my arm around her, and then roll her very slowly onto her back. Her legs lift to wrap around my hips. I push inside her, further than before but still not all the way in. "Oh, that's nice," she says.

I chuckle and bury my head in her neck. "Is this all right?" I whisper. I push in a little more and then pull back out. When I push back in I sink as far into her as I can go. She's so tight that I can barely breathe.

"Yeah." She whimpers when I tilt her bottom up and dig deep, taking everything she'll give me.

I'm going to come, and she's not. So I make some room between us, and my hand seeks out her heat, rubbing her clit. I take her nipple between my teeth and abrade it gently, and she starts to squirm beneath me. Her hips arch to meet my thrusts, and her cries are little noises by my ear. Her breath blows across my cheek, as moist and humid as her private place where I'm buried and fucking loving it.

Suddenly, she clutches my shoulders and stiffens beneath me. Her body quakes, and she starts to come. I rub her through it, and it's so hard not to push her legs back toward her shoulders and power through my own orgasm. But I force myself to keep it slow and soft. She quakes in my arms. And it's not until she's loose and languid that I take my own pleasure. I wrap my arms under hers and bury my face against her and thrust once, twice, three times. And then I pour into her as I come. I feel like my balls are trying to come out through my toes, and she just wraps her arms around me and holds me close while I lose myself in her.

I brush her hair back from her face, and her body starts to quake under mine. Is she crying? Oh fuck. But then she snorts, and I realize she's laughing. Almost hysterically. Her body shakes and rocks, and her tight depths grip my dick. I pull out of her, because I need to, not because I want to. My dick is so sensitive that I can barely stand the retreat.

She giggles, and I look down at her. Her eyes are dark in the dim light of the room, and they're shiny. But not from tears. From happiness.

"How did I do?" I ask. I kiss her cheek quickly with little pecks. She giggles again.

"That was a practice test," she says. "When can we do the final exam?"

I take a deep breath. "Any time you want, princess. I live to serve."

She laughs again, and I have never, ever heard a more beautiful sound. Ever.

Reagan

I wake up to the feel of my bottom nestled in Pete's lap, his hardness pressed against my butt. He rocks against me, and I come awake slowly. He pushes my hair from my nape, and his lips touch the sensitive place where my neck meets my shoulder. Strong fingers cup my breast, and he doesn't move. He doesn't inch toward my nipple, he just strokes his fingers lazily beneath the sensitive sweep of my boob.

"Pete," I whisper.

"What?" he whispers back, and I can hear the smile in his voice.

"Are you trying to put the moves on me?" I ask.

He chuckles. "If you have to ask that, I'm doing a really bad job at it." He rolls me to my back and throws my leg over his shoulder, and his breath is hot against my curls as he grins and says, "I'll have to work harder."

I gasp when he spreads me open with his thumbs and bends his head, his tongue lolling against my clit over and over. "I'll have you trained before I know it," I say. But I can barely get my breath. I reach a hand into his hair and hold him tightly, pushing him where I want him. He latches onto my clit just as he slides his finger inside me. He's less careful with me today than he has been in the past. He seems less afraid to try something new with me, but he's still gentle and slow. I know that he holds back for me, and I wonder how long he'll feel the need to do that. Forever?

I'm not afraid of him or what he does to me, and I never have been. I grip the sheets in my hands and squeeze tightly as he crooks a finger inside me and reaches a spot I didn't know existed. I cry out, and he gently and rhythmically sucks my clit in time with the movement of his fingers until I spiral out of control. I come so hard I can barely breathe, and he drinks in the power of it. I push his head back when I grow too sensitive, and he unlatches from my clit and licks across it. I tremble with aftershocks.

Pete wipes his face on my inner thigh and then crawls up my body. He reaches over me and grabs a condom and sheathes himself quickly. Just when I think he'll settle between my legs, he doesn't. He rolls my body over slowly, and slides a pillow beneath my hips, "This all right?" he asks. He puts his weight on my back, and his lips touch my shoulder again, just like he did a few minutes ago, and he gently bites down. "I need you," he says.

I nod. "It's all right," I say. He sinks into me from behind. It's one slow thrust until he's fully seated inside me. "Are you sore?" he asks.

"A little," I admit. There's a little pinch, but I welcome it because Pete's inside me again, and that's right where I want him to be.

"I'll be careful," he whispers. I know he will. I don't want careful. I want Pete.

He takes me with lazy strokes, filling and then retreating, pushing and then pulling, riding me with care and caution. I came with his mouth between my legs, but I feel a build-up again. It's a completely different feeling. It's more of a warm wash of heat rather than a raging, quaking orgasm. I come, and he grunts and pushes himself deep inside me, his body shaking as he comes with me. He grunts and makes a noise low in his throat. It's a noise of completion. All too soon, he pulls out, and stands up, removes the condom and cleans himself up. Then he hands me a towel and turns his back. I wipe off really quickly, and then he's back in bed with me, drawing me in to his chest.

"You okay?" he asks, pulling me down to lie in the crook where his arm meets his shoulder.

"I'm not going to break, Pete," I say quietly. "You don't have to treat me like I'm made of glass."

He startles and looks down his nose at me. "I'm not."

"You are," I say quietly. I hate that I'm doing this. But I can't have a relationship based on fears he thinks he wants to avoid with me.

My phone dings, and I reach for my pants on the floor because I know it's in my pocket.

I pull it out and read the screen.

Dad: *Where are you?*

Me: *I'm at Pete's.*

Dad: *Why?*

Shit. What do I say?

Me: *Can we talk about this later?*

Dad: *Sure, we can. As soon as you arrive at your apartment where we've been waiting since last night.*

Shit, shit, shit, shit.

Me: *I'll be there in a few minutes.*

I heave a sigh and lay my head on the bed. Dad is going to kill me. Or kill Pete. "My parents are at my apartment," I say.

"Oh no," he breathes. He rolls to the edge of the bed and starts to get dressed.

"Where are you going?" I ask.

He looks up, his brow arched. "I'm going with you."

"That's not necessary," I say. In fact, I'd rather he not. Dad's going to be pissed and seeing Pete is only going to make it worse.

"I don't mind," he says, and he keeps getting dressed.

"Pete," I call. He finally looks up at me.

"What?"

"I'd rather you stay here."

"Why?" He looks confused.

"It's Sunday morning. My parents are probably going to stay all day. I need to spend some time with them." I really just want to spare him my dad's wrath.

He nods. "Okay," he says slowly. He kicks his shoes back off.

I get dressed and go over to give him a kiss. "I'll call you later?" I ask.

He nods. "Sure."

I need to deal with this situation with my dad so that I'll never have to deal with it again.

Pete

The phone rings, and I jump to grab it. It's six o'clock on Sunday evening and Reagan has been gone all day and hasn't called even once. "Hello?" I say. Sam chuckles into his fist. He's taking the bus back to school late tonight, so he'll be here until around eleven. He says something about my balls being in a vice, and I throw a pillow at him.

"Pete?" a male voice says.

"Yes," I say.

"Pete, this is Phil." I must be too quiet because he goes on to say, "Your parole officer."

"Yes, sir," I say. I sit up so I can pay close attention.

"Pete, could I come and pick you up and take you somewhere with me? It's kind of important."

"Of course," I say. I don't even hesitate. "Can I ask where we're going?"

"I'll tell you more when I pick you up," he says. He sounds like he's upset, and I want to know what's going on. "Can you be ready in ten minutes?"

We hang up, and I go get dressed. I wonder what could be important enough to make Phil need to see me on a Sunday. But I guess I'll find out.

Phil pulls up outside my building in a black Ford, and he motions for me to climb in. "I have some bad news, Pete," he says. He doesn't look at me.

"What kind of news?" I ask.

"Edward, the boy from the youth program, he got visitation yesterday with his sister after group. He was doing so well, I felt like he was ready, particularly after he spent so much time with you at camp. There was an altercation, and his sister's foster father was badly injured. Edward was stabbed, and he just got out of surgery. The foster father died in the fight."

"What?" I breathe. "How could that happen?"

"Apparently, Edward's sister told him that the foster father wasn't treating her well. Edward lost his head, and he snapped. He attacked him, and the two fought over a blade the father had. Edward spent the whole morning in surgery."

"Is he all right?" I ask.

Phil shakes his head. "I'm not sure. That's why I'm going to see him. He won't see anyone else, and you seemed to have a real connection with him at the camp and even at group yesterday. So, I thought you might be able to talk to him."

"What's going to happen to him?" I ask.

"Hopefully, this is going to be a self-defense case. The last time he got in trouble, he was a juvenile offender. He's eighteen now. He'll be tried as an adult if there are criminal charges." He shakes his head and blows out a breath. "I need for someone to get his story, so Caster can help prepare his defense, but he won't talk to anybody. I already talked to Bob Caster, and he's coming to talk to him, too."

"He's at Reagan's," I say.

He cuts his eyes at me as he puts the truck in gear. "Yes, I heard."

I sit back and scrub the back of my head with my hand.

"I told you to be careful with her," Phil reminds me.

"I have been," I say. "Very careful."

"He's pretty pissed," he tells me. I am sure of that already.

"I love her like crazy, Phil," I say.

His thumb taps on the steering wheel, but he doesn't say anything else. When we get to hospital, they let us into the room when Phil flashes his identification. He walks in and I see Tic Tac, no *Edward*, in bed. He has tubes and wires sticking from his body, and he looks so frail. There's a young lady in a chair beside him holding his hand, and I can't help but think this must be his sister. She hops to her feet when we come into the room.

"I never should have told him," she says. "I never should have told him, and then this wouldn't have happened."

Phil hands her a tissue, and I jam my hands in my pockets. I'm not sure what to do with them. "Hello," I say when she stares at me.

"You must be Pete," she says. She smiles. "Edward told me all about you."

"What happened?" I ask, nodding toward the bed.

Her eyebrows arch with feigned amusement. "He gave up his life for me. Again. He did it before when he went to the detention center, and he did it again today."

Phil turns her with a hand on her shoulder. "I could use some coffee," he says. "Walk with me?"

I think she knows that I want to talk with Edward. She nods and looks longingly toward the bed. "Please make him fight," she whispers. "Don't let him give up."

She leaves the room with Phil, and I go sit in the chair where she was sitting. I nibble absently on my fingernail, wondering if I should wake him. "I'm so pretty that you can't catch your breath, right?" he asks, his voice quiet. I didn't even know he was awake. "Deep breaths, man," he says. "You can push through it."

"How are you?" I ask. I force some joviality into my voice. "You look like shit."

"Thanks." He groans as he pushes himself up in the bed. "They say I'll live." His gaze roams around the room, and I wonder if he's thinking about the man he killed.

"I'm glad," I say. I don't know how to talk to this kid. I really don't. I'm floundering here. "Want to tell me what happened?" I ask.

He shakes his head.

"Why don't you do it anyway?" I ask.

"He's dead, right?" he asks. A tear rolls down his cheek, and he swipes it away.

"Yeah."

"Some people need killing," he says. He doesn't crack a smile, and his voice breaks. He's hurting, and I can tell.

"Did he need killing?" I ask.

"He was hurting my sister," he says. "I knew it the minute I walked into the room." He squeezes the bed rail until his knuckles turn white. "She didn't even have to tell me. I could see it in her eyes. Just like before."

"There was a knife?" I ask. I try to remember everything he's telling me, and I wonder if I should be writing it all down.

His gaze snaps to mine. "It wasn't mine," he says. "It was his. He came at me with it, and I couldn't stop him." He lays a hand over his stomach. "He jabbed me with it. I pulled it out, and he jumped me and fell on it." He's openly sobbing now. "I swear to God that I didn't want to kill him."

I reach out and clasp his hand, squeezing hard, our thumbs crossed the way men shake hands. "It was an accident."

"Do you think they'll believe it?" he asks.

"I don't know," I say quietly. I don't want to give him hope if there is none.

"I had plans, you know?" he says. He sniffles. "I wrote them down."

Jesus Christ. This kid had plans.

"I wanted to be somebody my sister can be proud of. I wanted to be for her what no one was for me."

"You can still have those things, Edward," I say.

He shakes his head. "Will I go to prison?" he asks.

"I don't know," I say again.

"I don't want to go to prison," he says.

"We need to get you some tattoos," I say. "Nobody fucks with you in prison if you're all tatted up." I squeeze his hand. "I need for you to do me a favor," I say.

"What?" he asks, his eyes wary.

"I need for you to remember that you're just as important as your sister."

"I'm not," he starts.

I get in his face this time. I can only think back to when I used to call him Tic Tac in my head, and I realize what a disservice I did this kid. He's better than that. He's good on the inside, and I could try to be more like him. But I judged the outside, and I feel terrible about it. "You're just as important as she is, and you never had anybody to fight for you." I feel my eyes filling with tears, and I blink them back. "But you have somebody now, dummy. I'm here. I'm not going anywhere."

"They told me my whole life that I'm not worth anything."

"They lied," I grit out. "They lied to make themselves feel better." I shrug my shoulders. "It's up to you if you believe them." I let his hand go because holding it is getting awkward. "You're pretty fucking amazing," I say.

"My sister needs to go to a group home until I can get her out of foster care," he says.

"We'll talk to Phil and see if he can help." I heave in a deep breath. "Don't give up, okay?" I say.

He doesn't say anything.

"Look what you've been through, Edward," I say. "How many people could have survived it? You did. So, don't throw it all away now. Have hope."

"I can't afford any hope." He snorts. "That shit's expensive."

"Then you can have some of mine. Hell, you can have all the hope I have for you. Because there's a whole fucking lot of it."

"I never had anybody on my side before," he says.

Phil and Mr. Caster walk into the room. Mr. Caster glares at me, and Phil looks curious. "The guy fell on the knife," I say. "Edward didn't do it on purpose."

Mr. Caster pulls out a notepad and starts to write. He motions for Edward to continue, and he goes through the whole story while Reagan's dad takes notes.

Phil claps a hand on my shoulder. "Thank you," he says. "I really think you could be successful in this line of work."

"I'm not sure I can take the heartache," I admit.

"He sobbed like a baby," Edward tosses out. He laughs and then clutches his side when it hurts.

"I didn't sob," I grumble. I point to his side. "And that's what you get for being a smart-ass."

"Better a smart-ass than a dumb-ass," he says. I flip him the bird.

"I should get you home," Phil says. "It's almost nine o'clock."

Shit. I almost forgot. I nod and clasp hands with Edward. "I'll see you tomorrow," I say. He smiles and nods. Watching him is like watching a flower reach for the sun. It's like Reagan's tattoo.

"Mr. Caster," I say, and I extend my hand. He takes it, albeit reluctantly. "It was good to see you again."

"You'll be seeing a lot more of me, Pete," he says, and he grins. But there's no mirth in it. It's all warning.

"Wouldn't have it any other way, sir," I say.

Phil nods at me, and we walk out to the truck. My emotions are on overload, and I want to hit something. "What happened to Edward, that happens to a lot of kids?" I ask.

"More than you could imagine," he says. "All variations of the same scene." He looks up at me. "I wasn't kidding when I said you'd be good at this line of work."

"I know. I'm thinking about it." I don't know if I want to be on the front lines the way he is. Or if I want to be a lawyer like Mr. Caster. I'm still deciding.

"Thanks for going with me," he says.

"Anytime," I toss back as he stops the truck, and I get out. I really want to go to Reagan's, but with this damn tracking bracelet, I can't. I don't need to be there with her anyway. I'm too emotional right now. I could never be what she needs in this state.

I run up the stairs. I really need a good workout to get rid of this energy. I feel like I am two steps from losing control of myself. I'm angry. I'm angry at myself for ever fucking my life up. I'm mad at cancer for getting Matt sick. I'm mad at my life. I'm mad at me. I'm mad at a system that couldn't protect Edward or his sister. I'm just mad in general.

I walk into the apartment and the lights are out. Thank God, nobody's home. A sliver of light shines from beneath my door. I open it and see Reagan sprawled across my bed reading a book. She sits up and brushes her hair back from her face. "You're home," she says. She smiles at me. It's so pretty and so sweet and so not what I need right now.

"You shouldn't be here right now," I say.

"What?" Her eyebrows scrunch together.

"You should go back to your apartment," I say. I mess with things on the dresser so I won't have to look at her.

"No," she says. "What's wrong?" she asks.

"I had a long day. I don't particularly want any company." I know that I'm hurting her, but if she stays, I can't be what she needs.

"Pete," she starts. "Tell me what happened today."

"What happened with you?" I ask. "Was your dad pissed you spent the night here?" With the ex-con. I don't say the last part, but I think it.

"He was," she says with a nod. She's choosing her words with care. "But he's my dad. He's supposed to act like that."

Her hand lands on my shoulder, and I flinch. She flinches too, but she doesn't draw it back. I squeeze my eyes shut and rest my hands on the dresser, my elbows locked. I want to crawl into a ball in the corner and rock myself to sleep. No, I don't. I want to draw Reagan into my arms and sink inside her and make her a part of me and let her take all this. But she can't. She's not made for that.

"You should go, Reagan," I say again.

"No," she replies. She tries to turn me to face her, but I won't budge. She blows out a breath and ducks down to slide under my arm, getting between me and the dresser. I back up. I can't be this close to her. I can't. It's not all right.

"I can't be what you need right now," I say quietly. My voice shakes.

"What do you think I need?" she whispers.

I swallow past the lump in my throat and flex my fingers, making fists over and over. "You need to be loved calmly and carefully. And I can't do either tonight. You need to go." I can't even look at her. I can't.

"You think I need to be loved calmly and carefully," she says slowly.

I nod, sucking my piercing into my mouth to toy with it.

"You want to know what I think?" she asks.

"What?" I grunt. Apparently, I've turned into a caveman who can only speak in monosyllables.

"I think I need to be loved…completely."

My gaze jerks to hers. Her eyes are soft, and a smile plays around her mouth.

She walks to me and takes my face in her hands.

"I do love you completely," I say. "But…"

She shakes her head. "No, you don't. You hold back because you're afraid to hurt me." She wraps her arms around my neck, and her lips hover an inch from mine. She whispers. "Love me completely, Pete."

I growl and jerk her shirt over her head and pull her pajama bottoms down, her panties going with them. She doesn't shy away from me, so I walk her backward toward the bed. She takes a step back every time I take a step forward, until she has no choice but to sit back on the bed. She scoots to the center of the bed, and I drink in my fill of her as I watch her undress really quickly. "I can't be calm or careful," I warn, "but I'll stop if you tell me to. Just say the word."

"I know," she says. She crooks a finger at me, but I don't let her take charge. I grab her foot and jerk her to me. I immediately worry that I'm being too rough, but she just laughs.

"I need to be inside you," I say as I grab a condom and roll it onto my dick. "I don't think I can wait."

She doesn't say a word.

I spit into my hand because I'm afraid she'll be dry. I rub my dick with it and crawl to lie between her legs. I palm her ass and tip her toward me, and then I surge inside her in one hard push, hitting it hard enough that she moves on the bed, her head pushing toward the headboard. She cries out. But she's not crying out in pain.

"Don't stop," she says. She yanks my hair in her hands and forces me to look into her eyes. "Let me be what you need, so you can be what I need, too." Her breaths stutter from her as I stroke inside her. I can't get enough of her. I can't get deep enough. I push both her legs toward her chest, which tips her bottom up higher. Her hands clutch my ass, pulling me in, deeper and harder with every thrust. I am fully inside her, taking every inch of her silken sheath as she accepts me. She accepts my anger. She accepts my helplessness. She accepts my love for her.

"Pete," she cries. She breathes out my name, over and over, and I feel her pussy contract around my dick, milking me as she comes. But I'm not ready to be done. I flip her over and pick her up on her knees and then I'm inside her again. I grab her thighs and pull her back to me, and she feels even tighter this way, if that's possible. She lies down, her face against the sheets and her ass in the air. She lets me power into her from behind. I'm rough and abrasive and I fucking love her so much. I roll her hair around my fist so I can turn her head and kiss her. Her tongue touches mine, and she her lips quiver. I reach around her and find her clit, rubbing it the way I know she likes. I slow my movements and bring her to orgasm until she's quaking in my arms.

I roll onto my back and pull her to straddle me. "I don't know how many more times I can come, Pete," she says. She draws her lower lip between her teeth and worries it.

"Ride me," I say. She reaches between us and takes me in her fist, giving my dick a slow pump. It's slick with her juices. I stop her hand, and she balances on the head of my dick. I take her hips and draw her down on me, until she has all of me. Then I bring her down to lie on my chest and I fuck her hard from below.

She cries out my name between whimpers, and I fucking love that she'll let me love her like this. Her breaths move by my ear and she says, "I love you, Pete," over and over and over and I can't believe how fucking lucky I am.

She comes apart in my arms, and I hold her tightly as I come, too. I pour myself into her, and my love for her overflows my heart. I wrap my arms around her, and she's still quaking. I brush her sweaty hair behind her ear. "Are you all right?" she asks. She rests her chin on my chest and looks up at me. I slip from inside her, and I can't bite back a groan as we separate.

"I'm fine," I say. I look up at her and suddenly feel very sorry for doing that to her. "What about you?" I ask. "Please tell me I didn't hurt you."

"Pete," she breathes. "You have to get over your fear of hurting me."

"I'm pretty much over it," I say. After that, I don't have a fear left in my body. I chuckle. "I'm all the way over it."

She lies there draped across me, and nothing ever felt so right. I draw little circles on her back.

"I love you completely, princess," I say.

She accepts me like no one ever has. She accepts me as Pete. She accepts me as that ex-con. She accepts me as a brother to four men who will love her because I do. And I hope one day, she'll accept me as her husband because I don't think I could live without her at this point.

She giggles, and the feel of it rolls through me. "I think I'm going to be too sore for you to love me completely again tonight."

"I can think of some ways to work around that."

I hear a plaintive little *meow* from the other side of the door and look over to see a tiny paw sweeping back and forth in the gap where the door doesn't quite touch the floor. "Go get my cat," she says, shoving my shoulder. "You wore me out. I can't move."

I laugh and go let her kitty into the room.

Epilogue: Matt

Reagan is teaching a class on self-defense at the recreation center, and all of us Reed brothers were told to be there. None of us knew she wanted to use us as practice dummies. "Aren't we supposed to get face masks and some padding for this?" Paul asks as he tries to block a kick to his groin from Friday. He succeeds but only barely.

"I could have so had you!" Friday cries. She pumps her fist in the air, and Paul wraps an arm around her waist and swings her around playfully. She shrieks and bats at his hands, but he doesn't let her go.

Reagan looks at Pete and winks. She's not afraid for any of us to touch her anymore. She's never been afraid of Pete, but now she's calm and content around us all, and sometimes I pick her up and hug her just because I can. She makes Pete so fucking happy. "Come attack me," she says. "Pretty please?" she adds when he hesitates.

He groans and pushes to his feet. He's still on the ground from the last time he pretended to attack her. He comes at her, and she spins around and flips him onto his back. He groans and rolls into a ball. "Enough," he cries. "Someone else has to take a turn."

Reagan's dad laughs. Her parents are here for the weekend. Pete is kind of pissed because he had to come home while they're at her apartment. He lives with her almost all the time, now that he's off house arrest. Reagan's dad is enjoying Pete's discomfort way too much. Her little brother, Link, is pretty good at martial arts, too. He goes at it like he goes at everything else—with passion, forethought, and caution. He doesn't speak often, but we're all okay with that. He is who he is, just like the rest of us.

Sam steps up, and Reagan works out some moves with one of the girls from the assault program. Sam takes what Reagan gives him, and the girl grows more confident with each move. It's good to see this. It's good to see Reagan in her element, and I know she's doing good work with these girls.

One of Pete's friends from the prison program, Edward, came with his sister. He's wasn't charged for his participation in that man's death, and he's spending a lot of time with his sister, even though she can't live with him. He keeps an eye on her. She's timid as a mouse, but she's a sweet girl, and I feel like she can get through this. She's not participating in class yet. She's sitting on the edge of the row of bleachers beside a boy in a wheelchair. I think his name is Gonzo. He's another of Pete's foundlings. They hang around him like they need him. Maybe they do. I know I do. Pete has become the man he was always supposed to be now that he has Reagan. I have never been so proud of him.

Gonzo laughs, and I know the boy can't talk because of his trache. So, Gonzo is using a computer so he can communicate with the Edward's sister. I wish I could remember her name. She speaks to him, and he grins and types something really quickly. Her face colors. They're the same age, and there's definitely a spark there. There's a lid for every pot, Pete always says. I mentally shrug my shoulders.

Reagan motions me forward. I see Sam lying on the floor in a heap. Shit. She's going to emasculate all of us. "I had cancer," I toss out, as she smiles at me. "I almost died," I remind her.

She laughs and uses me to show some moves. She goes easy on me. Or so I think. Then I'm on my back on the floor, too. She puts her hands on her hips and grins down at me. "You didn't really think I'd go easy on you, did you?" she asks.

Logan tosses Emily over his shoulder and starts to run around the gym with her squealing. Paul does the same with Friday, and Sam comes to stand beside me. "Something going on with Paul and Friday?" he asks.

"Paul still thinks she's a lesbian," I say.

"Should we tell him she's not?" Sam asks.

I shake my head. "Nah." I grin. It's more fun this way.

I look toward the door and see Skylar, the woman who is taking care of Kendra's kids. She'd promised to bring Seth today, and I'm glad to see her. My heart stutters at the sight of her. She's wearing gym clothes, and I can see her belly. I want to lick it. Or pierce it. Or climb on top of it. My dick twitches, and I walk over to her. "Hi," I say.

She blows her bangs up with an upturned breath. "Hi," she says.

"Things going okay?" I ask. She shoots a glance toward Seth.

"Not really," she says on a heavy sigh. "I was hoping I could ask you for some help."

"For those kids?" I ask, jerking a finger toward them. "Anything."

I look around the gym. This is my life. And I fucking love it.

Dear Readers,

This book was a journey but I hope you remember that this was Reagan's journey, and every victim of sexual assault will have a different one. No matter the story, we all should be aware of the facts:

- 1 in 4 college age girls will be sexually assaulted during her college career
- 20% of women when asked if they have ever been forced to commit a sexual act will say "yes."

If you have been assaulted or know someone who has, there are national resources you can contact for help.

The National Rape, Abuse and Incest National Network can be reached at 1800-656-HOPE.

Remember, even if you've never been assaulted, you can volunteer to help someone who has. Your local rape crisis center will have more details.

I hope you enjoyed Reagan and Pete's story.

Please remember that silence changes nothing.

Best regards,

Tammy

Made in the USA
Lexington, KY
19 July 2014